PHIL

EARTH JUMPED BACK

Black Rose Writing | Texas

©2024 by Philip Reari
All rights reserved. No part of this book may be reproduced, stored in a retrieval system or transmitted in any form or by any means without the prior written permission of the publishers, except by a reviewer who may quote brief passages in a review to be printed in a newspaper, magazine or journal.

The author grants the final approval for this literary material.

First printing

This is a work of fiction. Names, characters, businesses, places, events, and incidents are either the products of the author's imagination or used in a fictitious manner. Any resemblance to actual persons, living or dead, or actual events is purely coincidental.

ISBN: 978-1-68513-448-8
PUBLISHED BY BLACK ROSE WRITING
www.blackrosewriting.com

Printed in the United States of America
Suggested Retail Price (SRP) $21.95

Earth Jumped Back is printed in Minion Pro

*As a planet-friendly publisher, Black Rose Writing does its best to eliminate unnecessary waste to reduce paper usage and energy costs, while never compromising the reading experience. As a result, the final word count vs. page count may not meet common expectations.

All extracts in this novel are from real articles first published in the UC-Santa Barbara student newspaper, El Gaucho, 1969-1970.

PRAISE FOR
EARTH JUMPED BACK

"*Earth Jumped Back* is an audacious novel of time travel and terrorism, of environmental peril and uncanny nostalgia. With shades of DeLillo's debut, and sometimes reminiscent of Vonnegut, Philip Reari's alternate history of Santa Barbara and the 1970 Isla Vista riots is convincingly evocative, compassionate, and finely written—a fantastic Californian kaleidoscope."
–James Reich, author of *The Moth for the Star*

"*Earth Jumped Back* is an engaging time-travel yarn strung between the massive Santa Barbara oil spill of 1969 and the bustling University of California of 2023. Philip Reari has a keen eye for the foibles of college idealists of both decades, and for the cynicism of their faculty counterparts. The prose is light and spirited but the dark side here—not quite obscured by the sometimes-stoned and often goofy students—is how earnest activism can turn violent."
–T. Jefferson Parker, author of *Desperation Reef*

"A wonderfully weird adventure through time, disaster, and youthfulness. Philip Reari weaves an energetic story that, at its core, probes our connection and responsibility to our environment and to each other."
–Irina Zhorov, author of *Lost Believers*

ACKNOWLEGEMENTS

This book has been a labor of love and I need to acknowledge first and foremost those I love for providing time and space for the labor. My wife, who takes my writing seriously but not too seriously and is always game to offer her thoughts, which always make me think and rethink. And my kiddos, for getting me out of my head and for not staying home sick too much.

The first chapter benefited greatly from The Shit No One Tells You About Writing Beta Reader Match Up, and I hope my feedback was similarly useful for the four other participants in my group. Listening to the TSNOTYAW podcast also filled me with ideas and made me feel like part of something greater than a desk in a sunny nook. James Reich provided a critical developmental edit that was equal parts encouraging and insightful, and the shape of the final manuscript owes much to him. Greg Theilmann and Christian Alexander graciously agreed to read drafts of the novel and their notes were much appreciated.

The University of California Daily Nexus archives helped construct the scaffolding for this story, and I thoroughly enjoyed the ink-stained wormhole those old newspapers took me down. I'm also grateful to have finally read some Edward Abbey, whose idiosyncratic style stimulated me to pursue my own.

EARTH JUMPED BACK

"It was fun to have that sense of engagement where you jumped on the Earth and the Earth jumped back—the sense that you were a part of history."
–Abbie Hoffman, member of the Chicago Seven

"I don't like to call it a tragedy because there has been no loss of human life. I am amazed at the publicity for the loss of a few birds."
–Fred L. Hartley, President, Union Oil, 1969 Congressional Hearing

"In the midst of one Isla Vista riot, a philosophy professor saw a sweet-faced girl hurl a rock toward a sheriff's deputy. The professor carefully placed his glasses in his coat pocket, pulled her by the ear to a nearby bench and methodically spanked her a dozen times."
–*The Isla Vista War—Campus Violence in a Class By Itself*, Winthrop Griffith, The New York Times, August 30, 1970

CHAPTER ONE
ISLA VISTA

Ethan Trousock taps his fingers to the lapping of the waves against the inflatable raft. Effervescent thoughts swim a few laps around his waterlogged cranium before exhausting themselves. The Channel Islands serrate the distant horizon, suspended between the midnight sky and the ocean. In the foreground, the flickering lights of long-abandoned oil platforms cry out to be noticed. His flip-flop squeaks against the raft's interior. He observes his legs as if they are somebody else's. They are the legs of a healthy young man, and they are wet, but not soaked.

"I'm dying," Ethan says as the raft rises over a shallow ridge of water. His thick dark hair is matted to his forehead. A budding rattail slithers down the back of his neck. Moonlight graces his cheekbones before concentrating on the blunt tip of his nose. His sleepy eyes, burrowed beneath bristly eyebrows, pivot towards his companion on the raft, Paul Parfitt.

Paul slowly shakes his oblong head. His brown eyes, rounder than Ethan's, rise from their previous preoccupation with a scab on the outside of his knee. In the shadowy night light, Ethan is almost his mirror image. Two young men with similar physiques, speech patterns, humor. It's been commented on before. The main difference between them might be that Ethan is dying.

"Dying of…" Paul replies.

"I can't seem to pass gas," Ethan says. "How long can you go without farting, before, you know, it becomes a problem?"

"I'm no gastroenterologist, but from experience, more than a few hours would be unusual."

Ethan shifts his rear up in the raft and assumes a more flatulence-inducing posture.

"You're no what?"

"You mean you haven't been to a gastroenterologist yet?" Paul says with mock surprise.

"Farting's not my main problem anyway."

"You can say that again."

"It's time."

"It's time for what?"

"Time is my main problem. It's too…strict. It's a problem for everyone. It's got us all on a death march, but we act like it's just a pleasant stroll. And anyway, all I do is waste it."

Paul nods, picks at his scab. "Sure, time is a bitch. But we're young. For now, it's on our side."

Ethan winces and twists his torso. "Also, I think I might have cancer, in one of my organs."

In lieu of responding Paul looks inland towards the coast. For a second, he thinks he spots a wisp of smoke rising ominously over the mountains in the near distance. A bolt of panic shoots through him as images of the previous summer and the wildfire evacuation take hold. But it is quickly relinquished. It's just a smudge. Some sort of smudge in his eye or in the sky. He exhales, breathes in the fresh air with relish.

They sip their beers in harmony with the playful splish-splash of the ocean. A hundred yards away, Isla Vista's colorful, shoddily built houses line the bluffs. Each year they erode further, daring the student ghetto's oceanfront real estate to plunge balcony first into the sea. Ethan's gaze rests on a light blue, two-story rowhouse with crumbling paint under the gutters. He shares the house with 11 other juniors (some of them fourth-year juniors), at least seven of whom are there now hosting an impromptu party. His eyes wander up the coast towards campus, where Storke Tower juts into the sky like a piston frozen in time. Ethan finds it hard to believe that the blocky clock tower was ever considered architecturally inspiring, even when it was first built. It looks like it's seen better days, like his parents. He guesses they might be around the same age. In fifteen-minute intervals, the clock tower counts down existence, or maybe up? Ethan shivers and looks away, inviting the shadowy ocean surface to flood his thoughts and drown them out.

"Anything left in that piece?" Ethan asks.

"Nah, it's cashed." Paul turns the pipe over to punctuate the statement. Silence ensues as the two friends retreat into their respective wormholes.

"So glad we got the raft operational this semester," Paul says eventually, shifting his weight and gesturing towards civilization. "How many people do you think are over there getting fucked up right now? Thousands?"

"Not as many as Halloween."

"Halloween was crazy," Paul says. Paul slept with his second person ever on Halloween, a friend of a friend in town from UC-Merced. He'd been dressed as Roy from Ted Lasso and she as Keeley. Their entanglement was fated from the moment they identified each other's costumes and began role playing. "Just totally wild," he adds.

Ethan smiles. He knows given the slightest provocation, Paul will launch into the details, followed by his scruples, and ultimately, his indecision about how to feel about the encounter. The airing of Paul's problems is often therapeutic for them both and constitutes a significant component of their friendship. Ethan wishes he could be so straightforward with his issues, just put them out to dry like laundry and then collect them the next day, cleansed of all impurity and ready to try on again. But he can't seem to, they're too stained and gnarled and hopelessly soiled.

"What was her name again?" Ethan asks.

"Milo," Paul responds, his voice acquiring a willing edge. But then his pocket buzzes. Ethan takes in the salty breeze as Paul reaches for his phone. Even though it's only late January, he catches a whiff of spring. It reminds him of his childhood in Monterey, of planting flowers in the backyard with his dad or being chased around by his older sister, the moon-shaped bay always just over the hill. Last week his dad forgot his sister's birthday. Samantha told him this, a worried undercurrent in her voice. It's 3 a.m. in New York, but Samantha could be awake. She's always been a night owl. He hopes she's taking better care of herself since her convalescence back home.

"It's Greggy," Paul says, slipping the phone back into his pocket. "I told him I'd discuss his stolen scooter with him tonight."

"Paul Parfitt on the case."

They each grab an oar from the center of the raft and begin paddling in. They row harder and harder as if under pursuit, their slender arms burning from exertion. The water splashing Ethan's back doesn't feel wet, only weighty. They reach the ribbon of beach in under five minutes. As they pull the raft in, Ethan tells Paul to go on ahead. Paul shoots him a squared-jawed look of parental concern.

"I gotta pee," Ethan says. "And I might just chill here for a few minutes. Get my bearings. I can carry the raft up myself."

They glance up and down the beach in unison. Fifty yards to the left, a young man and woman lean stiffly against the cliffside. Judging by their body language they might be breaking up. To the right, close to where the beach narrows as the coastline approaches campus and the lagoon, half a dozen skinny guys, probably freshmen, wander around like seagulls.

"Alright, I'll see you up there," Paul says, his heel digging into the sand as he turns to go. "We're still studying anthro tomorrow at noon, right? At my place."

Ethan blows air through his lips. It's too early in the semester for an exam, a fact Professor Bourman apparently hasn't grasped, or perhaps is grasping onto with a death grip. Ethan signed up for HIST4A: Ancient History hoping it would be an easy, intro-level elective to go towards his core PoliSci curriculum, and he could lean on Paul, an actual history major, for help. But from day one, the humorless

Bourman, who is himself ancient, has been relentless, almost possessed; like he gets a kick out of force-feeding them material.

"Ugh, yeah," Ethan responds. "Bourman needs to retire, maybe go live in an RV in the desert or something."

"Yeah," Paul says. "I feel bad for the guy. He's like, so clearly unhappy. He's got a reputation for being a crank, but I didn't think it'd be this bad."

"Maybe I'll switch to pass, not pass."

"Yeah, or maybe our studying will pay off and you'll ace the test."

Paul aces most of his exams without much studying, and unlike the other guys in Ethan's complex he doesn't waste a lot of time going through the motions of studying either. Ethan is curious to see if Bourman can dent his friend's GPA.

Paul trudges through the sand away from the water.

"Anything could happen," Ethan calls to the back of his head, but a gust of wind carries his words out to sea.

Left alone, Ethan urinates into a crevice along the steep wall of earth that erodes further into the town every year. Currently a handful of oceanfront properties stand empty, evicted for lack of safety. Literally falling off the cliff, they are a reminder of something, but no one pauses for very long to consider what. Pulling up his hood, he returns to the raft. Carrying it up the couple dozen steps and down the block to their residence suddenly seems an impossible feat. He sits in the sand and admires the waves as they gracefully self-destruct, their cascading repetition the most calming sound in the world. If anything knows how to die, it's a wave.

In the distance, a luminous puddle appears on the water. Ethan rubs his eyes and stares intently. It's as if the bright spot is lit from below; as if rather than setting over the horizon, the sun has shrunk to a few meters wide and been placed on the ocean's surface like a gold coin. He contemplates the phenomenon, which gets him to his feet. The beach is now empty. The couple has broken up, or stayed together, and the buddy group has staggered forth. The Big Dipper sits low in the sky, pricks of light thrust through the canvas of an unknowable universe.

With one foot in the raft, Ethan freezes, giving anyone, or anything, one last chance to deter him. Stepping into the raft and raising an oar, he momentarily attunes to the music emanating over the bluffs—something that sounds like Drake. And then, with the crash of a wave, the connection is lost.

CHAPTER TWO
EL GAUCHO

Denise Pirouet pulls back her flaxen hair, tightens her backpack's shoulder straps, and takes a final bite of a nail as she approaches the student newspaper office for the editorial meeting. Passing the nearly completed Storke Tower—the gray edifice emerges from its cement platform like a cuboid tumor—she scrunches her lips in disapproval. UC-Santa Barbara is such a beautiful campus. Now the powers that be are messing it up, as they seem to mess everything up.

The morning dew burns off the flowers lining the main pedestrian walkway, which reach towards the azure sky endowing the ocean-side campus with a spring eagerness. Students pass by in their long skirts, colorful blouses, khaki pants, and button-downs, looking pleased with themselves, as if they all got laid the night before. After an uncharacteristically rainy spell, Southern California is living up to its reputation again. Nearing the subterranean headquarters where her connection with the sun will be abruptly terminated, Denise picks up a copy of the student newspaper, *El Gaucho*, and checks the date: Monday, Jan. 27, 1969. Before departing her house, she perused the national news in *The Los Angeles Times*: more mudslides along the coast; a new president in office, Richard Nixon, whose appeal to Denise begins and ends with his birthplace being within an hour's drive from hers; continued escalation of the war in Vietnam and increasing protest against it. She scans the *El Gaucho*, which is devoted to the treatment of minority students on campus and minorities within academia—a current flashpoint—and contemplates the relationship between local and national news. If, perhaps, someone perusing all the school newspapers in the country could spot forthcoming national headlines based on what's trending on campuses. Journalists write the first draft of history, as one of her freshman-year professors loved to espouse, but what about the stuff that comes before the drafting? The stuff of ideas and seemingly random connections where human events are outlined before the filling in. It's beyond human ability to document that, even beyond human comprehension. She learns so much every day—takes in so much information—but instead of synthesizing into some greater knowledge or understanding, it feels like it's just piling up, taking up space that might otherwise be valuable.

She pulls a chair out with her long fingers and sits down. Joining the newspaper was supposed to help, and on good days it does, but it also stretches her thin and fills her not with self-worth, but a sense of inadequacy. She feels claustrophobic and it's not just because of the slate-grey office walls now boxing her in. There's a tightness in her chest. She loves the newspaper, but it also weighs her down, constricts her breathing when what she needs is to take in more air. The world turns so fast it's dizzying. Not for the first time, she wonders if she's cut out to be a reporter.

Editor-in-chief Becca Wildman shakes the dark curls from her face and calls the meeting to order. Denise slides the slender paper under her notebook, recrosses her legs, and adjusts her skirt. The clickety-clack of the aging typewriters peters out and the room goes silent aside from a conversation in the photography corner that loosely echoes across the low-slung space. The photographers are always the last to tune in and Becca proceeds without them. Denise assumes the editorial calendar will resemble the previous day's. She expects to shortly depart to work on her feature about the youthful and affable anthropology professor Bill Allen, whose willingness to engage students in counterculture discussions, and even insert his own radical opinions, is making waves across campus—waves the students are eager to surf. But something in Becca's severe stance gives Denise pause.

"Listen up everyone," Becca says. "I just got a call from *The Santa Barbara News-Press*. Apparently, there's a problem at one of the offshore oil platforms. There's some kind of leak, and there may have been an underwater explosion. I don't know how big or how long it's been going on, but from what I can gather the oil is already making its way towards the shore."

Everyone is paying attention now, even the photographers—especially the photographers.

"Obviously the oilmen are trying to limit leaks to the press," Becca says, eliciting a few wincing smiles from the underclassmen. "But we need to see what we can find out. For the time being, I want Denise and Steven to take the lead on this."

Becca glances at Denise before shooting Steven a look. He's sitting ramrod straight in his chair, smiling smugly like he's already won a Pulitzer for his reporting on the unfolding catastrophe. They both nod.

"Great," Becca says. "See me after the meeting."

Denise met Steven when they joined the paper as freshmen two years ago. They've worked side-by-side for most of that time, yet they remain like two ingredients that don't mix well but also don't react much when put in contact. Like oil and water. Denise can't help but judge Steven's prim coif of hair as a stand-in for his personality: sleek, inflated, anal, and a little unconvincing. But the hair also bestows him a pointy edge to lead with, which greatly behooves a reporter, and she gives him credit for not being afraid to stick his nose into things. Her lightly freckled nose, on the other hand, is almost allergic to anything too messy, or, as is often the case in the course of reporting, confrontational.

Denise catches Steven's attention and he smiles at her, lips zipped, just as Becca wraps up the meeting and beckons the two of them over.

"Listen," she says. "I don't know much more than I've already told the staff, but the guy who called this into the *News-Press* said, 'The ocean is boiling.' And frankly, that makes me shudder."

"Who called it in?" Steven asks.

"They don't know," Becca says. "But there's a hell of a lot of oil under the seafloor out there. And what I want to know now is how they're going to plug this leak. Go downtown and see what the buzz is. If this oil starts washing up on the beaches…"

"I've got a friend whose dad works for Union Oil," Steven says. "Maybe I can get something from him."

"Not if your friend's dad wants to keep his job, but it's worth a shot."

With that, Steven decides he's through debriefing. "I'll check in later," he says before heading back to his desk.

"Anyway," Becca continues, watching Steven go with an expression caught between curious and amused. "It's probably best if you pursue separate angles. Denise, you're good at ingratiating yourself. Maybe you could stop by the *News-Press* and see if they need any help. If this story is going to be as big as I think, there'll be more than enough to cover for every reporter in this puny town."

Denise likes the idea, especially since she's getting overwhelmed by the implications of the spill. Emerging from the dimly lit newspaper office, the outside feels different than when she left it a half-hour before. The contented students, picture-perfect landscaping, and jumble of angular buildings now feel small and staged, unsteadily poised between the vast ocean and the ridge of mountains to the east. Usually, she's the one who feels inadequate, but right now, it's her surroundings. She heads towards her anthropology class and arrives early. Seated on a bench across from several rows of overflowing bike racks, she returns to the *El Gaucho*, and lands on an editorial, "The Place is Here, the Time is Now:"[1]

> The purpose of the University, when one gets right down to it, is to serve the people of California. Ask Ronald Reagan, ask any of the legislators, ask any University administrator, and he will tell you that the privileges of the University are a "sacred trust" from the people of California.

This reason, this excuse, is given any time any program which might tend to limit the power of the great white majority is proposed. "The people of California do not approve of this," comes the sanctimonious reply from Sacramento. How does the Governor know? Has he been out talking to all the people, one by one?

Students, faculty, and administrators, please note this point: The University is not serving the needs of almost one-fifth of the people of California at all. Blacks and chicanos make up approximately 17 percent of the state's population, and what do they have to show for it in the higher education system of this state? They are oppressed and harassed people in the "Land Of The Free."

They come to the University to work towards the real emancipation of their people, and they do not find anything here that can help them in their struggle...

Her concentration is interrupted by the enthused yelps of two guys engaged in a hand-swatting exchange; Denise observes the overwhelmingly white river of students heading into the lecture hall for Prof. Allen's anthropology course. The editorial's rhetoric is powerful if a bit clumsy. She wonders if she could have made it stronger. She knows if she'd asserted herself, she could've been the lead editor. But she didn't assert herself. She's a sucker for high ideals and fighting for what one believes in, but what's required to live up to them daunts her. She looks around again and wonders what real emancipation would look like. Some days simply reading the student newspaper makes her heart ache over everything that needs doing and everything else that makes doing things so damn hard. Almost despite herself, her chest rises hopefully as she observes the onrush of students. She spots the guy she's dating and calls out to him.

Leroy snaps to attention at the sound of his name and jogs over to Denise. He looks happy as a dog, his wavy brown hair glistening in the morning light, his pronounced jaw bobbing up and down. Even though he's an inch or two taller than the average guy, and 15 or 20 pounds heavier, he weaves through the crosscurrent of bodies with childlike ease. He embraces Denise and she buttons his top shirt button for him before realizing the whole row of buttons is askew. He unbuttons and rebuttons his shirt as she tells him about the morning meeting.

"Oh my," Leroy says, and Denise can see the gears churning behind his penetrating brown eyes. He's always onto something, always caught up in whatever he's thinking about, often one step ahead of himself and stumbling forward in enthusiasm to catch up with his thoughts. Denise blames this unusually intense disposition, at least for a beachside university, on his San Francisco roots. She intends to inquire about borrowing his car, a mustard-yellow Plymouth Valiant overdue for a trip to the mechanic, to head downtown after class, but what he says next forces her to recalibrate.

"You know my friend from the dorm whose house I went to downtown for his family's weird autumnal gathering? Well, they keep a little fishing boat docked at the wharf. I can ask if we can use it to get a closer look. He knows I can handle it; we took it out together before."

CHAPTER THREE
ANCIENT HISTORY

January 20, 2023
Today was a bad day. Every morning, I look out my car window at the perky palm trees and smiling coastline and tell myself, I'm going to feel like that looks today. And if I can't feel that way, at least I'll act like it. But by the time I arrive on campus, my resolve is already broken. The morning news certainly doesn't help. I can barely stomach NPR anymore. The hosts increasingly remind me of my students, full of indignant, "woke" opinions and a self-righteousness that makes me want to just turn them off—which at least with the radio is an option. And then later, between classes, I read the news online and become even more furious. I can't even visit The Times or The Post anymore, they've become so opinionated and blatantly biased. This anger can't be good for my blood pressure, I remind myself. Take a short walk, I tell myself. So, I stroll around campus, doing my best to look up at the sky, which at least hasn't changed since my days as a student. Although, even then, I can get worked up over all the fuss about climate change. As if we really know what we're talking about. As if it's just about the science. A close look at the actual data should be enough to convince even the laziest scientist that the planet isn't heating up. I mean, there's more polar bears around now than there were 50 years ago. But no, the media buries that information because the media has a climate agenda. I miss Walter Cronkite.

I'd love to tell the students how I feel, and maybe I will one day when I'm finally ready to retire. I know that's what everyone is waiting for; they're probably as tired of looking at my aging face and protruding belly as I am. But I'm still the seniormost tenured anthropology professor and I can still teach a damn good course—I can even keep up with the latest studies. Although, I often think, What's the point? So many of them are mediocre with little hope of making a lasting impression in the field, perhaps a dozen citations at most and the data's not very robust anyway. Makes one wonder how these things get published, although that's obvious enough. Scientific progress is just as subject to external pressures—peer, politics, bias, background—as anything else. And to think I used to give scientists the benefit of the doubt.

But why am I wasting my time writing down this stream of drivel? I've never kept a journal before, never saw the point. I always had something more meaningful to apply myself to. My hand is already sore from writing after only a few minutes, do I need more reason to quit? I definitely don't need to devote more effort to documenting my ever-expanding portfolio of gripes. I'm too old to dwell on that stuff, although of course, I do dwell on it. I can see that. I'm not completely self-absorbed, nor am I senile.

No, I'm writing because of a strange dream I had, a dream in which someone I hadn't thought of in a very long time was once again by my side. For one, this worries me, because I've noticed that after people pass away, they often appear to me in a dream. And even though I'm estranged from this person, I can't tolerate the thought that she might be dead. But now I'm wondering if this morose, agitated state I'm in, triggered by today's youth, today's culture, today's world—and yes, there is irony in using that most reviled campus term of triggering—if all that's not so much the cause of my malaise, but a symptom. If this undesirable future is more connected to my past than I'd ventured to fathom. As you age, the length of your life contracts and you come to understand that much of the past is still acting upon you—in obvious ways, but also subtle and mysterious ones. At least that's how I've been feeling.

I'm not up to writing more details of the dream or even the woman's name. It's been a long day. I've had enough.

• • •

January 23, 2023
I smiled in class for the first time in a long while today and for the most unexpected reason. As I was lecturing about the recent discovery of Queen Nefertiti's tomb and how it relates to Egyptian social anthropology, I observed a chipper young woman pass a note across the aisle to a guy in a tank-top, after which they exchanged a smile. My initial instinct—after wondering why they didn't just text—was to scold them for not paying attention, distracting the class, leeching off society, being spoiled, and any other indiscretions and shortcomings that came to mind. But a distant memory burst into my mind with such force as to cause me to lose my train of thought. The time required to regain it was so long that some of the students eyed me with concern, no doubt praying to themselves that I wouldn't croak right there and then but do them the courtesy of waiting until after class. But I managed to continue lecturing, only permitting myself another reflection, this one so indulgent that I smiled, several minutes later as they watched a brief video.

The memory itself is scarcely more than an image. Junior year of college, in a small lecture hall not far from the one I taught in today, I was in class with…Oh, heck with it. I've got to write her name. If I'm going to gain anything from this painful and painstaking exercise, I've got to shed some of this repression, which grips me like a boa. Denise was her name. I mean, is her name, assuming she is still alive, and I haven't yet worked up the courage to look into that. She was my first love, and, well, my most intense love, although these two descriptors—first and most intense—surely almost always accompany each other.

Who knows if the intensity would've lasted? Nobody knows and nobody ever will.

Anyway, the memory: It must've been the end of January 1969, or maybe early February, because I remember as I accepted the note, I thought it would relate to our discussion prior to class about taking a boat out to investigate the oil spill. Oh, just remembering those days before the spill is surreal, perhaps similar to how Southerners recalled the last days of antebellum America. Everything was about to change, and not just for us or for the greater Santa Barbara community, but across the country. At least, that's where I pinpoint the moment America began its long political and cultural crumbling, which is now cratering so hard that another civil war appears a realistic possibility. The Santa Barbara oil spill was eye-opening for us, and the remainder of my university experience, up through mid-1970, was, frankly, a wild ride, even if I did my utmost to keep my head down in my study books. In some ways it's hard to believe I lived through all that; that the person that experienced it was really me. That the withered, speckled hand I'm looking down at now is the same one that was covered in an oily slick of water while helping clean up the spill's devastation; the same one that pushed recklessly through strangers during the Isla Vista riots; the same one that received that note from Denise.

And as for the note, what did it say? For the life of me I can't remember, but I know it was inconsequential. Simply receiving the precisely folded piece of paper, of brushing fingers with the woman who increasingly transfixed me, is what mattered. Of course, at the time I thought none of this. At the time, well, what did I think? My main memory from that class, aside from anything involving Denise, is that I found the professor to be both effective as an educator and "groovy." Oh, what was his name again...he later became pseudo-famous for his stand against the administration and his role in the riots. Bill Allen, that's it. I can see now that he inspired me to pursue an academic career as well as to fortify my ideals. I used to have ideals. I wonder what ever happened to him. I wonder what happened to everyone from back then, in a way, except for Lonnie. I'm happy to never hear about Lonnie until the day I die.

It strikes me that if my 20-year-old self enrolled in my course now, he'd detest everything about me. Although, I think he'd learn a lot. Still, that's a depressing thought; to think that your younger self would hate you now. Unless you've got reason to dislike your younger self. Which I don't. I do have occasion to, but I feel more pity about the regrettable decisions I made then, or failed to make, than anything resembling anger or hatred. Pity for me then as well as for me now.

I've taken a break and refilled my tea. Hopefully my hand can tolerate another spell of composition before entirely pooping out. I've got another dream I want to document while it's still fresh, a dream that somehow fits into all this, shall we call it, unpacking. One of the first classes I took in college—before deciding I wanted to major in anthropology, before I even knew what anthropology was, before I'd ever kissed a girl, before most of what I now consider my life—was a writing elective. Going into college, I briefly entertained the idea of being some sort of writer for a living. My dad was a salesman and my mom a bookkeeper, and while I loved them, I did not look to them for career guidance. So, I sort of pulled writer out of the air, because, why not? Hollywood was just down the road and look at the crap those people were churning out and getting rich from. I remember telling some of my friends about this pursuit, sort of sounding it out, and while they may have pinched their eyebrows a bit, nobody scoffed or thought it unreasonable.

The writing seminar, which focused on science fiction, was a one-credit affair held once a week in a small, squarish room on the bottom floor of a building off the main campus corridor. I remember thinking, This must be what it's like at those small liberal arts colleges out East. All I recall about the teacher is that he wore a lot of black and was stout and balding. I remember much more clearly what we read: Excerpts from Herbert, Asimov, Bradbury, Huxley, Kafka, even Orwell. I loved it.

Every week, or maybe every other week, we got a writing assignment. Most of what I wrote is long forgotten (and deservedly so), but I remember one prompt, I think it was the final one, to write a story set in the year that you'll be 75 years old. I remember the year being 2023, which I can now confirm, is the year I will turn 75 (assuming I make it to September). The twenty-first century seemed incredibly distant then, and the middle of its third decade truly like a science fiction world. This was several years before we landed on the moon. Some people still didn't even have landlines. The idea of a cell phone was incomprehensible. The details of the plot—which probably barely held together—are lost to the immense chasm in time between now and then, but I do remember my characters flying around in cars, engaging in some kind of telepathy, and living to be several hundred years old. I remember highly intelligent robots and even a human colony on Mars. In short, a lot of things that seemed perfectly reasonable to imagine occurring over the next half century, and not just to me. Of course, later as an anthropologist, I learned that progress is hardly ever so straightforward or predictable, or rapid, and as I look back now it's quite fascinating (that's one word for it) how things have turned out. It's not much of an exaggeration to say the future is not at all how I expected it to be. And in my lower moments, I might even think it's not how it was promised to be. In fact, it's much more disorienting than much of the science fiction I read, which at least attempted to make sense.

And in my even lower moments, I might conclude that this confusion, this burning unease, this disorientation with the way things are oriented, might be more internal than not. Most of the time I'm convinced I've got a problem with how things Turned Out To Be. But actually, I've got a problem with myself; I can't make sense of myself. Why not? Being young makes sense, being old doesn't. Could it be as simple as that? According to Occam's razor, sure it could be, the simpler the better. But—as much as the tech brothers would have us buy into it—humans are not just some amalgamation of data so easily distilled. I am large, I contain multitudes, as a writer much more successful than myself once stated. Life never really made sense; I just didn't used to dwell on that inconvenient fact so much.

In my dream the other night, I inhabited the world I created in that short story so many decades ago, whose outlines I only vaguely remember. But that's all you really need for a dream; your subconscious can fill in the rest. It was a glorious dream. Denise was at my side as we—the young versions of ourselves—navigated by hovercraft a sprawling city of glass towers, verdant greenery, and impeccable cleanliness. Also notable is how at peace I felt, which is very unusual for a dream. Typically, at least for me, in my dreams I'm constantly chasing after something or struggling with some dilemma, but not on this occasion. This dream really was a dream, but also, it was only a dream. I awoke refreshed and even a little uncertain about what was real—when was real—but only for a few seconds. Unfortunately, while history might be up for interpretation, and the future up for debate, the forward passage of time is fixed.

CHAPTER FOUR
GENERATION

Ethan scans the horizon as his heartbeat slows. He swears the Big Dipper isn't at the same angle as minutes before. And there's something off about the water, about the way it absorbs the starlight rather than reflecting it. Something dark and murky that he hadn't noticed before. Breathing in is no longer a salty delight, the air is unpleasant, even noxious. He doesn't trust his senses, it's as if they've gone haywire. He starts to worry he's having some kind of breakdown. Mental illness runs in the family, and he's always assumed it might be running after him, especially since his sister's nervous breakdown. He attempts to piece together the preceding few minutes. He rowed out to the bright beacon in the water with a dream-like determination he hardly believes, as if in a trance. Upon reaching the luminescent blob, he leaned over the raft and stared into a deep well of light. He sensed a storm brewing within the water, like lightning might erupt upward towards the sky. The last thing he remembers is reaching over the rim of the raft towards the water. And after that, a loud noise like a book slamming shut. Then he awoke with a start.

And now, he's in the raft, reclining and with an increasingly severe headache. Everything is familiar, explainable, and yet not. He scooches up to get a better view. The bright spot is a couple dozen yards away and harder to discern, as if it's being ripped apart by sharks. He considers rowing back over to it, but suddenly he's exhausted.

Whatever just happened sapped his energy down to the core. He slumps over and submits to the wave of sleep knocking him out.

He awakens to a bubble of pale light ascending from the horizon to the east, over the mountains. It's beautiful, but the beauty is offset by the same acrid smell invading his nasal passageway. He hears voices, somewhat faint, one male and one female. He doesn't move, worried the voices might be in his head.

"Jesus Christ, this is so much worse than I imagined," remarks the female voice, which is muffled, like it's talking through a filter.

"I know, I almost can't believe it's real," says the male voice. "And we're not even that close to the platform."

"I'm not sure we should go much farther; I'm starting to worry about your friend's boat. And it's getting light out."

"You're right. Not sure what we'll learn pushing through more oily water anyway."

"Hold on," says the female voice, now more clearly and with a degree of disbelief. "What's that floating on the water over there? It looks like some kind of raft."

Ethan tenses. It's unlikely voices in his head would be surprised by his presence.

"You're right," says the male voice. "I think I see an oar, too."

The revving of a motor overpowers the voices. Forcing his damp, achy body up from the floor of the raft, he spots a white boat with a yellow hull and vintage wooden siding about 50 yards away. A young woman standing on the stern gazes towards him. She calls to the guy in the cabin and then waves in his direction. Ethan waves back. The woman comes into view. She's dressed like a mannequin in front of a vintage clothing store. Maybe she lives in one of the co-ops. When the boat is about 20 yards away, the engine cuts. The man joins the woman on the stern. He's wearing corduroy pants and a turtleneck. Ethan decides they must be foreigners, perhaps from a small, Mediterranean country.

The woman cups her hands around her mouth. "Are you OK?" she yells.

Ethan slowly raises a hand and gives a thumbs up.

"What are you doing out here?" the man asks.

Ethan pushes himself up and rows closer to the boat. "I…I rowed out here last night. I thought I saw…something. And then I guess I passed out for a little while."

"You what?" says the female voice.

"I fell asleep," Ethan clarifies.

Shock crosses both their faces. "You fell asleep in the middle of the ocean?" the man asks incredulously. "You must have some sort of death wish."

Ethan can't explain it either, but death wish doesn't strike him as out of the question.

"What's that horrible smell, by the way?" he asks.

"There's been an oil spill," says the girl. "That's why we're out here."

Ethan almost says he didn't think there was offshore drilling anymore, but he stops himself. Maybe an oil tanker crashed into the islands. Maybe the captain had a heart attack or died of some sudden-onset cancer. Those things still require humans to steer them, right?

"Look," says the guy. "We've got to get this boat back to harbor. You'd better come with us."

After a brief hesitation, Ethan paddles over. His arms, sore from rowing and whatever else his body just went through, give out just as the man and woman reach him and pull him and the raft into the boat. Seated on a wooden bench, Ethan begins shivering. The woman sees him eye a canteen and a partial loaf of bread. She offers them to him along with a ragged blanket. He eats and drinks and they both observe the open water, the oil platforms penetrating it, and the faint crest of the Channel Islands beyond. They don't question him further and he's grateful for that.

Before too long, Ethan passes out again. When he awakens, they're approaching the coastline. Like everything else, something about the view of Santa Barbara is off, as if the sun melted it down a little. But he hasn't ever taken it in from this vantage point, so that might be it.

"What's your name?" the woman asks. Ethan tells her his name. The woman's face shows surprise. "Ethan, that's a nice name. I don't think I know any Ethans."

Ethan, who knows at least a half dozen other Ethans, finds this hard to believe. She really must be foreign. And yet, something about the woman is very American, very Californian. He asks her name, and she tells him Denise.

"I'm not sure I've met a Denise before either," he says. The woman smiles and laughs a little, adding, "Well, that's hard to believe." She introduces Leroy, who's busy navigating the small vessel into the docks. They watch Leroy bring the boat in, kill the engine, and tie up.

"It's strange, none of these people knowing about the spill and all the oil out there yet," Denise says. "I don't like being the one to bear the bad news."

"Either way, they'll know soon enough," Leroy says. "I'm sure most reporters would kill for this kind of scoop, though."

His eye catches Denise's and he smiles. Ethan realizes that these two odd ducks are dating. Denise lifting her backpack off the deck reminds Ethan of his study session with Paul later that morning. He needs to cram to have any hope of passing Prof. Bourman's exam. That old bastard. He takes his phone out of his pocket to check the time, but the battery's dead. He interrupts Denise and Leroy to ask the time. Leroy pulls up his sleeve to reveal a stainless-steel watch and says it's almost 8 a.m.

Denise observes Ethan strangely. "Are you a university student, then?" she asks.

"Yeah," Ethan says. "What about you guys?"

They nod and Denise asks him if he needs a ride back to campus. Ethan says that'd be great. Leroy hops out of the boat and helps Denise and Ethan onto the wooden pier. Ethan's legs are rubbery. He walks hunched over behind the two of them. Feeling sturdier as they approach the beachfront, he looks up and his legs go wobbly again. The cars are all classics and the people dressed funnily. He must be on a movie set.

"Hey," he says to Denise and Leroy. They look back. Earlier he overheard them saying maybe he was on drugs, which wasn't inaccurate. "What movie are they shooting here? Something from the 60s?"

Their expressions indicate that they don't comprehend. "They're shooting a movie here?" Denise asks, looking around.

"If they are shooting a movie, it's probably set in the 60s," Leroy adds.

Ethan pulls his phone out of his pocket again and tries, somewhat desperately, to turn it on.

"What's that?" Denise asks. He shoves it back in his pocket. "Oh, nothing."

"Some sort of recording device?"

"Yeah," Ethan says. "But it's broken."

Denise doesn't look satisfied, but she lets it go. They walk along an uneven strip of sidewalk between the beach and a row of palm trees stopping in front of a yellow car that Ethan thinks could've used a better restoration job. Leroy unlocks the passenger-side door and Denise hops in the back. Leroy opens the front door for Ethan, who decides to stop trying to make sense of anything for the time being and just go along for the ride. Maybe this is all a dream, he thinks, his eyelids still heavy from the long night asea.

• • •

Dover O. Sharpe rises before dawn each day. He has a long list to get through to open the Faculty Club on time, and he doesn't like to rush. In those calm, quiet minutes, when only the birds are stirring, he often thinks of his son, three daughters, and six grandchildren. He likes to imagine them waking up, likes to imagine them living even better lives than he has, one day at a time.

He used to think of himself as the maintenance man, but most people refer to him as the caretaker and he likes the implication of that, that he takes care of things, things that people care about. Although they might not always show it. Most of the faculty members treat him respectfully, some hardly notice him, and some are, it must be said, rude. He doesn't mind. He's been around long enough—55 years—to know that it doesn't pay to take things personally. Most people don't mean any harm by the things they do. Although some of what he perceives in students these days, and what he reads about students at other universities like Berkeley, worries him; increased agitation, combined with a rebellious attitude towards power. Not that they aren't justified in demanding change, in wanting to improve things, that's what he wants after all, mostly for his kids and grandkids. He fears the situation could spiral out of control, though, leading to more strife, less progress. He wonders if anyone is really in control. Whenever he worries like this, he thinks of his own children, and rests assured that their fine attributes—respectfulness, loving natures, good work ethics—can be extrapolated to the generation as a whole.

He pauses for a whiff of the morning mist over the lagoon as he gathers the mail at the club's rear entrance, adjacent to the pool and the patio. It's hard for him to imagine a more beautiful scene, at least it used to be before he started reading that new book he found. A grassy hill leading down to the lagoon, and beyond that the ocean. Mighty eucalyptus trees lining the path up to the University Center in the near distance. That's another reason he likes to wake up early, it allows him to appreciate what he has—and gratitude, that's another fine attribute.

The thought reminds him of something he overheard one of the most amiable professors, Bill Allen, say the other day as he read by the pool. Talking to another young professor, Prof. Allen said, "When students at a university in as idyllic a setting as this, with every distraction in the world, start getting pissed off about the state of things, then you know it's real. We're not Berkeley down here. This is a surfing haven. A party school, even. But I sense an awareness growing, really coming on, and if I contribute to that, man, then so be it. I don't want to be like some alien lifeform to these kids."

Dover wanted to continue listening to Bill—the professor insists he call him that—but he had to run inside to help one of the housekeepers prepare for a distinguished guest. Still, those few sentences lodged in his mind. He never went to college and doesn't feel he can relate to what the students are going through. He can't quite comprehend what it's like to possess the wide-open futures they have, and the opportunity to focus, almost exclusively, on learning. Although he knows the students at UCSB aren't always so focused. But they do try, lugging around backpacks full of books and staying up all night to write papers. He can see it in their eyes in the mornings when they pass by the club; there's a certain dry redness that indicates an all-nighter of the studious sort. He can't help but grin when he sees that. Then there's the wet redness, usually from a hangover. Sometimes he smiles at that too, but often he shakes his head in disappointment. He likes to imagine his grandchildren one day making that walk from Isla Vista to campus after a long night, term paper in hand. They'd feel both exhausted and exhilarated, a perfectly fine combination of emotions for a young person to possess.

The sun is rapidly burning away the fog now, ushering in clear views of the pale blue sky and deep blue sea. Dover loves the damp coolness of the fog, and the way it shrouds the landscape in mystery. And when it rises, he's never disappointed with what it reveals. But this morning, his nose is twitching. There's an unfamiliar harshness to the air. He worries it will disturb some of the guests and that they might think it's emanating from the club. He'll have to double check that it's not. He walks to the edge of the property and sniffs again, assuring himself that the prickly stench is coming from afar, and not within—an assurance that isn't very reassuring.

Back inside, shielded from the ominous odor, Dover eats his simple continental breakfast and continues reading *Desert Solitaire*, an odd little book left behind by a philosophy graduate student the other week. Dover loves to read whatever visitors to the Faculty Club neglect to take with them. While some of it is far too technical or dense for him to understand, he always gets something out of it. In a way, he considers this undertaking an informal education. He lives on a state university campus after all, one of the top ones in the country. It makes him feel more a part of the ecosystem.

Reading Edward Abbey's book—and this Abbey is quite a character—Dover can almost feel the heat of the Utah desert scalding his shoulders. The scorching sun in this Arches National Park sounds like nothing Dover's ever experienced—or even really considered—and the idea of it, of the power it has over your body and the way it can dictate your actions, is something he's surprisingly drawn to. The weather in Santa Barbara is so accommodating. He wants to feel this overpowering heat, to succumb to it, and has decided that when he retires, if not before, he will make the trip to Arches. He will become one of the growing number of tourists to the remote area of the country that Abbey so ruthlessly laments. While he strongly relates to the tourists that Abbey pillories, just hoping to get a few days off and see something new—something spectacular even—he sympathizes with Abbey's critique of industrial tourism and relentless growth. He gets the way he so despises all the big cars and wide roads made to accommodate them; he's witnessed many of these roads and the cars they transport like ants on the march take over the landscape during his lifetime, and it hasn't been pretty. And he has an almost innate understanding of Abbey's desire to live simply and naturally. Some days, when Dover's out of sync with the campus vibe, he feels alienated from his surroundings, as if he might be rejected as an outsider. On days when he's beat down like this, he strolls over to the lagoon and hikes along the narrow bluff trails, which offer both isolation and expansive views. At these moments, he feels in touch with something much more ancient and formidable than the university and its inhabitants, older even than the Mission downtown. And as you age, it's nice—necessary even—to connect with things much older and more enduring than yourself.

Dover takes one last sip of his coffee before closing the book and slowly rising from his seat. He can see Storke Tower now that the morning mist has cleared. He's still adjusting to the intrusion of the square column, but he knows he'll get used to it. Soon enough it will seem like a natural part of the landscape, for better or worse. He wonders when they'll start using the bells. When the tower will commence keeping time. That will lend it an air of authority, the gravitas to watch over everything, to assume a stoic figure as the surrounding world passes from one moment to the next. He looks at the clock on the wall. It's just about time to unlock the front door.

CHAPTER FIVE
PROPERTY THEFT

When Ethan doesn't show up for the study session, Paul thinks little of it at first. Seated at the small table on the second-floor balcony off his two-bedroom apartment's main room, he's having trouble thinking much about anything at all. He sips a day-old iced coffee and watches the bikers cruise by, the skaters skate by, and the walkers walk by as he nurses his hangover. There's also the occasional runner, not to mention all the cars, mostly hand-me-down sedans and SUVs, but every so often a glistening Tesla silently slips by. Isla Vista's half-dozen long, straight streets that parallel the ocean and dead end into campus lack adequate sidewalks to accommodate all the non-vehicular traffic, and so function less as car-centric roads than all-purpose thoroughfares.

Thinking of Ethan reminds him of their curious exchange the night before about time. Paul was prepared to spar with Ethan over his hypochondria. He knows that almost like a child, Ethan can't suppress his fear of death, so he finds creative ways to vent it. Paul appreciates this irrepressible urge, finds it refreshingly human. He seeks out unconventional conversation and the best way to do that is to make friends with the slightly unhinged. That's how his friendship with Ethan initially kicked off in the dorms, a shared smirk over something Ethan said, Paul can't remember what, but it cut against the grain. Three years later, they're best friends. Not that they'd ever say that to each other. That'd cross a threshold of intimacy that would almost paradoxically violate the intimacy of their friendship. In friendship, the unsaid matters almost as much as what gets spoken. That's why Paul was surprised when Ethan ventured into the territory of time, and not just time, but encroaching time, the inevitability of death—the reality that they will die. In his mind, that's rarified subject matter, suitable for tripping on mushrooms or when someone close passes away. Ethan obviously knows this, and Paul can't remember him crossing the threshold before, even if it was only a momentary transgression of the norms of male friendship.

Paul played it cool, kept things low-key, acted like because they were young time was on their side. He could've pushed Ethan, seen how far he wanted to take the inquiry, perhaps turn it into an intervention. That wouldn't have been out of character for him. He likes to make people squirm a little, hold them accountable for their words, and their actions too if possible. But he was stoned and couldn't see the point. Out there on the raft, lolling on the surface of such an immense belly of water with its unfathomable depths, death seemed both remote and accessible. Talking about it felt like talking about the air they were breathing. It's better to just breathe it. If Ethan wants to tell him something specific, he'll just have to spit it out.

But now, squinting into the noonday sun, life and death are once again irreconcilable opposites. He can almost feel the seconds of his time on Earth counting down, as if he was just some gussied-up clocktower, his head empty but for a pendulum. Instead of the rays of sun warming his body, they seem to be extracting his lifeforce. He gets up, goes inside, and forces himself to focus on the material for the Ancient History class. Before long he gets the urge to masturbate. This is not surprising, he's unable to press pause on his sexual drive; his body seems to need this release to function properly, like a car requiring a daily oil change. Nor can he go more than a couple days without watching porn, which disgusts him. Watching porn when you've hardly had sex strikes him as almost immoral, and certainly against the laws of nature. But technological progress has done away with so many laws of nature, what's one more? He knows the healthy thing would be to pursue more girls, have more sexual encounters like the one on Halloween, but he doesn't really enjoy the undertaking. The meeting, greeting, flirting, planning, intriguing. The baggage and the collateral damage and the unforeseen externalities. It exhausts him. Which is strange, because he wants it so badly, and also because he generally likes people, but thinking of them as sexual objects puts him off. Unfortunately, it also turns him on. His sexual drive confounds him, it's an endless source of frustration, a reminder of his shortcomings and of his mortality, of the youth he's squandering and of the years and decades ahead in which he'll have to find a way to come to terms with all of it.

He returns to his books, hoping that putting things in the perspective of several thousand years of human civilization will make his dilemmas seem less acute. But no, reading about the Trojan Wars does not diminish the swell of emotion he's feeling, does nothing to disgorge the growing discomfort. If anything, it makes him feel even more shackled to his humanness, at once irrelevant and part of something profound. What he does for the next fifteen minutes doesn't matter, but what he does with his life matters. There's an inconsistency in this attitude, but people are nothing if not walking contradictions.

With a knowing shake of his head, he forbids thoughts of masturbation for the rest of the day. But first, he masturbates. Then, it's back to the patio and the Egyptians and Greeks, and finally he can focus. After a half hour, he takes a break and texts Ethan, *u coming?* Twenty minutes later, his phone lights up. He's certain it's Ethan, but no, it's Greggy asking if Paul can come over to check out the scene of the scooter theft. Paul welcomes the opportunity to focus on an endeavor he feels no guilt about pursuing.

Isla Vista is a campus-adjacent, ocean-adjacent, highway-adjacent community made up almost entirely of students. A geographically isolated student slum that happens to also be scenic as hell. Many students take advantage of this separation from society and remove from societal norms to devise their own schedules revolving around class, partying, hanging out, and maybe working part-time. So basically, they are college students but a little more blessed. Paul has decided to take advantage of the unprofessionalism of the place and fill a niche solving minor crimes. And so far, everyone he's told has taken him at least partly seriously. Because it goes without saying that anything goes in I.V.

Greggy is his third case. The first involved a stolen phone, which was hopeless, and he almost gave up the private detective charade entirely after failing to track down any leads. But he kept advertising his services, usually while partially inebriated, and was offered a second case involving a missing cat. Deploying a handful of strategically placed motion-sensing cameras and bowls of wet cat food, he located the cat. For his efforts, he made several hundred dollars and walked around with a sober buzz for a few days. So, he decided to keep up the low-key self-promotion, and thus caught Greggy's attention.

Greggy, Paul, and Ethan lived in the same hall freshman year on the upper floor of the two-story Santa Rosa building across campus. A large contingent of the hall's residents that year now live with either Ethan in the Del Playa Duplex or in Greggy's standalone house on the far side of I.V., which if you squint at almost resembles a residence in a normal suburban neighborhood. Paul studied abroad sophomore year in Budapest, and rather than attempt to squeeze in with any of his old dorm buddies, he lives with a guy he met in a history seminar on the French Revolution. They still get into heated arguments about Napoleon's legacy, often when they're both raiding the fridge. Other than that, they don't interact much.

Paul heads to Greggy's house and walks right in the door, a privilege reserved for former roommates and current girlfriends. Greggy tosses down his video game control, rises from the forest green couch that's nearly swallowed him whole, and gives Paul a one-armed hug. He sips his energy drink and precariously places it on the overcrowded kitchen island, slips on his flip-flops, and leads Paul back out the front door. Paul observes from the driveway as Greggy rolls up the garage door with a heave of his chest, which is thick and would sit well on someone a decade older than him. But on Greggy, whose legs are skinny as stilts, it makes him appear top heavy. Sunlight floods the room, which looks perfectly in order, meaning just about as disordered as you'd expect in a group house of five college males. Steel metal racks lining the walls overflow with gear for everything from gardening to spelunking, straps hang loose like vines, and weights lay strewn about like a gym had a fire drill. The side of a chair peeks up from a pile of discarded items that past residents didn't care about enough to move.

Greggy steps into the few feet of open space in the garage, kicks the stray parts of a roof rack aside, and gestures towards the side door. "That's where I had it locked up, next to that bike."

Paul approaches the spot and squats, stepping into some decaying pet foot pellets left over from the last time anyone owned a pet in the house. The cable lock is on the ground, cut right through. Paul fingers it. It's not very high quality, and therefore not that hard to cut through.

"The scooter is electric, right?" Paul asks.

Greggy nods.

"And you said the internal-locking mechanism wasn't activated?"

"Yeah, I don't think I had it on. But I did have it locked up."

Paul nods. "So after cutting the lock they could've just rode away on it?"

"Yeah. Pretty hopeless case, right?" Greggy, who's naturally mopey, does a great impression of a hopeless person.

Paul doesn't respond directly but asks if the garage side door is usually locked. Greggy says he's almost positive it was locked, so they must've picked it somehow.

"They?" Paul asks.

"Well, I did find some footprints, I think. You have to walk through that mud spot to get to the door, and it had rained the day before, so it was extra soft. I got a couple photos."

"Cool, I'll check those out in a minute," Paul says as he scrutinizes the door lock. Greggy's mention of the footprints inspires him to more closely inspect the ground around the door, even if any prints have been trampled over several times by now. Bending down, his sunglasses fall from his shirt pocket. Retrieving them from the tall, weedy grass along the garage wall, his hand grazes against something sharp. He yanks it back but then reaches down again more cautiously, picking up what looks like an open flip knife, but rather than a blade, there's a curving hook, almost like a broken fishhook. On the other side of the hand grip there's a long piece of metal with several swivels.

Not even attempting to withhold a smile, Paul presents the item to Greggy. "It's a lock-picking tool."

"Fuckers," Gregg says, holding the silver item in his hands. "Feels, like, old-school."

"Yeah," Paul says. "But also, in great condition."

"Nice find," Greggy says. "That's like a real clue. Not sure where it'll get us though."

"It might not get us anywhere," Paul says. "But it might entice the perpetrators to return."

"You think they're going to come back looking for this lock pick?"

Paul fingers the lock pick, rubbing the sharp end of one of the tools with his thumb. "I think it's a classic, maybe even a family keepsake of some sort. So yes, I think there's a chance."

Greggy nods, then nods more adamantly in response to Paul's next question. "Is it cool if I set up one of my motion cameras out here?"

CHAPTER SIX
EVEN DOONESBURY IS BANAL NOW

January 27, 2023
I'm not sure what's going on with me these days. Long-forgotten memories are being dredged up from the muck that constitutes my subconsciousness on a regular basis and being spliced into my thoughts as if they were movie reels in need of flashbacks. Today's example: After class, I was reading news in my office, attempting to decompress from another unpleasant lecture (I nearly blew a gasket when a student blew a bubble and let it pop—and looked like they enjoyed hearing the pop echo through the acoustically resonant lecture hall). I got drawn into a story about a human skeleton in a barrel being discovered by some unlucky tourists around Lake Powell. It turns out the water is getting so low that murder victims left to rot at the bottom of the lake are now turning up on a regular basis. It's like archeology clickbait, which no anthropologist could resist. I guess my news algorithm is finally getting to know my sensibilities. The article asserted that Lake Powell has reached an all-time low. Well, "all-time low" is a little misleading since up until half a century ago there was no Lake Powell. There was a river, a stunning river at that, and a seemingly endless maze of mesmerizing canyons (at least from what I've heard). But then they dammed it just like every other river in the West with enough water to generate electricity.

I remember reading Edward Abbey's *Monkey Wrench Gang* and getting riled up about what we were doing to these treasured Western landscapes. It's hard to believe, but blowing up the dam as the book's protagonists strive to do seemed like a reasonable approach to me for a few years. Now I see that I let my idealism carry me way too far back then, almost like a fever dream. Luckily one that broke after just a few years and was always pretty limited in scope anyway. I was never on board with the wholesale revolution agenda that took over the left, and nearly became mainstream, before the economy cooled off and people realized they had more pressing matters to attend to. And, it occurs to me, I perhaps had trouble processing my associations with that place—that man-made lake in the middle of the desert—which I tried for so long to suppress, and which are now bubbling up with the force of magma. I maybe mistook the idea of blowing up the dam with blowing up my memories.

Anyway, a half a century later, Glen Canyon Dam and the reservoir it established are as much a part of the southwestern landscape as the Grand Canyon, and many of my students probably think of Lake Powell as a fun place to water ski, nothing more, nothing less. Although it's becoming something less as the water depletes. How unbecoming are those crusty white mineral lines that reveal how far the water level has fallen. Must be a depressing place to visit now, and not just for me—but for everybody.

The point being, reading that article evoked another memory, one I haven't thought of in years: The only time I visited Lake Powell, back when it was still filling up in 1970, was with Denise. I know, I know, all rivers flow to the reservoir of Denise; it does seem that way right now. Even though I lived a rather full life since then—an esteemed career, a wife, raising a boy and a girl—as I look back at that trip, I can see it was a turning point in my life. Some part of me got left behind there, along with the ring. And was I crazy for bringing that ring, for keeping it within arm's reach for days in case the right moment arose before I anticipated? And for expecting Denise to react differently? I was. But we were all a little crazy then. And that's what made America great. We were crazy in love, or crazy adamant about one cause or another, or crazy focused on solving the problems of the future or understanding the past. Now everyone's preoccupied with angry finger pointing but there's no substance behind the fingers. It's all about the pointing and the signaling. About identifying who you are just for the sake of asserting that identity. The tree now matters more than the forest, which, to me, simply seems crazy unhealthy, especially since all the trees are behaving the same way. Nonetheless, there was doubtless a fair share of nonsense back then. I mean, I don't think I could get through a page of an Edward Abbey book anymore without tossing it across the room and cursing it as the rantings of an eco-maniac, and also an egomaniac. At least the man thought for himself though, a quality that's becoming ever rarer as we all donate our brains to the internet. For God's sake, even Doonesbury is banal now.

The stock market took another hit today. I've stopped following my investments too closely. Anyway, I'll be fine. I've got a pension. One thing that's nice about living alone is that my expenses have gone down dramatically, and the kids have finally stopped leeching off me. Another year or two and I really ought to retire. Maybe I'll go visit the grandkids once the market settles. At least, once I finish a draft of my book.

· · ·

February 1, 2023
It's been an eventful 48 hours, to say the least. I came home from a highly satisfying, if a bit over-indulgent, steak dinner two nights ago to find my house had been broken into and my study thrown into chaos. Initially, well, initially I ran to the backyard and called the police. Then, convinced the perpetrators had departed, I cautiously reentered the house and surveyed the damage. Aside from my study, only a few drawers and cabinets had been accessed, and most of the house looked to be in order. Curious, for sure, but I'm not harboring anything of great value, so not too surprising that a criminal would leave empty

handed. Although I couldn't shake the thought that they must've taken something, if only to make the risky endeavor worthwhile. Only upon reviewing the scene with partially fresh eyes the next morning did I notice what had gone missing. And boy, I would never have guessed.

I'd picked up an old photo album that had been tossed aside during the raid, one of those fake leather ones with the three rings. Paging through it casually as I went to reshelve it, I noticed a half-dozen photos missing. Now, the photos in this album are about twenty years old, from just before everything went digital, and they are family photos, featuring me, Gabe, and Laurel (my ex-wife was holding the camera). The captions underneath the missing photos, for which I also have my ex to thank, describe one of our family trips to Arizona to visit Aunt Mira. We'd stopped for a night in Flagstaff and the ex took advantage of the soft high-desert light to snap some flattering portraits.

I can't for the life of me guess what someone would want with photos of me and my kids. To be honest, I barely want them. I've never been much of a sentimentalist; I've rather always avoided nostalgia like the flu. And anyway, there's no shortage of photos for that rare occasion when I do want to look back, or, more likely, show off my family to someone else. Ideally, someone who doesn't know the full extent of how ostracized we've all become. This theft is certainly a mystery, and one that will most likely remain unsolved. If the photos weren't so personal—if, say, landscape photos had gone missing—then I'd be ready to write it off as incidental. As it stands, it seems there's got to be a reason behind it. Possibly one endangering me. And perhaps even my family.

This invasion of privacy has seriously disturbed me, to say the least. I live in the hills, and while my small house is not along any main thoroughfare, it's possible criminals of the everyday variety might target it if they were surveying the area. For one, I've let my alarm system lapse. And my door locks are nothing special. So, another thing for me to take care of—increase the security of my residence. Santa Barbara is no longer safe from the crime wave sweeping the nation. I remember back in Isla Vista…here I go again…maybe I am becoming a nostalgic person. Anyway, we often used to leave our doors unlocked. I'm sure that's no longer the case there. I'm sure crime there is much, much worse now, as it is everywhere.

Another surreal thing about the past 48 hours—I relayed this experience to my class. I could discern their amazement at my personal anecdote by the stunned looks on their faces. At least they were paying attention. Not all of them, of course. There's a few who'd find a way to zone out a magnitude 8 earthquake. In my defense, I didn't present the story as a diatribe against lazy, drug-addled youth, California's homeless crisis, or the disappearance of neighborliness. In fact, I attempted to inject it with some humor, pausing on the part about what got stolen and wondering aloud, Who on Earth could want such a thing? This happened about two-thirds of the way through class; I segued to it during the discussion of mummy tomb robbing. Which in itself was somewhat humorous. I have to admit, the atmosphere in the room lightened after this spontaneous outpouring and I rather enjoyed the remainder of the hour. Quite a pleasant surprise, considering I'd been dreading teaching the class after getting so little sleep and already being on edge.

Then, after class, yet another curious thing happened. A student named Paul, who's come to my office hours once or twice in the past, and who seems to have a decent head on his shoulders, approached me and asked if I had motion cameras installed at my house. I told him no, and then immediately wished I did. Sometimes technology can serve a purpose, rather than just creating more hoops to jump through and making everyday tasks less intuitive. He told me that was too bad and that he could recommend some for me if I wanted. Then he asked if I knew how they'd entered the house. I told him the police said the locks had been picked. He seemed to process this for a long moment. I thought he was going to ask another question, but instead he thanked me and offered a nice condolence for what I'd been through. At that moment, I swear, he reminded me of my younger self. The thought gave me goosebumps, as if maybe Denise would walk around the corner the next minute. Time really is playing games with me.

Before departing, he added that his friend Ethan had been too sick to make it to the exam and that he hopes to schedule a make-up test. At that, I stiffened and told him that it's his friend's responsibility to look after his own affairs. Then this young man, Paul, said he knew that, and a worried expression crossed his face. And I daresay, one crossed mine, too.

CHAPTER SEVEN
THE CULTURE IS SICK, BUT HOPEFULLY IT'S NOT TOO BAD FOR CIVILIZATION

Denise turns towards Ethan in the backseat, a question half formed on her lips, as Leroy eases the Plymouth Valiant onto Embarcadero del Mar in the heart of I.V. But seeing his mouth agape, a different question emerges.

"Hey, are you alright?" she asks.

Ethan's distant stare zeroes in on her wide, curious eyes. "Ummm, yeah," is all he can muster.

"Where do you want to be let off?" Leroy asks, adjusting the rearview mirror.

"Oh, just…I'll walk from wherever you're going." A perfectly reasonable response for a town as compact as I.V.

"Sure," Denise says, still craning her head around. "We're just down Trigo. Are you sure you're OK though? You look a little pale."

"Yeah, yeah," Ethan says, as much to convince himself as Denise. "Just a little dazed and confused."

"I like that," Denise says. "Dazed and confused. I think I feel the same way after that trip out to the oil. At least I would if I wasn't so upset about it. You must also be exhausted, too. Even that short boat ride took it out of me."

Ethan nods his agreement as Leroy brings the car to a halt alongside a compact, brown-shingled bungalow occupying a corner lot. Ethan thinks he must really look out of sorts, because they both insist he come inside for a drink of water and maybe a nap. Fair enough, he muses, they did find him floating aimlessly on an inflatable raft in the middle of an oil-slicked ocean. He's surprised they accepted his flimsy explanation of having rowed out overnight and fallen asleep, but also, it's the truth. In their position, he would've called the police, or maybe a hospital. Denise and Leroy seem at once more mature than him and more innocent.

Getting out of the car feels good. He's back in touch with the ground. That familiar Isla Vista air, tinged with salt, dust, and that mild aroma of semen put out by some horny budding tree in the first part of the year revitalizes him, even if it is a bit more acrid than usual. He's hesitant to venture out but also eager to be on his own. Just as he's about to decline their hospitality, a disheveled figure emerges from the garage next door. Denise and Leroy, so attuned to their puzzling new friend a moment before, lose interest in Ethan and instead fixate on the glowering man with an oily mop of dark hair and an untrimmed beard, who trudges by them with a heavy step. Nobody says a thing until Ethan breaks the silence.

"Wow, serious Charles Manson vibes on that one."

"Who?" Denise and Leroy respond in unison.

"Never mind," Ethan says, realizing he expected they might not get the reference, that maybe he was testing them. He decides to accept their hospitality, if only out of increasing curiosity "Fine, I'll come in for a drink, but then I've got to get going. I'm already late for a study session."

When Denise asks what class, he responds, "ancient history."

"Oh, that's sounds interesting," she says. "I love history. Who teaches it?"

"Professor Bourman," Ethan says. "A real hard ass. I also thought it'd be a fun class, instead it's turning into a slog."

With his key in the door, Leroy turns around, a peculiar expression on his face. Denise also looks taken aback.

"Bourman?" she asks. "That's Leroy's last name. Leroy—did you know there's a professor here with your last name?"

Leroy now looks peeved. "What are you talking about, man? I'd know if there was a Bourman in the history department, I can assure you."

On his heels, Ethan thinks fast. "Oh, sorry, did I say Bourman. I must've just seen your name on something in the car. It's Parfitt. Professor Parfitt."

The downturned curve of Leroy's mouth is suddenly unmistakably that of his professor's. And the way his shoulders slouch into his movements—he's watched this person lecture for hours, from within a different body, much altered by years of heavy use, but also, in essence, the same. Ethan does his best to mask the sinking feeling in his stomach with an apologetic expression. "As we've already established, I'm pretty out of it."

"Yeah," Leroy says, still looking unconvinced. "You must be fried."

Proceeding with caution, as if guarding a senior from falling and breaking their hip, Denise accompanies Ethan into the house, which is sparsely furnished and messy, as expected of an I.V. dwelling, but with a conspicuous lack of screens. Ethan sits on a firm couch, downs a glass of water, and does his best not to stare with astonishment at Leroy. Leroy and Denise, satisfied that Ethan is recuperating, return to the topic of the unfriendly neighbor.

"Actually," Leroy says, "We had a decent discussion the other night after he finally turned the music down. He's got some far-out ideas about government spies embedded within the student body and the rise of the police state, but after a few beers I managed to steer him to more neutral territory. He's like obsessed with the Beatles."

"He's just so creepy," Denise says, scrunching her button nose. "I can't get past that scowl."

"Well, I'm pretty sure he's harmless," Leroy says. "Although some of his friends give me the heebie-jeebies. I haven't seen them around for a few days though."

"There's something off about that house," Denise continues. "Hopefully they move out soon. It's two guys, right?"

"Yeah," Leroy says. "Russell and his diminutive sidekick, Lonnie."

Feeling himself drifting off, Ethan jumps up from the couch as if awakening from a bad dream. He needs to get back out in the open. He thanks them for the water and Denise inquires again to make sure he's OK.

"I'm fine," he says. "I learned my lesson, don't pass out on a raft in the ocean."

He immediately regrets drawing attention back to the circumstances under which he was discovered. Denise winces a bit, then asks about the raft, which is still back in the boat, and what they should do with it.

"Oh shit," Ethan says. "I'll, um, can I get back to you about that?"

Denise and Leroy exchange a glance, and Leroy nods slightly.

"Sure," Denise says, pulling out a pencil and paper from her bag. "Here's my number at the newspaper. Just give a call and we'll figure something out. Or stop by. I'm usually around in the morning before ten or in the late afternoon."

Ethan takes the paper, folds it up, thanks the two of them profusely and heads outside fully aware that he's leaving a trail of concern and confusion in his wake. He wanders down the street towards downtown, everything so surreal it's almost like he's floating. Then his stomach growls angrily and his head starts feeling light, like it might just detach and lift off his body. He walks into a sandwich shop and orders a hoagie loaded with cold cuts. The impossible truth hits him as the clerk hands him back his credit card and asks, "What is this? Some kind of joke?"

Ethan responds with his own question, but he knows perfectly well what the clerk means. His face is contorted in perplexity, as if it can't quite process the sensory inputs it's receiving, which suits the moment fine.

"For one," the freckled cashier says, "We don't take credit cards. Also, this says it expires in 2027. That's like, 60 years from now."

So there, someone said it out loud. Said what he suspected about halfway through the twenty-minute drive from the Santa Barbara marina to Isla Vista. What he could no longer ignore, as hard as he tried, unless he fixed his gaze exclusively on the sea or the sky or the mountains. Everything else was unsettling. Everything else was part of that old movie set, but no movie set occupies an entire county. Entering Isla Vista restored a slight sense of familiarity. The place has always been stuck in its own sort of time warp. Some of the housing appears much newer than he recalls, while other lots are bare, as if what sat atop them the night before has been washed away by some tidal wave of the fourth dimension.

But even more urgent than figuring out what the hell is going on is eating the hoagie. With the bucktoothed clerk eyeing him suspiciously, he reaches into his wallet and thankfully finds a few bills. The sandwich costs $1.85. He takes two dollar bills out, slyly looks at the years they were printed, 2019 and 2017, and holds his breath as he hands them over to the cashier. The kid is distracted by some passing ladies in skirts, and he doesn't more than glance at the currency.

A few minutes later Ethan is stuffing his face on a sidewalk bench cursing his luck but also feeling unusually, almost insanely, invigorated. His thoughts seem to tear down the middle almost as soon as they emerge, reforming in ridiculous permutations. He searches for a way to describe what he's experiencing, some kind of manic episode perhaps. He's not quite ready to believe he's gone back in time, but he's also not able to deny it. Could it be true that, for once, he's defeated time? He chews with even more vigor as a sense of invincibility overcomes him. But it's quickly usurped by a dark wave. Like the oil bubbling to the surface, he doesn't belong here. "Fuck me," he says aloud. He reaches for his phone, as everyone from his time does when in need of diversion, but it's as dark as the oil.

Flailing around desperately for something, anything, to ground him, he notices a stack of *El Gaucho* newspapers beside the bench. He's not familiar with the publication, but there's a clear connection to the university, as the UCSB mascot is a gaucho. A gaucho is an Argentine cowboy as far as Ethan understands it. A strange choice for a mascot and one that might come up for replacement before too long, he thinks, along with the wave of other mascots relegated to the history bin for their lack of cultural tact. *El Gaucho* looks like it should be the student newspaper, and flipping through a copy, it's obvious it is. At some point, he supposes, the paper must've been renamed *The Daily Nexus*, which is what he's familiar with. Well, mostly he's familiar with the crossword.

Shoving the full width of the hoagie into his mouth and chomping down, Ethan watches students stroll towards campus, the men with their shirts tucked into jeans, khakis, or corduroys, the women in checkered shirts and colorful blouses paired with and denim and pencil skirts. The scene is so pleasant, he entertains the notion that maybe he's died and gone to Heaven. Then he looks at the date on the paper. February 4, 1969. His mother's birthday. The actual day she was born, somewhere in the suburbs of Seattle. The reaction this triggers is so powerful that it short-circuits, leaving behind a raw numbness for him to grapple with, like he's just waking up from an operation.

He continues chewing and swallowing, strangely fixated on the phenomenon of the sandwich turning from something hand-crafted for human pleasure and sustenance into saliva-drenched mush before heading down his esophagus for a fateful encounter with the billions of bacteria lining his stomach, waiting to digest it into nourishment and waste. As the last bite inches its way into this unceremonious journey, Ethan's intestines relax. The situation is urgent. All that alcohol and marijuana and time travel must be evacuated to make space for the sandwich. He pushes up from the bench, his backside clenched, and heads towards campus, where he imagines there must still (Still? But this is the past…) be a network of public bathrooms, one of which he can't wait to meet.

• • •

The bulk of his responsibilities done for the day, Dover heads down to the lagoon with his book, *Desert Solitaire*. He can't seem to get enough of Abbey's colorful descriptions of the bleak, bewitching desert, and the desolate yet abundant life he leads there as a park ranger in a remote section of Arches. The words seep into him, altering him at the cellular level and heightening his senses. Seated beside a stunted pine on a bluff overlooking the kelpy beach, he relaxes into his surroundings. He only intended to read for a few minutes before returning to the faculty lounge to tidy up and prepare dinner, but becomes fixated on a certain passage—more intellectual than most—reading it over and over, trying to comprehend its meaning but also just appreciating its rhythm.

Cultures can exist with little or no trace of civilization; and usually do; but civilization while dependent on culture for its sustenance, as the mind depends on the body, is a semi-independent entity, precious and fragile, drawn through history by the finest threads of art and idea, a process or series of events without formal structure or clear location in time and space. It is the conscious forefront of evolution, the brotherhood of great souls and the comradeship of intellect, a corpus mysticum, The Invisible Republic *open to all who wish to participate, a democratic aristocracy based not on power or institutions but on isolated men—Lao-Tse, Chuang-Tse, Guatama, Diogenes, Euripedes, Socrates, Jesus, Wat Tyler and Jack Cade, Paine and Jefferson, Blake and Burns and Beethoven, John Brown and Henry Thoreau, Whitman, Tolstoy, Emmerson, Mark Twain, Rabelais and Villon, Spinoza, Voltaire, Spartacus, Nietzsche and Thomas Mann, Lucretius and Pope John XXIII, and then thousand other poets, revolutionaries and independent spirits, both famous and forgotten, alive and dead, whose heroism gives to human life on earth its adventure, glory and significance.*

To make the distinction unmistakably clear:

Civilization is the vital force in human history; culture is that inert mass of institutions and organizations which accumulate around and tend to drag down the advance of life.

Eventually, he gives up on it, unsatisfied. He's never much considered the distinction between culture and civilization, and he's not sure either one has much to do with him, or that he has much to do with either one. He concludes the chapter, which finishes with another high-minded digression into star constellations, and puts the book down, excited to see that the next entry returns to the desert and an adventure through something called The Maze.

By the time he gets up, the sun is millimeters away from dipping under the horizon. The way the ocean seems to swallow its glancing rays disturbs him, and he's also identifying that unpleasant odor again. But what to do? Returning to campus, he takes a less direct trail bordering the interior of the lagoon. At sunset, dozens of birds including his favorite, egrets and herons, flock to the lagoon, and this inward-facing trail offers a superb and sheltered view of them. About a quarter of the way along the trail, 30 yards from the opening in the foliage where he likes to bird watch, he hears a moan that halts his advance. Another person's inhaling and exhaling overlays his labored breathing. Looking around, he sees a young man lying on his side just a few feet into the brush and easily visible from the trail, his face covered by the hood of a sweater. Initially, Dover thinks it must be a drugged-out hippie, and that maybe he'll alert the campus police. But like the sea's opacity, and the air's odor, there's something unfamiliar about the boy, and he decides to speak up.

"Excuse me," he says loudly and formally, leaning over the edge of the trail and resting his hand on a juvenile oak tree. Alarmed, the young man hurriedly pushes himself into a seated position.

"Sorry to, um, disturb you," Dover continues. "But I thought I should check and see if you're alright."

The young man considers the question. "No, not really," he says at length. "I'm not really sure what I'm doing here."

"What do you mean?"

Again, the boy takes longer to respond than would seem necessary. "I guess I'm not sure what to do next."

"Are you lost?"

This time an affirmative response follows. Without hesitating, Dover asks if he needs a place to rest. The young man closely observes him for the first time.

"What do you have in mind?"

"I'm the caretaker at the Faculty Club," Dover says. "I could perhaps put you up in one of the spare rooms—we have some extra quarters—for the night."

"Oh my God, that would be amazing," the kid says, standing up and seemingly equipped with a new store of energy. Then he looks down at himself and his dirty clothes. "I know this looks pretty weird—and trust me, it is weird—but if I could rest and maybe shower…" He trails off.

"I can offer that, sure," Dover says without hesitation.

"I only have a few dollars on me. That is, unless you accept credit cards from the future."

"Excuse me?"

"Never mind. I'm wondering if I'll need to pay."

"Oh, no. The Faculty Club isn't any kind of hotel. This is just a favor. You look like you could use one." Dover thinks of his own kids and how happy he is to be their father. "What's your name by the way?"

"Ethan," the kid responds, reaching out a hand.

"Mine's Dover."

The next morning, the whir of a helicopter passing overhead awakens Ethan from a dream in which he's trying to take his father to the doctor but is being waylaid by a variety of outlandish obstacles and interruptions. Sitting up and rubbing his eyes, it takes him a moment to recall how he arrived in this cabin-like room, with its solid-wood bedframe and built-in shelves. Urgent voices and footsteps emanating from down the corridor compel him to get up and put on the clean clothes Dover left on the dresser. Observing himself in the bathroom's small, round mirror, he thinks he looks like he's part of the movie now—but what is his part to play? Noticing some hair mousse on the counter, he finger-combs his hair across his forehead. He smiles at his reflection and thinks there's nothing to suggest he's an interloper from a future generation.

As he's about to exit the room, someone slips a newspaper under the door. He picks it up and reverses into the sturdy little desk chair. Before he can check the date to verify that it is indeed the day after February 4, 1969, because who knows anymore, the headline grabs his attention: "Giant Oil Slick Spreading In Santa Barbara Channel."

He wonders for a moment about the coinciding timing of his arrival and the spill. Could it mean something? He'd forgotten entirely about the spill, but now remembers it vaguely. Images of struggling birds slathered in oil come to mind. He recalls that the spill was very bad, but just how bad he doesn't know. Bad enough that they don't drill for oil on the California coast anymore, anyway. A sharp pain shoots through his forehead. He needs some coffee, and then, like everyone else, he wants to go see the oil. He decides to head over to the newspaper office to check if Denise is around. It's amazing, the restorative power of a good night's sleep. It might be the most rejuvenating rest he's ever had, almost more like a period of hibernation. More encouragingly, he can identify no potentially cancerous aches or pains, no unusual twinges in his joints or worrisome rough patches of skin or rashes.

On his way to the complimentary breakfast, he sees Dover, who breaks from his duties and greets Ethan, asking him how he feels. Ethan says like a new man, and then holds up the newspaper.

"Yeah," Dover says with a frown. "Looks like our industrial greed and failure to properly account for potential consequences is already causing us major trouble. The culture is sick, but hopefully it's not too bad for civilization."

Ethan is taken aback; not what he expected to hear from the genial caretaker, but also right on. He wants to tell Dover about climate change but can't figure out a way to do it without getting into the whole time-travel thing. "Yeah," he says. "Seems like a pretty big deal."

Dover shakes his head remorsefully. "Oh, I don't doubt it."

"I think I'll go see if I can get a closer look," Ethan says, eyeing the trays of food. "Is it OK if I stay another night?"

Dover is distracted by the arrival of a youngish professor with blond hair down to his shoulders who's clearly outraged over the news of the oil spill and whose voice carries across the room. He tells Ethan that should be fine, but that hopefully he can "find more long-term accommodation" soon. Ethan hopes so too, and he's already formulating a plan to ensure that accommodation exists in the year 2023. But first, he's got to lay eyes on this catastrophe. He's almost thankful for the oil gushing from the seafloor and blanketing the coastline, although he knows that's completely selfish. It's unexpectedly exciting to be present for an event of this magnitude, especially when bestowed with the knowledge, if only loosely, of how it's going to play out. He wishes he'd paid more attention to the history of the place he's called home for almost three years. He thinks of Paul. Paul would know like ten times more about the spill than he does. But nothing compares to living through it. By the time he finishes breakfast, he's buzzing with anticipation as he departs the Faculty Club into a world not only unrecognizable from the time before he encountered the portal, but from the day before when he'd hopelessly thrown himself into the decaying leaves and damp dirt of the lagoon at wit's end. He wonders if these manic highs and lows are similar to the ones his sister described the year before when he visited her in New York. If he could have one person by his side right now, it would be her. He imagines she'd appreciate witnessing the spill more than he would; she's the one working towards a low-carbon future. She might like to take a few swipes at the oil.

CHAPTER EIGHT
CRAZED, WACKO KIDS

As he's biking home from campus for lunch, Paul's phone dings, notifying him that the motion camera outside Greggy's house has been triggered. Pulling over to the side of the bike path, he checks the still image preview in the app. A skunk just skuttled across the side yard. In the two days since he installed the cameras, Paul's been pinged by a squirrel, a possum, a cat, a mouse, and one of Greggy's housemates taking a piss. A half-hour later, he's sitting on his balcony eating lukewarm leftover spaghetti when he receives another notification. He finishes scarfing down the final remnants of the pound of pasta before clicking open the app. The still image shows two college-aged guys in funky clothes and overdue for haircuts standing near the door engaged in what, from their body language, appears to be a heated discussion. These two guys are definitely not Greggy's roommates, and they definitely look sketchy. Paul leaps up from the table and jets out the front door with his bike, doing his best to ignore the heavy load of carbs weighing him down.

He stops half a block short of Greggy's house and props his bike against a parking sign. Setting off at a run, he doubles back, unlocks the U-lock, and slips it around the bike's crossbar and the signpost. He doesn't want to create another case for himself that he won't be able to solve. Looking up, he spots the two guys from the video frame leisurely walking from Greggy's house towards a small park across the street, where two scooters await them. One of the scooters has a grey stem and a blue deck—Paul is certain it belongs to Greggy. Brazen bastards. This would be a good occasion to have an actual badge, and some actual authority, Paul laments as he jogs towards the two guys, who look like they might be part of a folk-rock band.

"Excuse me."

The odd duo freeze in the middle of the street.

"What were you doing at that house?"

An intense exchange passes between the two shaggy characters. The taller one responds.

"What's it to you, bud?"

Paul has a little mantra he deploys sometimes when he's feeling overwhelmed: Don't be a pussy. He says it now, under his breath, before asking, "Where'd you get those scooters?"

That gets their attention, and after another look, they dash across the street and down a dirt path bisecting a grassy strip that connects to the park. Paul repeats his mantra and gives chase. The shorter guy, who is quite short, is lugging a worn leather shoulder bag that's disrupting his balance. He trips over himself and careens to the side of the path, tumbling over. Paul catches up to him as he's getting to his feet and grabs hold of the flap of his bag. The taller guy circles back and comes to his friend's aid. He's fuming with anger and his wild eyes give Paul a fright. Paul yanks on the bag and the strap tears a seam. Seeing it rip open, the short guy lets the bag drop from his shoulder and fall to the ground.

The three of them encircle the bag, which judging by the vehemence of the stare down he's engaged in now, Paul decides must contain something important. Paul eases up a bit and backs away, weary that the two guys, who seem increasingly crazed and possibly on drugs, are harboring weapons. And he's right, the small guy pulls a knife from his boot and bares his teeth through thick stubble. He's trying to intimidate, but Paul senses doubt behind his eyes. The three of them remain tense and poised for action. Paul notices the guys smell strongly of the sea, like they went surfing in their clothing. In general, they could use a thorough washing. Looking down, he sees a photo of a man and what looks like his son and daughter has slipped from the bag's interior onto the grass. They're posed in front of a hillside of stout evergreen trees. Paul flinches. He knows the man. It's his professor, Dr. Bourman. Recalling the professor's uncharacteristic personal anecdote from class, Paul realizes these two sleazebags must be the guys who broke into Bourman's house and targeted his photo album.

Taking advantage of Paul's momentary distraction, the smaller one snaps up the bag and they take off towards the park. Paul stays put. He's not up for a knife fight, and anyway, he's no longer so concerned about Greggy's scooter, even if he could use the reward money. He watches as they mount the scooters and zip away across the park towards the opposite block, where they turn left and are soon out of sight. He smirks at their unnaturalness on the scooters, which they ride with a graceless recklessness suggestive of an overeager kid learning to ride a bike.

Paul nearly departs without scanning the area for anything left behind, but he catches himself, disappointed at his near display of amateur sleuthing. Squatting down near where the bag fell, he picks up a small piece of paper. An address is scrawled in cursive on one side: Denise Pirouet, 7479 Merle Drive, Palm Desert. Neither the name nor the address mean anything to him, but he knows who he wants to ask about it.

He walks his bike home, his mind running through various scenarios, none of which lead to anything very promising. Looking down Camino del Sur as he crosses the street, he catches a glimpse of the ocean and thinks of Ethan. He hasn't heard from his friend in almost three days. He should at least inform him that he told Prof. Bourman he was sick. He's about to walk over to Ethan's duplex on Del Playa when he remembers the motion camera footage. He needs to see what happened in those few minutes it took for him to bike over.

The motion camera came equipped with a crappy microphone. When Paul tested it, he could scarcely make out what he said, which was unfortunate, but he doubted much of significance would be uttered in the side yard along Greggy's garage. Back at his house reviewing the footage with the volume maxed out, he wishes he'd invested in a halfway decent recording device. Another amateur move. In the video, the two guys pore over the ground, clearly looking for something, which Paul knows to be the lock pick they left behind. The taller one becomes agitated when they can't find it and they spend several minutes bickering. Then they waste another few minutes urinating. If not for these delays, they would've been long gone before Paul arrived. The audio is fuzzy, like a radio station at the outer limit of its range, and Paul can only make out a small portion of what they're arguing about. There's something about the ruling class and demonic powers, something about the ocean, a name that sounds like Russell, and he swears they're also talking about time travel. He thinks maybe they're arguing over the merits of a movie or film. Then they both lean on the garage and the mic picks them up better.

"Let's not screw around here anymore, it's too easy to get into trouble—and then what?" says the shorter one. "We know where Leroy lives, and we know where Denise lives. That's enough. And we've got the photos. We have an extra lock pick anyway."

"Yeah, I know, Lonnie," says the tall one. "We can scram from this spot, sure. But don't you just want to explore a little more? Maybe try to score some weed…see what it's like here?"

"No, not really. I don't want to upset you, man, but this place bugs me out, Russell. Anyway, I think the hole is shrinking. Remember how it was smaller last time? Do you want to get stuck here? If we stay much longer, I'm worried someone will find the canoe we stashed."

"You are such a party kill," Russell says. "But we do have what we came for, and we're swimming in dope back home anyway." Russell laughs so hard he coughs. "I'd love to see what the ladies are like, but you're a natural female deterrent, so that'd be pointless as hell."

Russell runs his hands through his greasy hair. Paul can almost see the dandruff gathering on his shoulders in little white pixels.

"If I really had my shit together, I'd come back with some Beatles paraphernalia and make a killing off it," Russell says. "But I can't afford to get too distracted from our main undertaking—spread yourself too thin and you might disappear. Right, my man?"

"Sure, Rus," Lonnie says. "Best to stay focused."

Then the two of them start towards the park, which is where they encounter Paul. Paul shuts his computer, even more confused than before. On his way to campus to see if he can catch Prof. Bourman, or Leroy as the Woodstock lookalikes call him, he stops by Ethan's duplex. Ethan isn't around and the roommates are also getting worried, having not seen him since the night of the party. And the raft isn't anywhere to be found either.

CHAPTER NINE
WHEN YOU'RE OLD, EVERYTHING STARTS TO SEEM TREACHEROUS

Feb. 3, 2023
I met with Paul again today and what he told me, if I choose to believe it, is, well, confounding to say the least. My intuition is to trust Paul, and my research into his academic record reinforces this hunch. He's a straight-A student and he's not coasting through by taking only the easiest classes, clearly demonstrated by the fact that he enrolled in my Ancient History course. I graded his exam myself, in fact—shocking the T.A. with my request in the process—and he did quite well. His responses indicated a level of critical thinking far above most of his peers.

But that's just it. He's one of them, these Gen Z or whatever kids whose attention spans are shot and who seem several years behind the maturity of my generation at the same age, a gap that I fear won't close any time soon. I don't totally blame overprotective, hovering parents or the brain-zapping qualities of the internet and all the crap on TV for this generational shortfall. That is to say; it's not all nurture, there's also nature. I mean, who knows what cocktail of harmful chemicals we're ingesting these days, and in what concentrations. And we can't even begin to fathom how the consumption of this modern detritus is affecting human growth and development. I read that sperm counts are way down, and that girls are hitting puberty much earlier, and that's just the obvious stuff—the low-hanging scientific fruit that all the mediocre scientists holed up in university basements love to step on each other's toes to publish first. And then there's all these trans people. I mean, that's not natural. They're not natural. They're in even more trouble, developmentally, than the rest of their age group. Of course, nobody can say anything like that anymore or they'll be canceled, especially anyone like me held captive by a university. Sometimes I worry I'll be accused of doing something inappropriate for the mere fact that I'm old and white, to get back at me for my privilege, or however you want to justify it. That's the real prejudice problem now, against white people, especially the older male ones. I see it everywhere I look. Cleary, the solution to all this is to devote more taxpayer money and government resources to making sure anyone can use whatever bathroom they want.

Ok, breathe, Leroy. You're getting sidetracked. With everything going on, the disturbing dreams and the break-in, I'll admit, I've lost my bearings a bit. If I don't place some trust in Paul—if I write him off as another messed-up kid to keep at arm's length—I might end up even more untethered. Frankly, what he told me would be pretty outlandish to fabricate, and I'd have to worry about his state of mind and, who knows, he could be one of the criminals. But that seems paranoid. Whatever the case, I won't be able to move on from the information he gave me, so I might as well give him the benefit of the doubt. Right?

Maybe getting it down in writing will help. Earlier today, around four in the afternoon, Paul came by my office. Putting aside the academic paper I was reading, which was starting to disgust me with its unsubstantiated logic anyway, I half listened to what he was saying while I sipped my tea. It's become my default response to only devote part of my attention to students when talking to them, otherwise I get too upset at the way they stutter and ramble. Soon, though, I was totally absorbed by what Paul recounted.

Apparently, while helping his friend track down a stolen scooter—I get the impression he fancies himself a private eye—Paul came to fisticuffs with some scummy kids, probably high on drugs, one of whom dropped his shoulder bag. Out of this bag, according to Paul, slipped one of the missing photos of me and my kids. Initially, I was shocked Paul knew of the photos. But then I remembered I informed the whole damn class about the burglary. Next, he tells me the guys also dropped a piece of paper with the name Denise Pirouet on it and an address in Palm Desert. And I don't have to take his word for this, he shows me the paper—although of course he could've written it himself. But even if he did write it himself, how would he know about Denise? I've definitely never mentioned her in class. I hardly acknowledged her continued existence to myself until she barged into my dreams. I do, however, recall running into a former mutual acquaintance visiting campus some years ago, and, in a moment I'm not proud of, inquiring into how she was doing. Steven, I think, a standoffish kid who worked at the paper with her, told me she lived east of L.A. He was going to tell me more but I cut him off out of fear I might lose my resolve and look her up. That was back when I was entirely focused on my family, at least that was the intention—looking back I can see my focus was scattered all over the place. Well, according to Paul's note, Denise is in Palm Desert, which would line up with what Steven said. Not where I imagined her to be, so provincial, basically an outpost in the desert, but I guess she's nothing like I imagine her anymore. She used to love being a part of the action and getting involved in as many things as possible. That's part of why I thought she could make a good journalist. The industry has changed now, though, and instead of the most intrepid reporters, those with the biggest mouths, and even bigger egos, are the ones that rise to the top. That was never Denise, not by a mile. Is there anyone more reviled than reporters nowadays? They bring it on themselves, acting like experts when they're just as biased as the rest of us. And then all that moralizing. Makes me sick.

Anyway, after he was done, Paul pestered me about whether I knew Denise. Reluctant to tell him anything, I eventually relented, saying I knew her in college back around the time dinosaurs roamed the Earth. He didn't laugh at my admittedly poor joke, but looked reflective, as if he was integrating this information into some theory he'd been formulating. I then asked him, in a somewhat harsh tone, what he thought these guys were doing with my stuff. His theory apparently didn't extend that far yet. Probably he's way off base anyway with whatever he's working up. He may be an above-average student, but he's still only a UCSB student. I told him I might update the police. He said he'd be happy to provide descriptions of the two thieves, who from what he told me sound like bums, likely in town from one of the nearby urban cesspools, either L.A. or San Francisco.

What I just can't get over is Denise's presence in all this. First, she features in my dreams, and now she's playing a role in this nightmare. It seems to me that this psychological, almost existential, barrier impeding me recently—that's been making me so miserable—has got to have something to do with her. How that's possible, I'm not sure, but I'm no psychologist, and I don't plan to go talk to one about it. There are better ways to throw away one's money.

But now, it strikes me, I not only have her address, but also an excuse to visit her: To inform her that she may be in some danger. But what will I say? "Hi Denise, it's me, Leroy. How've you been since that time fifty years ago when you bolted as I prepared to propose? As for myself, I've been having vivid dreams about you. Oh also, some wacko kids who robbed my house dropped a piece of paper with your address on it. Would you like to get a coffee?"

Would I even like to get coffee?

• • •

Feb. 5, 2023

I asked Paul if he thought he could track down Denise's email. Less than an hour later, he had it. I didn't ask how, I don't even care. The internet has made a joke of our right to privacy, and it's well into making our entire society into a big joke. I often wonder how much strain our culture can take before it breaks, and what will come next. On the increasingly rare occasion that I'm not pissed off at the youth, I feel pity for them. It really is harder to find a decent job and live an upstanding middle-class life. Everything is just changing so damn fast, and I simply don't believe kids have the wherewithal or foresight to stop this great unraveling. I mean, most people are in their mid-30s these days before they can even take care of themselves. Americans' commitment to freedom and democracy are what helped ensure that the twentieth century didn't end up another dark age for civilization. We have a few great leaders to thank for that, but also the culture of sacrifice and unwavering moral commitment. I don't sense that same internal strength or moral compass in people these days, and I worry that the only way to acquire it will be through massive upheaval and loss.

Back to the point. I decided against making the trek to Palm Desert to visit Denise for several reasons, both emotional and logistical. For one, I don't want to drive through L.A., that ceaseless maze of traffic; all those angry drivers, and then the distracted ones, texting their friends or making hookup plans. Furthermore, unlike an in-person encounter, I can edit my emails, which will come in handy dealing with a situation so, shall we say, delicate. I might be able to pontificate in front of a hundred students for an hour without a second thought, but with Denise I could get tongue-tied.

I kept my email short, concise, and free from anything too evocative, and only read it once before pressing send, convinced I'd never get a reply. But astoundingly, she responded that very evening. Reading her email, I immediately recognized her in it and even felt a tremor of that ancient kinship we once shared. It's amazing how an emotion can catch fire after so long a dormancy, as if being fed oxygen after an extended period of asphyxiation. It really does warm one's soul, even if only briefly. And that's just it—with Denise, my soul is involved. Good to know it hasn't yet entirely shriveled up and died.

I've read over her email so many times in that last day that I might as well just transcribe it here:

Dear Leroy,

I can hardly believe these words I type now are meant for you. I was, of course, extremely surprised to hear from you. But also—like yourself—I've been having dreams, visions even, of the past lately, a few of them from our time together. So in a way, it felt natural to receive your dispatch. It's almost Jungian in its synchronicity: you thinking of me, me of you, and then my address turning up in your hands. Maybe the universe is trying to tell us something. I, for one, am listening.

Your house being broken into and the paper with my address on it being found along with the missing photos is highly disconcerting, and I appreciate you worrying over my well-being. I think you are right to have this concern, which I reciprocate. Just another potential danger I'll have to learn to live with. When you're old, everything starts to seem treacherous. Have you noticed that? I now worry about things like slipping on the grocery store tiles and cracking my head open. This kind of speculation is pointless though, even counterproductive. Which is why I do my best to vanquish it.

Haha. Can you decipher the Denise you once knew in these words? Perhaps. I was always a bit of a worrywart, wasn't I? Those who know me now might use words like serene or mindful to describe me, but that fretful Denise still lurks just below the tranquil surface I've worked so hard to cultivate. And sometimes, bang! Out she comes. For example, and speaking of dreams, I recently dreamt my present-day self was in a tizzy observing the mental health of my younger self deteriorate way back when I was a reporter at the school newspaper. I was looking through a portal of myself looking through a portal at my younger self. This younger self—oh, she was cute—was caught up trying to cover that terrible oil spill with little inkling of the toll it was taking on her. I tried everything to get her attention, in the dream, but it simply couldn't be done. I had a similar dream not too long ago regarding another episode I now see taxed me to the breaking point, but...that's not something I'm ready to bring up here.

Well, I've divulged too much and now I'm becoming cryptic. I'd love to hear from you again with any updates on the situation you describe, or unrelated thoughts and ramblings if you feel so inclined. Whatever happens, this has made my day. Has it really been so long?
With Love,
Denise

Writing it out like that, I have to wonder if Denise is totally lucid. Women often get carried away by their emotions and are much more likely to lose touch with reality. But, as with Paul, I've got to set my doubts aside, and, at least for now, try to place trust in her. And to be honest, I can relate to most of what she's saying. I am recalling now that I used to consider her to be my near equal in intelligence, not something I've felt about many women since then.

Still, I've got to be careful not to upset her too much in case she's unstable. That means shielding her from this more abrasive version of myself…which may prove impossible. My restraint is nothing close to what it used to be.

How to respond, then? As long as we're sharing connections with the past, maybe I'll write her back and fill her in on some of what happened right after she left. It'll be interesting to see how she handles that—and if it upsets her, so be it. If we're going to get anywhere, we'd better start at the start. Or, I guess, at the end.

CHAPTER TEN
CHEER UP,
YOU'RE LIVING THROUGH HISTORY

Ethan, Denise, and Leroy get their first view of the spill from a palm tree-lined hill overlooking the Santa Barbara waterfront. Black goo has taken over the beach like some ravenous fungus. The lapping of the waves is eerily muted by the oil's viscosity, which clings to everything it encounters with a suffocating finality. Hundreds of birds desperately half-flap their oil-logged wings and struggle to make use of their wobbly, wilted legs. Stranded and helpless up and down the coastline, their cries bring people wandering the shore to tears. The cloudless sky is choked with putrid vapor. For the first time since the pandemic, Ethan misses his mask.

"My God, this is awful," Denise says, her eyes watery. She accepts Leroy's arm around her neck. "The coastline is ruined."

"It looks like the cleanup is well underway," Leroy says. "Maybe…"

"What, you think all that straw is going to stop the oil?" Denise says. "Who knows how much more is coming?"

"No, but I'm sure they'll plug the leak soon."

Denise shakes her head in doubt before tossing Leroy's hand from her shoulder and walking towards the beach.

Ethan thinks of Dover, who he knows was bird watching when he first encountered him alongside the lagoon. He dreads telling his friend of the birds' undignified, excruciating, and mostly losing battle with the oil. He hopes the oil won't reach the beaches closer to the university, although he senses it will. From his current vantage point, the oil slicks coating the water might as well extend along the entire West Coast. He's witnessing a fissure in man's relationship with the environment. The excitement he felt about coming to ground zero drains away, hardening his intestines. But watching the chaotic crowd organize before his eyes into a formidable force against the oil, that inspires him. And soon he's excited again to be at this place, in this time.

Having steeled her nerves, Denise is interviewing those on the frontlines, some of them fishermen volunteering their boats, some of them veterinarians volunteering their services, some of them able-bodied residents trucking armfuls of straw to the beach to help absorb the oil. All of them distraught, many of them overwhelmed. Several bulldozers pile up contaminated sand like giant, crusty dinosaur turds.

Wandering down, Ethan lingers by Denise as she talks to a teary high school student.

"This is my life," the student says. "I come out here all the time to relax and look at the birds and the other nature. Now that seems impossible. I can't even imagine someday bringing my children here. I don't know how it will ever be the same again. How could it ever recover from this? It's the most horrible thing I've ever seen."

Ethan wants to tell her to cheer up, she's living through history. And look at all these valiant people doing everything they can to fend off the murky invasion, doesn't that inspire her? He wants to tell her it will be the same again, because even if it won't, exactly, that's what she wants to hear.

Denise glances strangely at Ethan before patting the girl's shoulder and moving on. Ethan realizes he was smiling as the girl expressed her deep sorrow. His cheeks burn red as Leroy approaches and they watch Denise seek out her next interviewee.

"I can't believe this is really happening," Leroy says.

"Yeah," Ethan says, "Neither can I." He wants to add that it's the second most unbelievable thing to happen to him that week, but refrains.

"I mean, I know these oil companies are all about profit, but I also assumed they knew what they were doing. And shouldn't the government have been monitoring this better? This feels like an attack, I feel attacked."

He looks like he wants to say more but instead runs over to the straw bales and starts distributing it.

Ethan can't bring himself to pitch in. It's like he's in someone else's house feeling vaguely guilty as he watches them clean up after dinner, but also convinced it's not his place to intervene. Also, he's been waiting for an opportunity to slink off to the marina and locate the boat that Leroy and Denise rescued him on. Walking up the aging dock, the oily water swashing against the wooden beams only a few feet below, he recognizes the yellow trim of the boat. He climbs on deck and is relieved to find his raft intact. His spine shivers as he reaches out and massages the raft like an inanimate pet. These bodily tingles reassure him that he really does need to navigate through the murky seawater that night to the bright spot in the water, his only hope of returning home.

He heads back to the beach, where the oil is piling up, the slick several inches thick in some places. At an improvised field hospital people work frantically decontaminating birds. More trucks with rain slickers, boots, rakes, food, and water arrive.

"I've never seen anything like this," Denise says, approaching Ethan from behind. "It's almost like I've been dropped into a war zone to report." Denise's jeans are smeared with oil and her bare arms are coated with black globs of sand. She is having difficulty pushing her bangs from her eyes with the back of her hand. Ethan gently aids her with his forefinger.

"Thanks," she says. "Where did you go, by the way?"

"I, um, I went out to the marina, to see if I could help with anything."

"Poor boats," Denise says, looking across the beach towards the stranded vessels. "Poor everything."

"Wow am I gross," Leroy says, his clothes caked in oil and straw. "I'd like to stay and help, but we should get back so you can file your story, Denise, right? Anyway, I have some work I'd better finish, if I can manage to focus on it."

Denise lets the awful scene sear into her memory for a few more seconds. "Yes, I guess I'd better get this story done," she says. She looks at Leroy and then down at her soiled clothes. "But how are we going to get in the car like this? We're completely disgusting."

Leroy starts to say they can find some blankets or towels, but Denise cuts him off. "We'll just throw our clothes in the trunk and ride in our underwear."

Ethan, who'd been running through his plan for that night, jars to attention. He's glad he's not dirty too; he'd rather not sport tighty-whities in public, the only underwear that Dover had available to Faculty Club guests. They walk the few blocks to the car, parked on a side street where it's almost possible to forget a tragedy of enormous proportion is unfolding just around the corner. Leroy pops open the trunk and the two of them remove their filthy garments and toss them in.

Seeing Denise's exposed body, her white bra and thigh-gripping underwear, Ethan realizes she's a secret babe. Or maybe everyone already knew it but him, so thrown off was he by the unfamiliar styles of the day. Her undergarments approach her knees, and if she threw on a halter-top, she could pass for fully clothed in 2023.

"OK, it's kinda chilly," she says, folding her arms across her body and becoming self-conscious. Ethan offers her his long-sleeved shirt. She accepts and he drapes it around her shoulders. Leroy, who still has an undershirt on, has goosebumps too, but he doesn't say anything. Ethan thinks Leroy might be observing him dubiously. It's a look he's familiar with after three years of scavenging the Isla Vista dating scene. Don't worry, he thinks, I'll be gone soon. Back to a female population that observes me with as much interest as a piece of washed-up driftwood. It's a painful truth that he and Paul have lamented over the course of many a drunken night. Although he suspects if they did less drifting and instead tried to pursue a member of the opposite sex, they might do alright for themselves. Sometimes he encourages Paul to try harder, and sometimes it's the other way around. Every so often one of them tries just hard enough to catch something.

They duck into the car and head back to Isla Vista. Leroy drops Denise off at her place. When they pull up outside of Leroy's house, the unfriendly neighbor is just entering his garage. Ethan sees Leroy tense up.

"That guy really gets on your nerves, huh?" Ethan asks.

Leroy clenches his jaw and wipes his hands along his bare thighs. "Well, can I be frank with you?" he asks. Ethan says of course. "I try to act like we're working things out, me and those guys, especially when Denise is around. But really, I don't believe it for a second."

Leroy turns towards Ethan, a seriousness in his countenance that makes Ethan lean away. "I haven't told anyone this, but I suspect them to be up to no good in that garage. I swear they're building something that they want to keep very secret."

"OK," Ethan asks. "Like what?"

"I really don't know," Leroy says. "It might just be a stereo or something like that, but it might be something like…" He trails off, but Ethan knows what he's thinking, and finishes his sentence. "Like a bomb."

Leroy nods subtly.

"Well, if that's what you think you ought to tell someone about it," Ethan says.

"No, no," Leroy says, waving his hand in dismissal. "The last thing I want to do is bring figures of authority into this, then those guys will really be on my case." He opens the door to the car and gets out. "Anyway, I'm just being paranoid."

Ethan isn't assuaged, he knows Isla Vista has had its share of deadly episodes over the years. But he doesn't recall hearing about any incidents involving bombs. Just guns, knives, cars, and angry young men. Always angry young men.

Walking towards the house, someone calls from behind.

"Hey, Leroy, did you forget your pants this morning or something?"

They turn around to see two guys in what Ethan considers full-on hippie garb approaching. "Oh great," Leroy says. "Russell and his roommate."

"Russell is the neighbor, right?" Ethan asks quickly. Leroy nods before turning his attention to the guys, whose clothes, upon closer inspection, are also dirty enough to be tossed into a trunk.

"We were down at the beach, helping clean up the oil spill," Leroy says.

"Well, good for you," Russell says, a wall of tangled bangs covering his face. "I'm sure your mom would be proud."

"It's quite bad down there, a real disaster," Leroy says. "Not something to joke about."

"Don't tell us what to do," snaps Lonnie, only a few feet away now. "In fact, you'd be wise to keep your distance from me and Russell, if you know what's good for you."

Lonnie pats the slim leather bag on his shoulder and the two of them laugh conspiratorially, which seems out of place to Ethan. They reek of brine.

"Were you two by the ocean, too?" Ethan asks. "You smell like it."

"What's it to you?" asks Russell.

"Yeah," Leroy says. "They have a boat, or they know someone that does."

"Shut up," Russell says. "Just because there's a bit of oil out there doesn't mean we can't go fishing. If you catch anything you can just deep fry it right there. Ha-ha."

Leroy gives a slight grin.

"Who's the nark?" Russell asks Leroy. "Haven't seen him around before."

"Oh, this is Ethan," Leroy says. "We only recently met. Ethan this is Russell and Lonnie."

Ethan doesn't respond. He's looking at Lonnie's shoes. A pair of Airwalks. He doesn't know much about Airwalk, but he's almost certain the company didn't exist in 1969.

"Hey bozo," Russell says. "You ignoring me?"

Ethan apologizes and the two guys push past him and Leroy, warning them again to mind their own business.

"I don't know why they'd threaten you like that if they weren't up to something," Ethan says as they head inside.

"Yeah," Leroy says, collapsing onto the couch in his underwear. "Seems that way, doesn't it?"

. . .

El Gaucho Writer's Impressions:
Union Oil's Hartley's—'Distinctly' Executive[II]
February 13, 1969

Before I met Mr. Fred L. Hartley, President of Union Oil Company of California, I was ready to hate him. I pictured him as an impervious man who would look at me as if he were looking into his trash can.

He would be a big man and at home with a fat cigar in his mouth. He would have several aides following in his wake, all neatly dressed and pressed and bringing up the rear would be a short bespectacled man—rather odd looking in fact. But who was probably the world's greatest attorney.

And when I saw his expensive Lear Jet, with its hideous orange and blue color, cruise into S.B. Airport I knew I had pegged my man. But I was wrong. The image was there, but the shine wasn't.

He wasn't a big man and he wasn't followed by any aides. He didn't look bold or impervious either. In fact, he looked rather frightened. And, it struck me that he probably had a wife and kids. And yet, he still retained that air about him that is distinctly executive.

Stepping from the plane, he was hounded by reporters. Trying desperately to avoid them, he walked briskly toward the exit. He looked like a nice gentleman. Meanwhile, the pickets, waving their "no more oil" signs began to heckle him.

He walked faster and appeared very uncomfortable, even scared—as if trying to escape a sinking ship. Well, by now my ship was sinking—cigar and everything. Later I talked to him personally. He was very cordial and friendly. I got the impression that I was talking to a close uncle. I asked him about the pickets and he referred to them as "wild animals and monsters." He was very apologetic about the oil slick. But he didn't think of it as a disaster.

"I think of a disaster in terms of people being killed," he later said before Senator Muskie. This bothered me. I wondered how he could be so blind, so oblivious to popular sentiment. Then it dawned on me that the upper echelon of the business world lead a restricted sterile life. And it does something to them.

It makes them bland where we're emotional and conservative where we're liberal. They're much more conscious of their achievements—conscious of what they've done, rather than what they're going to do. And worst of all, they can't identify with other people.

Thirty years ago, Hartley might have been in that picket line. But not now. The corporation-life had molded and shaped him, dressed and fed him. Words like "merger, tax reduction, and fiscal policy" had become "priority" words. ("Beautiful beach" is not a priority word.)

When I finally shook hands with Hartley and said "thank you" he added, "Tell your readers that I raised chickens to put myself through college." I don't know why he made that closing remark. Perhaps, he thought his wealthy position, and not the oil slick was on the pickets' minds.

• • •

Ethan departs Leroy's and heads to the Faculty Club fully determined to attempt time travel that night. He doesn't know how he'll track down the portal other than by harnessing that same magnetic pull that initially drew him to it. If he focuses on it, he thinks he feels the pull ever so faintly even now, as he walks, tugging him patiently towards the ocean as if he were on a gentle slope leading down to the water. He wonders, should he succeed in making the jump, if he'll arrive at the moment he departed—the night of the party at his house—or if several days will have passed, as they have in 1969. Or maybe none of the above. Maybe he'll transport to some ancient geologic age where the organisms that died and broke down over millions of years ago to form oil are still alive. He imagines he would perish quite quickly were that to happen, with starvation being a best-case scenario. The more he thinks about time travel, the less it makes sense. He tries not to think about it, but of course, he does.

Back at the Faculty Club, Ethan spots Dover swishing his pool skimmer along the aqua blue swimming pool water. The water mesmerizes him, appearing naked in its transparency, especially when contrasted with the grimy scene he just witnessed. He leans over the edge of the pool and catches his reflection. He looks a bit like Dustin Hoffman in *The Graduate*, at least he thinks he does. He remembers the line about the future being plastic. He wonders if there was a double entendre there: That plastics—petrochemicals—were the future, which was right on, but also that the future is malleable, changeable. The thought occurs to him to abandon his current plan and go seek out Dustin Hoffman to ask him about this ambiguity of meaning. If he's going to reveal that he's from the future, he thinks Dustin Hoffman would be a good person to grant the privilege to. He could tell Mr.

Hoffman all about the future, at least his little corner of it. They're probably around the same age now, maybe they could party together. For a moment, he feels like he could do just about anything. Then Dover interrupts him.

"Hey, son," he says, still swishing. "You look like you've seen a ghost."

"Not too far off." Ethan steps back from his reflection. Before Dover can react, he adds, "I went down to Santa Barbara, the oil's blanketing the beach there."

Dover removes the swisher from the water and balances the end of it on the concrete perimeter of the pool like a pitchfork. "I heard someone mention that it's causing a lot of trouble for the birds," he says. "Did you see anything like that?"

"Um, it didn't look too bad, for the birds I mean," Ethan says. "Anyway, there's an army of people trying to rescue them."

Dover nods. "I'd like to get down there myself, but I doubt I'll get the chance."

They both stare into the crystal-clear pool for a moment.

"Dover," Ethan says, "I want to thank you again for your hospitality."

"Are you moving on?" Dover asks with a dash of surprise and expectation.

"Yeah, after I take a nap, I'll be headed out."

Dover lowers the swisher to the ground and embraces an unexpecting Ethan. Ethan feels the stiff denim of his work clothes crease around him. The muscles in his shoulders and back release for the first time in days and he leans into the hug, half raising his arms underneath Dover's donut hold.

"I'm really glad I found you," Dover says. "I know it's silly, but I almost feel like in helping you out, I helped rescue one of those birds. And now you're going to fly away."

"Oh, I'm not going too far—definitely not flying anywhere," Ethan says. Dover gives him a soft, understanding look. "Well, if you're nearby come say hi sometime."

Ethan says he will before departing down the corridor for one last visit to his cozy little room. He thinks he'll never talk to Dover again and he's right about that. In just over two months, Dover will be dead.

CHAPTER ELEVEN
DUDE!

After tracking down Denise's email address in the contact info for a yoga fundraiser hosted by an influencer with silver-streaked hair and an Om tattoo on her inside bicep, Paul turns back to his books. But before long, he's distracted by the organ cushioned within his boxer briefs. He blames the influencer's evocative social media presence, which he couldn't help but click into, but he's almost always ready to go. His discomfort with his masturbation frequency is one thing he's never brought up with Ethan, in part because it's taboo, but also because he doesn't want to imagine anyone else masturbating and feels he should extend the same courtesy. He distracts himself by scrolling through his texts. Ethan still hasn't responded, so he shoots him another message, *ur phone dead or something?* Typing 'dead' sends a ripple of doubt up his arm, and he decides if he doesn't hear from Ethan in another day, he'll alert the authorities.

He elects to delay the inevitable ejaculation at least a few hours by venturing out on an errand; one that's demonstrative of his commitment to finding a way out of this libido-driven preoccupation. He heads towards the campus clinic to pick up a handful of free condoms. The other day, he noticed a condom wrapper in the overflowing wastebin in the bathroom he shares with his roommate, whose high school girlfriend visits every month or so. Aside from a pang of jealousy, it also served as a reminder that he never restocked his meager supply of condoms after the Halloween encounter, which required his last three Lifestyles Skyns, two of which were put to good use and one of which tore during the hurried and awkward unwrapping process. He intends to pick up several varieties to see if he can discern any difference in the experience. He has a premonition he might end up jacking off into them to find out.

Walking down Sabado Tarde Rd., he passes a cluster of fraternities. Tank-topped guys with glimmering, hairless chests play volleyball and Spikeball while beat-heavy music pulses from a balcony. Through the sliding doors, Paul catches a glimpse of a multiplayer video game, whose players splay on couches and chairs, their long limbs taking hold of the furniture as if it could be pinned to a mat. If those guys are masturbating as much as him, it's basically a semen factory in there. He wonders if they watch porn together, maybe even to the point of climax. And yet they want nothing more than to be in each other's company. Which he gets. What's the point of college if not to measure yourself against like-minded peers. That attraction is maybe not stronger, but perhaps deeper, than the sexual variety. For the first time, spurred on by his absence, he feels thankful that he found Ethan. Even if they don't live together, they're best friends. He wonders what will become of them after graduation. It's not something he's considered before, and he doesn't like the way it makes him feel; the way it truncates their remaining time in this liminal space called college. If Ethan were around at this moment of deferred masturbation, which seems to be infecting his emotions to the point of bursting like a whitehead gathering pus, he might've garbled something about his feelings and created some new sinew in the body of experiences binding them together. But with each passing step the prospect becomes unlikelier.

On the way back from the clinic, a brown bag of condoms swinging in his hand, Paul is hit from behind. The attacker fails to push him to the ground, though, and Paul swings blindly into the hazy early evening light, visions of the stinky, knife-wielding bohemians he encountered the day before slicing through his mind. Then a familiar voice punches him in the gut.

"Dude! chill out it's me," Ethan says, backing away. "Sorry for tackling you, I'm just so happy to see you. You have no idea."

Paul steadies himself. "What the hell, that ..." But Ethan's appearance is so startling that he stops mid-sentence. "Um, what on Earth happened to you?"

Ethan is dressed like he's trying out for debate club, but also covered in oily grime as if someone threw him in a fast-food dumpster for being a nerd.

"Shit, yeah," Ethan says. "I should've gone home and changed first but I needed to find you. I mean, I took a nap on the beach for a few hours because that trip just destroys you, but then I came straight here."

"Well, I've been trying to find you," Paul says, increasingly aware that Ethan is somewhat out of his mind. "You just sort of vanished for the better part of a week. I tried to cover for you with Prof. Bourman…"

"Oh, I did disappear," Ethan interjects. "And it's fucking amazing that I made it back. In fact, you're not going to believe where I've been."

Paul folds his arms across his chest. "OK, well, things have been pretty weird with me as well."

"Really?" Ethan leans in, his interest verging on extreme.

"Yeah, I tracked down the guys who stole Greggy's scooter and it turns out they also robbed Leroy's house. But they only took a few old photos. And I also got in a fight with them, or at least a scuffle that could've become a fight until one of the guys flashed a knife."

"Leroy?"

"Oh sorry, Prof. Bourman." Paul smirks. "I guess we're on a first name basis now. Anyway, these guys, they were super odd. Like, they don't fit any of the usual I.V. profiles. And they were gross. They kind of smelled, well, like you…but not as greasy."

Paul stops talking as Ethan's attention is clearly somewhere else.

"I freaking knew Leroy was Prof. Bourman," Ethan says, slapping his hands together.

"What are you talking about?"

Ethan pulls Paul's arm towards the apartment complex. "Let me take a shower and then I'll tell you everything. And do you have any boxer briefs I could borrow? These tighty-whities are chafing me bad. Also, I'm starving. Maybe you have some leftovers around."

Ethan's eye catches on the folded-over brown bag in Paul's hand. "What's in the bag? Anything I can eat?"

"No," Paul says. "Just some condoms."

"Hah, nice! I must've missed more than I thought."

"No," Paul says, shifting the bag to his other hand. "Nothing out of the ordinary on that front. Just realized I didn't have any around."

CHAPTER TWELVE
I'D LOVE TO REMAIN IN DENIAL

February 10, 2023

I slept in my office for the first time last night—the first time, I believe, that I've slept on campus since my graduate school days. When the usual time to head home arrived, I remained glued to my chair. It's not that I have security concerns about being home; I got a new alarm system installed just the other day. No, it's that—and this is hard to admit—I thought a change of scenery might be good for my dreams. I've spent the last few nights tossing and turning through restless sleep, and when I do fall asleep, I don't find much peace of mind there either. Last night, I witnessed someone—a man—being murdered in my dreams. Stabbed close to the heart by another man. Actually, the two men looked almost exactly alike. I don't know who they were, the whole thing is somewhat of a blur, but I do know I wasn't particularly set on saving the victim. In fact, I just watched it happen, at least until I awoke covered in sweat.

    And what should I take from this dream? I think I can confidently assert nothing good. I'm not killing anyone, but I'm letting someone get stabbed to death without so much as lifting a finger. One reflection I had is that I'll most likely go my entire life without witnessing a human being die. I wasn't at my parents' deathbeds when the moment came, and I hope to have passed on myself before any other immediate family members reach their last breaths. And I haven't been unlucky enough to be in the wrong place at the wrong time to otherwise see a friend or stranger pass on. It must be a unique circumstance for our age to live without ever getting close enough to death to observe it in real time. To watch as body and mind make that final transition. Not even for an animal, I don't think, have I been present to watch death set in. Throughout history, death has been as common, as, well, the common cold. Wars, illnesses, public killings even—to get through life without bearing witness to death via these commonalities of civilization would've been the exception not the rule. In a way, now that I'm approaching the average lifespan of an American male, I feel I've missed out on death. I feel, well, like I should be more prepared, more inured. Maybe that's all the dream means, that I need to better process my own impending death. I imagine Denise's letter may have opened this channel of thinking in my mind.

To be honest, I'd love to close the channel, to collapse it for good, bury it, and to remain in denial. That's the privilege of our era; denial. Denial of death, denial of responsibility, denial over denial, even. And no matter how much I can't help railing against the coddled youth, when it comes to death, I'll take what this moment in history has to offer.

So, the upshot for now is that sleeping in the office offered some respite from the dreams: No murder, but still chasing after someone, this time in the desert. And yes, probably Denise, although I couldn't get close enough to make out the figure. But it came at the expense of comfort. I awoke this morning with a crick in my neck and a sore shoulder. Unfortunately, the tradeoff is not worth it. I'm getting better at ignoring the aches and pains that accompany aging like reverse growing pains, but I don't need to be facilitating new ones. The residual mental and emotional hangovers from the dreams are easier to cope with, they're more intermittent at least. So tonight, I'm back home, with all the creature comforts that I so readily take for granted. Well, I do pay quite a bit for them, especially as taxes keep shooting up in this state, which is run by economic nitwits. And I don't take my money for granted, never have. Even if this frugality did ultimately contribute to the break-up of my marriage, I don't regret it. I earned my money, I should be the one that decides what to do with it.

Something else of note: Paul came by my office after class today to check on me and see if I had any updates. I told him, no, the police probably already filed the incident away as old news. No doubt they're preoccupied patrolling the streets looking useful while crime continues to escalate thanks to all the leniency with which we treat criminals in this state. I read an article about how stores are closing because they can no longer deter shoplifters—the state refuses to prosecute them for their crimes. Well, why not break the law if there's no real consequences? Of course, that's more appealing than finding a job, even a low-paying one, and accruing a bit of savings over time, maybe making some smart investments. That would require willpower and foresight, which are no longer in vogue. The temptation to steal is just too great. What next? Raping and pillaging?

In my office, Paul eyed the blanket on the couch. I told him I was fine, that I sometimes sleep on the couch when I'm busy. I don't think he believed me, but he didn't question it further. Only then did he introduce his friend, Ethan, who I guess had missed the last exam. I was going to lay into him for not notifying me ahead of time, but the disquieting way he stared at me threw me off. Instead, I told him we could do a make-up next week. I made sure to point out that I wasn't happy about it because it means I'll have to come up with a new version of the test. He nodded, but he remained somewhat dazed, and that's when I thought he seemed familiar. I asked if he'd taken one of my classes before. He said no. His unusual behavior was making me uncomfortable, which I think Paul caught onto because he interjected, remarking that they'd better get going. The whole exchange felt a bit like a dream itself, but once they left reality set in and I headed home to take care of a few things, most importantly responding to Denise, which I'd been putting off because of the emotional investment it demands.

• • •

Dear Denise,

I was almost as surprised to receive your prompt response as you must've been to get my initial note. I was very glad to learn that you're not also caught up in whatever strangeness I am, and I hope it remains that way. I must've read your letter over a dozen times since receiving it; it's amazing how much response it elicits from me. It's like it has access to remote slivers of my brain that've been lying dormant for years only to redolently blossom once nourished by your words.

I'm not exactly sure how we should proceed from here, but considering how long it's been, I thought indulging in some recounting of the distant past might be wise, or at least appropriate, to kind of jog the memory and keep jarring those neglected synapses. I thought I'd commence with those first moments after you walked out of my life for good, or at least until now. You may be thinking that it's a little soon for that, we should warm up first with more superficial or positive associations, and normally I would be in full agreement with you. However, I worry if I don't take the initiative now the opportunity might slip away into the past, as opportunities tend to do. I'll get lazy or distracted or fail to find a convenient time or tell myself it doesn't matter, and we may never clear the air. And then there's the curiosity I've been unable to rid myself of for half a century over why you left right then, and towards what end. I'll admit, this curiosity is aflame, having been fed some oxygen. To put it out would be suffocating.

So, the moment of separation. When you left me high and dry staring up some finger of Lake Powell with an heirloom ring in my hand, I had what I think could safely be referred to as a panic attack. I remember watching in disbelief as the van you'd so unexpectedly hopped into drove off around the bend, the midday heat lending the atmosphere that shimmering oasis effect that makes one distrust one's own eyes. This was the summer of 1970, a year after the oil spill and shortly after the campus protests, bank burning, and the interminable, insufferable police state in I.V. Just when I thought maybe things were finally settling down, settling into the new decade—and that maybe it was time for me to settle down. But apparently, we weren't on the same page there, and I see now that I should've just brought the topic up so we could discuss it like grown-ups. Not waited until a moment so fraught with potential meaning—literally balanced on the edge of a precipice—that letdown was perhaps inevitable. But we were just kids then, and I was somewhat of a romantic about all that stuff (hard to believe now). And I had yet to learn to thoroughly temper my expectations.

So, the van disappeared into the blinding desert sun (who was with you in that van is a question I'd really like answered if this exchange keeps up) and I screamed into the void. And it really was a void. I don't remember another living thing in sight aside from the brownish scrubs dotting the scrappy desert landscape. I screamed and I stomped around in a circle like some Native American dancer summoning the Gods, it strikes me now. I sure had a lot of questions for the Gods. For instance, what in God's name just happened?

But seriously, I was at a complete loss there in the middle of nowhere, the woman I thought I'd spend the rest of my life with climbing almost casually into a VW bus, leaving me alone in that unforgiving landscape, hours from what I considered to be civilization. Not that it would've mattered much if you'd done the same thing in midtown Manhattan or at a beautiful tropical resort. The emptiness emanated from within. Still, I cursed you for suggesting we take that trip into the heart of the Southwest, saying we needed to get far away from everything for a spell. I thought I knew what you desired out of it, but it turns out I had no idea.

I gripped that turquoise ring overlaid with my great-grandmother's initials like my survival depended on it; like maybe if I squeezed hard enough it would extract some of my pain and mold it into another jewel. Then, another fit overcame me, and I ran towards the edge of the canyon—at that time the drop to the water was at least fifty feet. Survivable perhaps because it wasn't a straight fall, but it would've involved some cascading, and could easily have been deadly, especially for someone inviting it. But my body's survival instinct kicked in and I skidded to a halt a few feet from the precipice. In my place, I hurled the ring towards the water's edge. As you can see, I didn't just lose you that day. I lost the chance to pass on one of my family's oldest, most cherished possessions. A ring that had been handed down at least three generations. Immediately afterwards, gazing down at the jagged topography, I thought I perceived a sparkle reflecting from a craggy outcrop near the water. The ring hadn't quite reached the lake, but as the dam filled and the water rose, I was sure it would soon be submerged.

After that, all life flowed out of me, and I returned exhausted and defeated to my car. I didn't even pack up our camping gear. In fact, I threw everything that wasn't essential—everything that reminded me of you—out of the car right there by the side of the poorly paved road. I drove back to Isla Vista for a day or two, gathered my belongings while numb with shock, and returned home, where my parents doted on me. Slowly but surely, with the help of everything from my childhood that still brought me comfort, I emerged from that deep, dark rut. By summer's end I was sick of being home, which meant I was feeling like my old self again, and I hit the road for graduate school with a renewed lease on life. Thinking back on it now, I am proud of the resiliency I displayed. I believe that all along I grasped that true love had slipped through my fingers, but I refused to become too beholden to the loss. There was just so much to look forward to, which is not something I say or think very often anymore. And I'm not just talking personally, but regarding the state of our nation right now—our moronic political class, the myopic youth, the hellbent focus on problems that aren't really problems. But I promised myself I wouldn't get into all that with you.

I knew recounting that episode would be draining but I didn't think it would leave me perspiring like a pig. That episode by the lake isn't something I've ever discussed, even with my ex-wife. I suppose it makes sense that the only person I'd want to share it with would be the person who was there, at least just beforehand. Otherwise, and I am just coming to this conclusion now, I'd be treating my most vulnerable of moments as a sort of cheap thrill, you know, to evoke a reaction. And there was nothing cheap about what went on at Lake Powell. It was both the realest and most unreal experience of my life. Telling you feels, I don't know, like something that had to happen, no matter how much time passed. I think a therapist might say I've made some progress. I guess we'll see if there's any discernable change in the content of my dreams. I'm no Freudian, but I think I might sleep a little better tonight.

I'm tempted to read this over, but I worry that if I do, I'll delete about half of it. So I'm just going to press send. How very bold of me.

Leroy

CHAPTER THIRTEEN
THIS IS HOW YOU MEET PEOPLE FOREVERMORE

After the awkward visit to Prof. Bourman's office hours, Ethan and Paul steer clear of each other for a few days. There's a tacit understanding between them that after telling someone you just traveled back in time through a wormhole in the ocean maybe you'll both need a little space to process.

Paul doesn't believe Ethan but doesn't let that get in the way of how, taken at face value, his story helps explain his encounter with the hippie-garbed burglars outside of Greggy's place and the photos they had of Leroy. If those two hooligans took the photos back to 1969 and showed them to Leroy, they could really freak him out. Why they would want to do that is a nut that isn't showing any cracks. Paul wonders if a young person can definitively recognize their older self, concluding that at the very least it would be highly unsettling and knock a few screws loose even if it wasn't exactly clear what was going on. Then there's the additional disturbance, of no small matter, that Leroy's unborn children are standing alongside him in the photos. Ethan, who swears he hung out with 20-year-old Prof. Bourman in 1969, said young Leroy is suspicious of the two guys Paul saw, who match Ethan's description of Leroy's neighbors. He told Paul that Leroy suspects them of being up to no good, with something violent in mind perhaps. Maybe they took the photos to have insurance against Leroy acting on his suspicions; to have recourse to blackmail. It's a flimsy theory, but it's all Paul can come up with.

Initially, Ethan attempted to convince Paul to take the raft out and see the bright spot in the ocean for himself, which he thinks is getting smaller and possibly sealing up, but Paul didn't accept the offer. For starters, he's concerned about Ethan's sanity and isn't keen to spend time with him asea in a tiny vessel. He knows freshman year Ethan's older sister was briefly hospitalized after some kind of breakdown in Central Park. Having been alerted by a sympathetic jogger, the police found her half-frozen in a t-shirt in the middle of winter, rambling incoherently. Ethan took a week off at the time to travel back to Eugene and be with his family while his sister recuperated and commenced a new medication regime. He only told Paul about the real reason for his absence six months later, once their friendship had solidified and they were in that short-lived stage, similar to dating, where divulgence is the norm rather than the exception. Ethan said his sister was doing OK by then, that her meds appeared to be working, and that she was planning to return to New York City and find another job in climate finance or carbon trading, Paul's not exactly sure what she does and he's not sure Ethan knows either. Paul was surprisingly touched by how openly Ethan spoke of his sister then, and with such obvious affection, but in the year and a half since, she's rarely come up. Now Paul wonders if maybe Ethan is prone to similar episodes of mental instability, maybe even of a hallucinatory nature. He wants to be there for his friend but doesn't know what that means. So he remains both available and distant.

Plus, he signed up for a dating app and it's taking up a lot of his time, although thus far it's only made his crisis of onanism more acute. There're so many cute girls, many of whom respond to his quips and pokes and a few who seem genuinely interested in physically meeting. He's enjoying this honeymoon phase with the dating apps, even relishing it, but not without a sense of foreboding. There's the inevitable disappointment he'll experience upon getting to know them, and the equally unpalatable disappointment they'll find in him. But what really disturbs him is the way the app feels like a gateway drug to the rest of his life. A message burned into the back of his mind by some subtle force emanating from his phone: This Is How You Meet People Forevermore. It doesn't seem normal to him, but maybe he's the problem, maybe he's the abnormal one. His phone disgusts him almost as much as his penis, and he's having a hard time figuring out what to do about it. They're both a part of his body, but also seem to have minds of their own.

Ethan, for his part, has a lot of catching up to do. If only he could focus. He keeps getting drawn back towards the water's edge, though. He walks around the lagoon one afternoon, admiring the birds and the lack of oily residue, and then the next day goes for a long hike through the nature reserve on the other side of Isla Vista. Sitting on the sand, he idly watches the surfers for an hour before trudging off down the beach, kicking clumps of stinky kelp as he goes and launching gnats in all directions. He feels somehow incomplete and whatever's missing is making it harder for him to do his homework.

He wishes he had someone else to talk to but after Paul's lackluster response to his time traveling—the more he replays the episode in his mind, the more he's sure Paul thinks he's full of shit—he doesn't dare broach the topic with anyone else, not even his sister, who's default response to most anything is skepticism. The only other time he really considered it was when they stopped by Leroy's office. But how can you tell someone that the day before they were driving you around in 1969? You can't. At least not with someone as unapproachable as geriatric Leroy. Ethan still can't get over the fact that the basically affable, only moderately conceited, young man he hung out with in 1969 matured into the crankiest professor he's ever had, no contest. Something must have happened to him, he thinks, or can people just calcify into assholes over the years?

By the time the weekend rolls around, Ethan is eager to get wasted and forget, at least for a night, everything that's weighing him down. Paul is eager to get too wasted to masturbate. The majority of Isla

Vista's residents are eager to get wasted for one reason or another. By 11:00 p.m. on Friday, Ethan's Del Playa duplex is the scene of a sort of half-baked party. A cluster of people dance to music in the shabby living room under exposed lightbulbs, another group talks loudly in the kitchen, the soles of their shoes sticky with beer and the linoleum streaked with dirt, and down the hall in a mold-encrusted bedroom, the new Zelda is being ravenously consumed. A steady stream of people make their way along the main drag outside, stopping off at friends' houses or friends of friends' houses to shoot the shit and scrounge for a drink before alighting again. Ethan started pre-gaming before seven, and only realizes how far gone he is when he loses his balance on the balcony upon spotting the raft tied to a post near the staircase to the beach. The salty ocean breeze, typically so cleansing, makes him gag with metaphysical indecision and angst. The raft symbolizes everything he's trying to blow to smithereens with alcohol that night; everything he can't understand and everything he doesn't want to think about. Something's always killing him, and right now it's the raft. He should puncture it and stuff it down a sewer somewhere. Steadying himself, he elbows his way into a semi-circle of a half-dozen people talking loudly and pulling heavily on cigarettes. Several pairs of eyes land on him but they quickly lose interest—he does live there and can impose himself as he chooses—and the conversation doesn't skip a beat. He's not on very close terms with anyone in the group, and nobody's making an effort to include him in the discussion. He should abort, go deploy his hosting privileges somewhere more advantageous.

As he's backing away, he faintly discerns the sound of his phone ringing in his pocket. He pulls it out and blurrily reads the name splashed across the screen: Samantha. A straitjacket of fear grips him, and he's floored by how the emotion dominates him; if the raft was surface level, this is deep sea stuff. The story hasn't changed—it's still the story of his life—but suddenly it possesses the gravitational pull of nonfiction, of something not even his mind will fuck with. But if Samantha's calling him, then she must be OK, at least able to operate her phone. The thought is reassuring. He answers, retreating to the quieter, far end of the balcony, where several steps lead down to a patio.

"Hey Sammy," he says. "You alright? Isn't it like 2 a.m. there?"

"It is." Samantha's even-toned voice echoes through Ethan's head, evoking an image of her soccer-player's build taking up a human-sized parcel of space somewhere in New York City. "You know I hate to call when it's convenient."

"You hate to do anything convenient."

"Full disclosure," she says. "I'm drunk."

Ethan thinks he hears a door shut, maybe she just got home.

"Full disclosure, me too."

"And I just got dumped."

"Oh shit," Ethan says. "By the artist?"

"Well, he's more of a UX designer moonlighting as a graphic novelist, but yeah."

"Oh, right, very New York. Well, that sucks."

"It blows because breaks up suck, but I'll be fine. And don't worry, I remain 100 percent committed to my meds. I actually wanted to ask you about something else." Samantha exhales heavily, as if maybe she just plopped down on her couch. Ethan wonders how his sister knew he was worried about her meds.

"Yeah?"

"Have you talked to dad much lately?"

"Not really, why?"

"This is weird, or it sounds weird, but I think he might be, you know, losing it a bit. I mean, he's getting up there, he was always an old dad. I'm worried he's showing signs of Alzheimer's, or senility, or something."

That same dry, nonfiction feeling clamps down on Ethan's kidneys. He hasn't noticed-noticed anything, but he can't deny something's been amiss in their correspondence. Ethan thought it was just part of growing up and growing apart from one's parents. As they become less formidable, they also grow more distant. He hated the separation taking place, but also knew it to be inevitable. But now he sees there might be something more going on. His body floods with adrenaline, preparing a fight or flight response that might last months or years.

"Why do you think so?" he asks. "Did something happen?"

"Well, he keeps repeating things to me," she says. "And then the other day he forgot where I lived, thought I was back in Boston."

As Samantha's talking, Ethan sees Paul's slender figure through the window on its way to the kitchen. He's distracted and his sister picks up on his pause.

"It sounds like you're at a party, but I guess that's every weekend in I.V." she says. "Anyway, I need to eat before I pass out. I'm getting brunch with someone tomorrow who might have a lead on a job for me, so I should minimize the hangover. As for dad, I could be overreacting, but I wanted to let you know since, I don't know, you know, siblings."

"Sibling thank you," Ethan says. "But it's true, the party is calling me."

"Yeah, it's probably on life support without you. Go give it some mouth-to-mouth."

"And you get some rest."

"Sure, sure," Samantha says. "Take care."

"I will." Ethan hangs up, feeling like an idiot for any number of reasons. Paul emerges from the kitchen beer in hand, makes eye-contact with Ethan through the window, and heads to the balcony.

"Who was that?" Paul asks. His cropped bangs catch the rising ocean air and reveal his dimpled forehead to the night like a partial moon. His sober eyes rest on Ethan.

"Oh, just my sister," Ethan says, not wanting a drink but feeling like he should have one. "Just a drunk sibling chat."

Paul nods. "Everything OK with her then?"

"Yeah, I mean, some guy broke up with her, but she doesn't seem too phased. Way better off than I'd be anyway."

From the photos Paul's seen of Samantha on social media, she's clearly attractive. She has a winning smile and the same wide nose as Ethan, but it fits her face better. Paul casts the image from his mind, worried it'll come back later and cause him trouble. He spent the last two hours going over his dating options with his roommate and his girlfriend, who seemed to enjoy the exercise significantly more than him. All the smiling female photos are starting to blend together into one uber-woman, at once always present and forever out of reach.

"She still liking New York?" he asks.

Ethan shrugs. "I think so."

"You still liking 2023?" Paul asks, immediately regretting the joke.

"Haha," Ethan says. "Let's go down to the raft right now and I'll prove it to you. I'll take you back in time, motherfucker."

Ethan yells the last sentence and they both glance around to make sure no one's listening. No one is anywhere near listening. They could jump over the balcony without causing a scene. The absurdity of the moment releases the tension and Ethan smiles.

"Sorry," he says. "To be honest, I'm not loving it."

• • •

Two months go by.

Ethan meets Samantha and his parents in Florida for spring break. They spend the week with his grandmother in the house his father lived in as a teenager before heading west for college. Ethan's grandfather taught at Florida State for two decades before retiring and his grandmother still lives in the three-story house in a suburb of Tallahassee where his father came of age. Ethan wants to ask his dad more about his life back then and at Berkeley for college; wants to know how he determined to go to law school, or if he dated seriously before meeting his mom. He wonders what his parents were like when they were his age, or more accurately, how they were different. But the right moment never presents itself. Instead, they watch mediocre movies on a large, plasma-screen TV, eat meals demanding minimal preparation, and visit lakes and wildlife preserves requiring long drives to get to and involving short hikes upon arrival.

Neither Samantha nor Ethan bring up their father's possible illness. To discuss, no matter how discreetly, something so grave within the hermetic confines of the family bubble would disturb a dynamic at least twenty years in the making, since Ethan's birth. Best avoided until unavoidable. A couple minor incidents do occur though, upsetting Ethan enough that he worries someone will ask him if anything's wrong. Many things are wrong, we're all dying, but he doesn't like to be asked about it. One night at dinner, Ethan's father puts his fork down and asks his mother how Tom is doing. Tom, one of his father's old friends from the neighborhood, died a decade before in a climbing accident. Ethan's father attended the funeral. Ethan's grandmother gives a worrisome look and after a few seconds a light enters Ethan's father's eyes and, looking down, he says never mind. His father is also driving slowly, like geriatric slow, and stopping at stop signs for multiple seconds. Ethan also notices his mom holding his dad's elbow whenever they step down a curb or traverse a patch of grass. And once, only once, does Ethan's father meet his eye with an expression of irrecognition. Like at the dinner table, after a second a light sparks and his dad asks him about his courses or whether he can help with a bit of yard work. Had it happened again, Ethan may have been disturbed enough to consult Samantha, which could escalate into a family discussion and from there, who knows, the end of the world. Fortunately, it does not happen again.

One night, Ethan and Samantha take their grandmother's Toyota Avalon hybrid into town in search of a decent bar. Ethan finds them all sufficient, and reminiscent of those in Santa Barbara, but Samantha can't stop comparing things to New York, and it takes half and hour to single out an establishment dark and dingy enough to meet her criteria.

"Sorry," Samantha says once they're seated at a two-top pushed up against an exposed brick wall. "I guess I'm a little nostalgic for New York."

"Nostalgic for New York? You just left a few days ago."

"Yeah," Samantha says. "About that. It looks like I'm moving to L.A."

Ethan is shocked.

"I'm going to try to become a movie star. You think I've got what it takes?"

"Shut up."

"Seriously, though, I accepted a job at a newish startup helping monitor and evaluate carbon capture and storage projects, and they're headquartered in L.A. They gave me the option of staying in New York, but I don't think that city is so good for me anyway." Samantha points at her head and twirls her finger. "Kind of makes you go insane in the membrane after a while. Not that L.A. will necessarily be much better."

"Wow. Congrats. Have you told mom and dad?"

"I will, I just hate that proud look they give, it's worse than the worried one. Makes me feel like I'm just some genetic spawn and that whatever I do, it'll all come down to procreation in the end."

"That's weird, but yeah, I'm sure they'll be happy to have you back on the West Coast. What's carbon storing or whatever anyway?"

Samantha flicks a loose bang around her ear. She's gone running every day so far in Florida and she's getting tan.

"Well, burning fossil fuels to make electricity or do other industrial stuff creates a lot of carbon dioxide, which as we all know, is warming the planet. Carbon capture and storage is when that carbon is captured, piped underground, and stored there so it doesn't go into the atmosphere. It's a new technology, and it's not ideal by any means, but it could prove helpful. Unless it all leaks out, which is what I'll be working on—making sure that isn't happening."

"I see," Ethan says.

"Fossil fuel companies like it because it's another source of revenue, government likes it because it's less polarizing, people like it because people like wishful thinking."

Ethan thinks of the oil spill, how it felt like it could've gone on forever if they hadn't plugged the leak. It never occurred to him that the space underground could be put to good use.

"Did you know there was a giant offshore oil spill in Santa Barbara back in 1969?" he asks.

"Look at you," Samantha says. "Starting to take an interest in your surroundings. I did know that, but I don't know much about it. Just that it got into a lot of environmental history textbooks, and I think Nixon made a trip out there. Why?"

"Oh, just wondering. Figured you would."

In Ancient History class, Prof. Bourman is intolerably grouchy. The March midterm is so challenging that the bell curve raises most grades a full letter. Prof. Bourman tells the class they deserve to fail but that the worthless academic grading system, in which students are all too pampered to suffer any setbacks, won't permit it. Stomping back and forth from his lectern, his slacks wrinkled and his shirt cuffs haphazardly rolled up, he lambasts the class for a solid five minutes. Paul is pretty certain Prof. Bourman is not long for the world of academia. Ethan thinks maybe he'll have a personality-altering stroke and return to being the decent human he was fifty years prior. They are torn whether to sign up for another of his classes, the acerbity is becoming an acquired taste, and there's something addicting to being demanded so much of and scolded so ruthlessly.

"It's masochistic, but I'm kind of getting used to it," Paul says.

Over spring break, Greggy's scooter is found along the beach by a principled graduate student who looks up the serial number in the campus's registration system. The scooter is returned to Greggy's garage the next day, and he rides it over to Paul's to celebrate with beers. The photos taken from Leroy's house make no further appearances and are all but forgotten about. Occasionally, when he's home alone at night, Leroy will notice the photo album lying on the shelf and wonder briefly about the missing images. But mostly he wonders why Denise hasn't written him back.

On campus in early April, Ethan notices a flier on a telephone pole promoting Earth Day, which falls on April 22 every year. A jumble of text and photos, it's almost punk in aesthetic. In the lower left corner, there's a black-and-white photo of an oily beach over which bold white letters announce, "Conceived in SB." Ethan stares at the photo, which looks like it's from a long-forgotten era. But in his mind's eye the same scene appears, this one fresh and vibrant with color and life. He steps back, snapping out of the vision. The overcast day around him is muted and pregnant with lethargy. He heads to class, unable to shake a sense of incompleteness that's been dogging him.

Seated in the second to last row of his 50-minute Media, Politics and Government course, Ethan reads on his phone about Earth Day, which he's always considered an extension of 4/20 and a day of happily celebrating the Earth. He knows it's intended to raise awareness about all the pollution plaguing the planet's health, but that's always seemed so, what, retrograde? Obvious? He's surprised to find the Santa Barbara oil spill at the top of the Earth Day Wikipedia page:

On January 28, 1969, a well drilled by Union Oil Platform A 6 miles (10 km) off the coast of Santa Barbara, California, blew out. More than three million gallons of oil spilled, killing more than 10,000 seabirds, dolphins, seals, and sea lions. As a reaction to this disaster, activists were mobilized to create environmental regulation, environmental education, and Earth Day.

Something about all the dead animals makes him viscerally ill, like biting into a piece of uncooked meat. He takes a swig from his water bottle. Waves of history seem to course through him. He clenches and unclenches his fist and thinks about the past.

Specifically, he thinks of Leroy and Denise. He never considered them activists, but maybe they are, maybe almost every student was back then. He wonders how they mobilized in the weeks and months after the spill leading up to the first Earth Day in 1970. Not for the first time, he registers a pang of regret for departing when he did. But for the first time, he allows the pang to ripple across his consciousness. It's like the color has been drained from his life in Isla Vista, meanwhile the black-and-white photo on the flier was saturated with it. He lazily takes notes and doodles, unable to muster the motivation to pay much attention to the lecture. Wondering how anyone can pay attention to it.

After class is dismissed, he wanders campus through a stubborn fog apparently intent to hang low for the duration of the afternoon. He habitually takes out his headphones, but slips them back into his pocket, not in the mood to listen to anything. Students on bikes and skateboards emerge suddenly through the haze only to disappear back into it seconds later, the whir of their wheels skimming playfully through the mist. Tree trunks melt away into the pervasive white blanket as if they might rise for miles.

He pauses in front of the main library, a blocky, eight-story edifice that might benefit aesthetically from being shrouded in fog. He walks up the crescent staircase leading to the main entrance and through the building's double doors. The musty smell of book stacks mingles with the plastic clickety-clack of computer keyboards. He takes the elevator up to the seventh floor and sits down at a vacant cubicle next to a large window. The fog presses against the outside of the pane, resembling a gray canvas waiting to be stroked to life.

Ethan opens his computer and navigates to the UC-Santa Barbara archives, where he reads through *El Gaucho* issues from the weeks after the oil spill. The spill rarely makes the front page. There's so much else happening—so much activism. No one comprehended how long the spill would go on for, or how impactful it would be; how it would contribute to the rise of the environmental movement, or even what environmentalism meant. Also, Ethan notices, the paper took several weeks off from publication for spring break. On March 31, there's a passing mention of President Nixon's trip to survey the damage. Ethan tracks down a quote from Nixon during his brief Santa Barbara visit from another webpage:

"It is sad that it was necessary that Santa Barbara should be the example that had to bring it to the attention of the American people. What is involved is the use of our resources of the sea and of the land in a more effective way and with more concern for preserving the beauty and the natural resources that are so important to any kind of society that we want for the future. The Santa Barbara incident has frankly touched the conscience of the American people."

Ethan observes the accompanying photo of Nixon, who looks less aggrieved, and less jowly, than he recalls ever seeing him. Nixon is standing on the beach a few feet from the water flanked by men in dark suits on either side. His receding hair is combed back in waves. His probing nose evokes a beak. He's talking to members of a clean-up crew in clear hazmat suits. He looks relaxed and confident, and so do the clean-up crew, like they really are going to contain the spill and do whatever the environment requires to be preserved and stewarded through the upcoming centuries of human onslaught. Reading on, he sees that Nixon did accomplish a lot towards these ends. He passed the National Environmental Policy Act, the Clean Air and Clean Water Acts, the Endangered Species Act, and the Marine Mammal Protection Act. That seems like a hell of a lot. Ethan looks again at the photo capturing this moment very early in Nixon's presidency and shakes his head. He doesn't think anything like that is possible anymore. But is it the politicians' faults or the American people? Or somewhere in-between?

He doesn't know. He has no idea. He moves on.

He opens the April 8 edition. News of the spill makes the front page, or at least a feature on the growing outcry against oil drilling in the area:

700 Demonstrators Fight Off-Shore Oil Drilling[III]
By Larry Boggs
EG Staff Writer

Approximately 700 Santa Barbara citizens and University students gathered at the beach near Stearns Wharf in Santa Barbara Harbor Sunday to hear speeches against off-shore oil drilling. Immediately following the speeches, the crowd (spurred largely by acting Santa Barbara Mayor Vernon

Firestone) surged onto the wharf to demonstrate against the presence of platforms in the Santa Barbara Channel.

Chanting "Get oil out," and "Spirit of '76," members of the crowd wrote their names and smeared grease on several cranes operated by Standard Oil Company at the end of the wharf. The high point of the afternoon was reached when demonstrators confronted two oil supply trucks. As the trucks drove onto the wharf, a large part of the crowd immediately sat down in their path, blocking any further entry.

Tossing a wreath of flowers around the hood ornament of the lead truck and hooting catcalls at the driver, the demonstrators began again their chant of "get oil out." Police reinforcements soon arrived, only to become the target of the crowd's taunts.

At one time the harassed driver climbed out of his truck, yelled at the protesters, climbed back inside and attempted to force his way through them. No one moved. When it became apparent that the police would soon arrest the protesters for unlawful assembly, Dr. Harold Boughey of the Sociology Department of UCSB became the temporary spokesman of the demonstration. Boughey stated, "This wharf is owned by the people, and these trucks exceed the legal load limit. Therefore, we have the right to stop them."

When the police persisted, he retorted, "If you're going to arrest one of us, you'll have to arrest all of us." Mayor Firestone quipped, "It's probably costing the company 20 dollars an hour to have the trucks sit there." After a few minutes the trucks backed off the wharf to the wild cheers of the demonstrators, who immediately cleared a path for the normal flow of traffic onto the wharf.

"Nothing like this has ever happened in Santa Barbara history," Mayor Firestone noted. He continued, "We're not going to stop until those platforms are out of the

Channel. These companies and their elected representatives have demonstrated that they are irresponsible."

Such revived public outrage has been stimulated by the recent news that drilling will resume in the Santa Barbara Channel. The wharf, where Standard Oil Company maintains a marine oil station, has become symbolic of the oil controversy which has been raging since February.

The article continues for another couple columns, but Ethan stops reading. He's losing steam, his connection with the past dissipating somewhere in his gut, which is growling for food. He's preparing to shut his computer and head to the Wendy's in the UCen food court for the second time that week when he clicks open the April 11 edition of the *El Gaucho*. Across the top there's a big, black banner reading 'Extra' and an accompanying story that erases his appetite.

CHAPTER FOURTEEN
IF HE DIES, THAT WON'T MAKE HIM ANY LESS DEAD

Denise is still in bed when the bright blue phone in the living room rings, rattling the uneven stool where she and her roommate placed it months ago and never got around to finding a better spot. By the third ring, she's up, glancing at the clock on the wall as she clumsily makes her way towards the ear-piercing disturbance. It's only 7:30 a.m. She clears her voice and answers.

"Denise, it's Becca. Sorry to bother you so early, but there's been an incident on campus and I need people in the office now."

Denise adjusts the phone in the crook of her neck, which is stiff from sleep. "Oh, OK, I'll be right over. What kind of incident?"

Becca pauses. "A bombing, with a possible fatality."

"Oh shit," Denise says.

"I'll tell you more when you get here."

Becca hangs up. Denise slowly replaces the handset. Still woozy, she tries to make sense of what she just heard, but mostly her chest just aches. She goes through her morning routine in a daze, freezing midway through organizing her schoolbooks to contemplate if perhaps classes will be canceled. She considers calling Leroy, but the idea seems indulgent, and she knows his morning's booked up with study groups and a T.A session. Looking in the mirror, she straightens her blouse and tells herself she can handle another crisis. She imagines Leroy encouraging her, not that he's so good at that kind of thing. Sometimes she just needs to hear a different voice than the one inside her head, which can otherwise resemble a broken record; loud, scrambled, repetitive, mind-numbing. Becca always sets her straight, lends her some of her confidence, somehow, almost like it infuses the air around her. It's life outside the office, beyond Becca's aura, where she needs additional support. She pops her lips, the silly sound of it soothing. She's as ready as she'll ever be. Out front, she straddles her aqua-green cruising bicycle, her hands gripping the pollen-dusted handlebars. She hasn't ridden it in a couple weeks and the tires bloat underneath her weight. She could still call Leroy and ask to borrow his bike pump. But no, she'll fill the tires at the communal bike station and meet Leroy at 4 p.m. as previously planned.

The morning fog prickles her warm cheeks as she rides down Isla Vista's slumbering streets and the cool breeze makes her eyes water. Her tastebuds rise eagerly, giddy goosebumps on her tongue. The odorous oily aftertaste present since early February has finally dissipated. It's her favorite weather—jean-jacket weather she likes to call it. She wants to smile in awe of Mother Earth, but she won't permit herself that. She's too disgusted with father Shithead or whomever should be held responsible for bringing society to such a low point that bombs on campus and bloodshed in the street are everyday occurrences. There are occasions, however fleeting, when she feels like her generation can rise to meet the demands of the moment; like all the little things will add up to something much greater, something that can deal with the world in a herculean fashion. And then there are moments like this, when everything seems broken into shards, impossibly sharp and impossible to form into anything whole or even coherent. Typically, the future looks most promising in the morning, but not this morning.

For the second time in two months, Denise arrives at the newspaper office amid an unfolding emergency, this one so nearby that she hears a cacophony of police sirens rushing through campus. She drags her bike into the bustling room and leans it on a far wall alongside two other bikes. There's an open pizza box on the long wooden meeting table left over from the night before. Several people munch on greasy slices that catch the glare of the low overhead lights.

Becca waves Denise over as she places her overstuffed bag at her desk. Of course, Steven is already by Becca's side, his neatly parted hair also catching a glare and his posterboard smile as posterboarded on his face as ever.

"Thanks for coming in early," Becca says. "Steven is about to head over to the Faculty Club to meet up with the photographer. They'll get what they need—what they can—from the scene."

"I'll make sure to get *all* the details," Steven says. The way he emphasizes the word 'all' grates Denise's nerves, which are already frayed.

"Denise, I need you to stay here and help me clean copy," Becca says. "We're short a couple editors today."

Denise nods. She's disappointed, relieved, and pleased all at once. She's been waiting for a chance to take on more editing, and while she wants to want to be on the scene of the crime, that's one too many wants. Becca is summoned to the phone. She lifts a finger indicating Denise hold tight and retreats to the back of the room, waving Steven towards the door as she goes.

Steven gathers his notebook and double checks that the pen in his breast pocket is up to the job ahead.

"Have fun down here below ground," he says to Denise, his black leather satchel neatly tucked under his arm. "This could be national news, you know?"

"Just like the oil spill was?" Denise shoots back. Steven was disappointed his oil spill coverage didn't get syndicated by any more widely read publications.

"You know there were dozens of reporters on that story, I…I mean, we just don't have the resources to compete with those papers." Steven leans heavily into his palms, which are planted on the desk. "If we get this first, it could catch fire on the wires."

"Well, you'd better get out there and report it then," Denise says. Steven responds with a humph and turns towards the door, his gait quick and tight like someone who wants to run to the bathroom but isn't sure they'll make it.

• • •

El GAUCHO EXTRA:
Home-Made Bomb Damages Faculty Club[IV]
Blast Critically Injures Resident Custodian, 55

A home-made bomb, which exploded in the courtyard of the Faculty Club at 6:23 this morning, critically injured Dover O. Sharp, 55, maintenance man of the Faculty Club, and caused $1,000 worth of damage.

The bomb was contained in a cardboard box and was placed in the north-east corner of the patio, next to the dining room. It apparently went off when Sharp attempted to open the box.

Sharp lived in the building and was probably on his way to the kitchen to fix breakfast. The explosion blew him 20 feet toward the center of the patio. Sharp then evidently pulled himself another 50 to 75 feet to the wading pool in order to extinguish his burning clothing.

Students in San Rafael dorm, located over 200 yards away, were awakened by the blast and two reported hearing "the most horrible cry for help."

Several men residents of the dorm ran to Sharp with blankets. They helped him out of the pool and covered him until the campus fire department and rescue squad arrived.

The squad arrived within a few minutes of the explosion and immediately transported Sharp to the Goleta Valley Hospital.

Sharp was reported to be in extremely critical condition with burns over 80 percent of his body, severe lacerations, and a fractured leg. He underwent immediate surgery.

The blast shattered four sliding glass doors, ripped screens, charred walls, and caused an estimated $1,000 damage, according to William H. Steinmetz, Manager of Safety and Security Services.

Although authorities had not determined the precise composition of the bomb, Fire Chief Arthur T. McGarry stated that it was a fairly sophisticated device, consisting of "a half gallon wine jug filled with a volatile liquid, such as gasoline, a timing device, a battery, and a piece of six-inch pipe packed with an explosive compound."

• • •

EDITORIAL[v]
April 11, 1969

What the hell kind of campus do we have?

Just why do some people think they have to destroy and maim before they believe they have gotten their point across?

We have no idea who was involved in this act—no idea at all, and the last thing we want to do is point the finger at any political faction, at any group, or at any individual. That is for the proper authorities to discover (if they can) in due time.

But we are frightfully concerned that others will believe that this is a proper course of action—that bombs and mutilation are the tools of political power.

This campus has been relatively free from violence. There has been no violent confrontation, no real destruction of property, nothing more dangerous than threats—up until now.

We believe it is probable that this act may have had nothing to do with anything political that has gone on at this campus. But we feel it is incumbent upon all those involved in the political activity on this campus—and that includes everyone from the Young Americans for Freedom through the Associated Students and on to the Black Student Union and the Students for a Democratic Society—to publicly and forcefully denounce this act, for if this is not done, we lay ourselves open to the charge of endorsement by inaction.

Right now a man lies in a hospital with burns over 80 percent of his body. He may be dying. He had nothing to do with anything that has happened on this campus, except that he cleaned up the Faculty Club on the night shift. But if he dies, that won't make him any less dead.

• • •

Denise is exhausted by the time she arrives at the three circular grass embankments, each about 20 feet in diameter, at four o'clock to meet Leroy for their prearranged rendezvous. Seated on the knee-high wall surrounding the middle embankment, she watches students pass by along the wide sidewalk abutting the utilitarian sculptures. Some of them appear zombified and depleted, like her; others relaxed, maybe a little high, and ostensibly unaffected by the news of the bombing; and a few have determined expressions, steeled for some arduous undertaking, whether that be securing their own safety, the fight for women's rights, or the need for a passing grade, Denise doesn't know or much care right now. She lays back on the grassy mound and lets the sun burn away her wearisome thoughts as she awaits Leroy.

They got the special edition of the paper out at noon, a major feat with a skeleton staff. Becca, as she always does, rose to the occasion, dispatching assignments with a fluidity as if requesting ingredients for a beloved recipe, and finessing disagreements and copy with unimpeachable authority and little unnecessary attitude. Becca has an internal reserve of courage, or conviction, or both, that Denise is realizing she herself may not possess, now or ever. The emotions and beliefs of others penetrate her skin all too easily, diluting or concentrating her own in equal measure. She is too easily influenced by others, she knows this, and she's unable to do anything about it. In fact, she frequently courts it, as the alternative of looking inside herself reveals a cluttered mess. Occasionally she finds a gem, but often, just more mess. Closing her eyes under the midday sun offers temporary relief though. For a minute, everyone disappears, including herself.

She hears a soft thump next to her.

"What a Goddamn horrible thing," Leroy says as Denise sits up and rubs her eyes. "Sicker than sick. Pointless violence. I don't understand how anyone could ... it's got to have something to do with the war. Fighting violence with violence. But the choice of target ... Maybe I should've said something when I had the chance ..."

Denise puts her hand around Leroy's upper arm and tightens her grip. Leroy looks into her moist eyes and shuts up. They listen to the wind blowing through campus, rustling leaves, hugging buildings. The sun is casting long shadows on the slender trees and squat buildings lining the central campus corridor, longer than usual it seems. All the fog has lifted only to be replaced overnight, as if people need to be shortsighted in the morning in order to start going about their days.

"How were things at the paper?" Leroy asks, tenderness in his voice.

"Busy as could be," Denise says. "Becca had me editing."

"Oh, that's good. Isn't it?"

"I guess so, but it didn't feel very good."

"I'm sure nothing felt very good today." Leroy turns his head towards Denise's. "At least almost nothing."

Denise knows what's coming and she wants to hear it. "What do you mean?"

"Well, it felt good to see you just now. Really good."

Denise swings her other arm around Leroy's bicep and gives it a bear hug. "Yeah, I guess that—this—does feel good."

A dozen or so female students walk past, their conversation bubbly. A handful of guys trail behind, scuffing the soles of their shoes on the cement as they proceed towards Isla Vista.

"So I guess Steven went down to the club, then?" Leroy asks.

"Yeah, there was no holding him back—he's dying for a national byline. Becca knows that. I don't know how she deals with him so well, he's just like, so rude. And he's always pestering her."

"Pricks like him are willing do to whatever it takes to get ahead, no matter how obnoxious," Leroy says. "They know that you don't succeed in society by coasting along. You've got to be an asshole, or a dick. Take our new president, Dick Nixon. Nothing nice about him, but he's on top. There's only so much the rest of us can take. After a while, you start to see how someone, someone already on the edge, you know, mentally, might decide to blow something up, even if it doesn't make any sense. Even if it kills an innocent person."

Denise is taken aback by Leroy's unhinged response. She sits up straight and observes him from arm's length. "Is something wrong? I mean something else other than what we're all dealing with."

Leroy stiffens like he's about to issue a total denial, but he lets his guard down as she embraces his hand. Denise feels a powerful current pass between them, feeding off their emotional vulnerability like electricity through water. She fleetingly thinks that it might be love, which makes her heart flutter but also pains her. Love is a very powerful emotion, too powerful for her to deal with right now.

"Well, actually, something is bothering me and I'm not quite sure what to do about it." Leroy looks in the direction of the setting sun. "I suspect my neighbors might be responsible for the bombing."

CHAPTER FIFTEEN
KNIFE EDGE

Lonnie Lazio sits alone in a dim room. Dust specs hang in the air in front of the sheer, off-white curtain draped partway across the only window. Lonnie watches them, wondering how they arrive at their next move as they dance effortlessly through space. They make it look so easy. Rising from the defeated beanbag that serves as chair and, many nights, bed, he slides the squeaky windowpane up a few inches, hoping increased air circulation will alleviate the sensation that he's suffocating. He sits back down and observes the curtain waving delicately in the light breeze. He is envious of the dust and the curtain, just blowing in the wind. He messes with the laces on his Airwalks. Things are bad enough now that maybe he should just go back to the future if the portal's still open.

At least Russell isn't home yet. When Russell gets back from his three-day visit to the desert, Lonnie knows he'll be in big, big trouble. He'll be in Hell. Although, he already feels like he's in Hell, so he'll be somewhere worse than Hell when Russell gets back. It's too bad because usually when Russell returns from these spiritual sojourns—trips is a more descriptive word—the bliss lingers for a while. He's content listening to The Beatles, eating raw foods, and not ordering people around. Inevitably, though, the buzz wears off and his demanding, short-tempered, ill-humored self returns with a vengeance. Lonnie wishes he could wait a few days before telling Russell what he's done.

Then he could soak up some of the afterglow of the desert high before plummeting down to worse-than-Hell. He tries to envision feeling good, what could make him feel good. But he draws a blank, feels a blankness inside. Anyway, there's no chance of putting it off because the second Russell sees a newspaper, he'll suspect what's happened and then Lonnie will be in for it.

Lonnie thinks of the bomb, of it exploding in Dover's hands. He wonders why he didn't visualize this gruesome scene before he dropped the parcel off. That might've deterred him from his, what already seems in hindsight of just a few hours, extremely rash and extremely poor decision; a decision that's left Dover burned to a crisp and Lonnie locked inside his stuffy room in the back of his and Russell's house, afraid to venture out in the daylight like some defanged, diminutive vampire.

Lonnie liked some things about the future—the motorized scooters, the superior coffee that gave him a head rush, the way female students always dressed in pajamas or exercise clothing, and especially the shoes—but the future was, for the most part, terrifying. There were screens everywhere, which meant spies everywhere, linked up by some mystical connecting ether known as the Internet. And the people were all so big, especially compared to a small guy like him. And the prices were outrageous, almost unimaginably expensive. And instead of the flying hovercrafts he'd imagined, everyone got around in ginormous vehicles that didn't seem at all fun to drive. And the news, from what he could gather, was stuck in even more of a doomsday cycle than it is now, which is hard to believe. He'd spent an afternoon in the UCen watching the TVs looming over the cafeteria, which were programmed to some channel called CNN. He couldn't make heads or tails of most of what he heard, typical political mumbo-jumbo, but news of a major storm on the East Coast caught his attention. Scenes of flooding like he'd never seen—flooding of entire neighborhoods—filled the screen, and the anchors debated something called climate change, if it's responsible. They didn't sound like they knew what they were talking about. But still, it left him feeling adrift, like maybe the whole world was sick in some mysterious way. Like the oil spill was just the beginning. After that, he knew he had to say something to Russell about going back.

They'd discovered the portal one evening while out on a boat one of Russell's wealthy desert friends had given him the go-ahead to use. Lonnie's not sure of the details, as Russell keeps him out of whatever loops he can. Lonnie can still see Russell diving into the water from the boat's deck, as cool as a cat. At first, the two girls they'd brought along had been impressed, giggling almost uncontrollably. But then Russell didn't resurface, and their expressions morphed to horrified and, to Lonnie, it seemed almost as if their faces were melting. He jumped in after Russell as much to get away from the panicking girls as to rescue his pal. Then they both awoke washed up on an Isla Vista beach in the year 2023, which took them about 24 hours to figure out. After five more days of living like street rats, scavenging for food and sleeping on discarded mattresses—of which there seemed to be many in the future—they returned to the sea using an old canoe Russell commandeered from underneath a termite-infested deck off the side of a house. They somewhat miraculously relocated the bright beacon and entirely miraculously arrived back in 1969 after jumping through it.

Russell was eager to refocus on their bomb-making in the buildup to the big political explosion he was orchestrating. Only a few days after their return did a devilish grin emerge from within his wiry beard as his hands pulled and pinched wires on a long table in the garage. He called Lonnie over and informed him they'd be returning to the future in search of some collateral to use against Leroy should he become an obstacle to achieving their target. It was only by chance they'd learned Leroy was a UCSB faculty member all those years later. Russell had wanted to see what'd become of Bill Allen, the only professor he had anything resembling a modicum of respect for, so they'd toured the anthropology department. When they unsuspectingly came across a Prof. Leroy Bourman's office, Russell yelped. The door was slightly ajar, and when Russell pushed it open, Leroy scowled at him from across the room as an oblivious student rambled on about some ancient dilemma.

After that, they asked a few kids about Prof. Bourman, what his reputation was and what his classes were like, gleeful at the negative reactions they got.

Russell had long thought of Leroy as a nuisance, but mostly for his basic neighborliness, which he took as an affront and had no doubt was some passive-aggressive con. He could barely contain his rage at Leroy asking if they'd like him to cut their lawn along with his own. Or if they needed help getting the trash cans out to the curb. But unless they relocated to the desert, which didn't enter into things until much later, they'd always have to suffer neighbors. Lately, after months of giving him the cold shoulder, Russell had tried to ingratiate himself with Leroy to help allay any suspicions he might have about their banging around in the garage. He seemed to think it was working, but not well enough to avoid having a backup plan.

Lonnie shivers recalling Russell's reassurance to him before heading into the desert that the plan would come together before summer break. Now, he's gone and screwed everything up so royally that Russell is certain to explode at him. Lonnie pushes himself up from the beanbag and kicks at a corner of the room's peeling beige wall. Russell's plan is no longer on schedule and it's all his fault. Even if they could remake the bomb in time, which Lonnie thinks might just be possible, security around campus is sure to be through the roof for the foreseeable future.

But really, it's that girl Margaret's fault for resisting his advances, or the caretaker's fault for not minding his own business—for not just continuing his walk around the lagoon as if he hadn't seen anything. Because Lonnie could not forgive Dover for pulling him away from Margaret just as she was about to submit to him. He knew she wanted to lay with him there under the twilight, lay underneath him mostly. Otherwise, why had she agreed to accompany him on a stroll to that remote and romantic spot? The knife may have had something to do with it, although it's not like Lonnie threatened her with it, he just wanted to show it to her. Dover backed away and apologized like a coward after Lonnie flashed the knife, but it was too late by then.

Margaret was already up and running, most likely scared of Dover, who did look a bit menacing, hunched over them under the fading light, his hairy arms hanging down by his hips. By now she's probably back in Santa Cruz strolling around in one of her miniskirts, fuckall on her mind. Before Dover imposed himself, Lonnie hoped she'd let him visit her up there, especially if he got his hands on some of the high-quality dope that Russell typically brought back from the desert.

Lonnie kicks the wall harder and curses himself, because he sees now that he does forgive Dover. That he, in fact, might've done the same thing. That he should've listened to Margaret when she said she just didn't go for guys that were shorter than her, or that she was on her period, or that she was really, really hungry. But then she flicked his hair and laughed softly. Why couldn't he have been happy with that sign of affection? Taken it as encouragement that if he bided his time maybe he would get a chance to see what's up that skirt. Now he's gone and ruined everything twice over and most likely murdered someone in the process. Next time, if there is a next time, he'll be more cautious. He'll even be precautious. He'll be like a saint, as far as any woman will be able to tell. Saint Lonnie. He likes the sound of that, likes the idea of being the good guy for once.

Lonnie looks at his watch. More than eleven hours since the bomb detonated that morning and he's still a free man. He's probably not even a suspect. He hears something out the window, a familiar voice but not Russell's. It's Leroy, he realizes, the only person who might have an inkling that the bomb originated in this house. His restlessness given an outlet, Lonnie pulls on his fringed jacket and stomps out of the room, down the hallway, and through the front door. Across the yard, Leroy and the girl he's dating freeze along the sidewalk, cease conversing, and turn towards him.

"What a bummer of a day," Lonnie says, his voice catching in his throat. His chest is heaving. He bends over to try to calm it, and himself, down. Leroy and the girl stare at him funnily, but there's nothing too unusual about that.

"Yeah," Leroy says back, his hands in his coat pockets. "Can't believe something like that could happen at UCSB, you know. And for what?"

"I have no idea," Lonnie says, wiping his brow. Now that he's outside he feels faint. He realizes he's neglected to eat anything all day.

Leroy steps off the sidewalk towards him.

"You really have no idea? Can you guess?"

The girl nudges him in the rib with her elbow.

Lonnie's anger, which he thought was dead and buried for the time being, is exhumed.

"Why would I have any idea?" he says sharply. He walks forward but his Airwalk is untied. He kneels to tie it.

"Let's get going," the girl says to Leroy a bit anxiously. "We've got to get to that peaceful protest on campus." Then, a bit in his direction, she adds. "Whatever the reason—anti-war, equal rights, or even anti-nuclear power, as some people are saying the bomb might've been about—there's never cause for violence. We must remain peaceful. It's not usually the easiest decision, but it's always the right one."

Lonnie looks up and catches the girl's eye. She looks surprised, perhaps not sure where that monologue came from. He senses she's not usually so outspoken. Then Leroy's arm tugs her forward and the two of them head inside.

Seated on the cement step, Lonnie feels as if he's teetering on the edge of another portal, but one that can't be jumped back through. If he goes forward into the fading light, he won't return. He'll find some food and catch a ride downtown and begin a new existence. The word 'peaceful' reverberates through his head. Whatever he does, he'll make sure it's peaceful; if he can't be saintly, he can at least be peaceful. He thinks this is what he's wanted all along, some peace—inner peace or outer peace or just regular, epidermal-level peace—and instead he's found only turmoil, enmity, and now violence. He's got almost a year to set himself straight before a new decade commences. He recalls the early 60s as a kid in the Phoenix suburbs. He wanted nothing more than to be in California by the end of the decade. Everything used to be—or at least used to seem—so simple and straightforward. Now it turns out, what seemed like one thing, like one person's life or one's own decision, is in reality one million different and conflicting things and lives all interacting and pushing through time chaotically, maddeningly. He longs to see things as he did as a child before everything was corroded by time.

If he proceeds down the block, as in fact he's already doing, he'll have to cut ties with Russell, who he considered until just a few hours ago to be a brother for life. But life no longer means what he thought it did, and he never really knew what brotherhood stood for. Everything is suspended midair like those dust particles. Who knows what'll happen next? A police car siren shakes him from his reveries, and he drifts down the street and turns towards Goleta, where he'll catch a bus to downtown Santa Barbara.

CHAPTER SIXTEEN
GET AWAY

Ethan desperately skips ahead in the archives after reading the article about the faculty bombing. He's pretty sure Dover won't survive, and his hunch is verified a few days later. He hadn't thought much about the caretaker or the Faculty Club in weeks, but now it's like he's back there again, chatting with Dover over a casual breakfast or helping sweep around the pool. He envisions the shards of glass exploding from a few feet away, inches even, and carving into his friend's body. He imagines the haunting screams students reported hearing as Dover fought for his life, crawling towards the swimming pool as if the water could transport him back in time to before death visited his doorstep. A hell of a way to die, even to someone like Ethan who's considered many of them. He's glad his stomach is empty because he'd throw up its contents. He gets up and steps to the library window. The fog outside is finally rising and he can see across the UCen to the lagoon. He identifies the spot where Dover pulled him from the brush and got him back on his feet. He wonders where he would be now if not for Dover. Maybe 1969. Maybe dead. Maybe jail. The police sure seemed eager to arrest folks back then. He considers what would've happened had someone less fatherly, less accommodating of his peculiarity, perhaps more invasive of his privacy, found him in that vulnerable state. He shudders, feeling more gratitude than ever for Dover.

He departs the library and walks briskly to the lagoon. He walks the trail ringing the main hill, which is much less overgrown than in 1969. The steady stream of joggers huffing by disrupts his attempt at an impromptu memorial. He encounters a tour group of prospective students and their parents where the trail descends to the beach. The tour guide is overflowing with enthusiasm, expounding on the campus's natural beauty and his love of surfing. Ethan wants to slap him across the face and tell everyone to stay away; to never leave their childhood bedrooms; to remain high and in high school forever; to just kill themselves now and get it over with. He observes the students with a mix of disdain and awe. Some parents shoot disconcerted looks his way, probably hoping their kid gets into Berkeley. After passing he yells over his shoulder, "Come here and you might end up like me!" He doesn't turn to gauge the reaction.

Down the hill, he stops in a secluded cranny along the bluffs and watches the choppy waves crash into the rocky coastline and swirl into oblivion. One of the organs around his midsection is aching cancerously again, but it's not the only sensation demanding attention. He can't deny it, the waves are calling to him like they did that night back in January when he first took the raft out by himself. With each crescendo he feels a slight tug. Not exactly across the shoulders, but that's how he's interpreting it. He wonders if it could be his imagination, something to do with his mind malfunctioning, but he can't ignore the effect so what's the difference. He slides his phone from his pocket and calls Paul.

"Hello?" Paul answers after a couple rings with the expected confusion as to why Ethan—or anybody aside from a family member—would call rather than text.

"Hey, it's Ethan."

"Yeah, I know. What's up? Is something wrong?"

"Not exactly. I sort of need your help with something."

"Yeah?"

"I need to go back to 1969 again and I was hoping you could cover for me."

Paul scoffs, then turns serious. "Wait, are you serious?"

"I might be gone a little longer this time," Ethan responds.

Eight hours later, they're down on the narrow beach dragging the raft between them. The night is brisk and gusty. They're both underdressed in hoodies. Paul makes a point of not letting the weather dictate his attire and Ethan is too distracted to register how cold he is.

After Ethan told Paul about Dover, Paul asked the exact date of the bombing. When Ethan told him, he responded, "That's six days ago. Well, 54 years and six days ago to be precise. Anyway, you won't be able to save him, assuming this time travel thing takes you back to the same day of the year as you seem to believe it does."

Pulling the raft across the sand, Ethan wonders why he didn't even consider the possibility of saving Dover. It seems so obvious in hindsight. Survival should be his first thought, as it was Paul's, not death. It's something other than that anyway, something other than thought, driving him out past the waves towards the bright beacon, at least towards where it should be. That was Paul's next question.

"Are you sure the time travel thingy is still there?"

Disregarding Paul's sarcastic tone and its implication of disbelief, he answered. "No."

Paul then asked how long he wanted to go for.

"A week, I guess," Ethan said.

"And what's your plan for that? Like, what am I supposed to do?"

Ethan looked neutrally at Paul and took a sip of a beer as they sat on Paul's patio. Two squirrels barked at each other across limbs of a nearby tree.

"You have no idea, do you?" Paul said before emitting a drawn-out groan, standing up, and continuing. "Alright, a week is doable. Tell your parents your phone has been weird, and you might miss their calls. You can be sick for a week of school. I can try to tune in for some of the lectures remotely, so it looks like you attended. Any longer though and it'll fall apart."

Down at the water, Paul runs through the plan again. Then he surprises Ethan by announcing that he's coming too. Ethan vehemently objects.

"Just out to this portal," Paul says.

Ethan protests again, but Paul is adamant. "I've got to see this crazy thing if I'm going to go along with all this."

The wind is whipping in from the ocean. Ethan decides he could use some help getting out there.

"OK, fine," he says. "But you're going to do the paddling. Making the trip though the portal, like, saps you dry, and I don't want to already be beat."

Paul consents. He puts the raft down and removes his large hiking backpack containing an inflatable kayak for his return trip. He hands Ethan a fanny pack from around his waist.

"Take this," he says. "It's got some granola bars, a Swiss army knife, and some change from the 60s I found in my change jar."

"Wow, thanks," Ethan says. "Good ideas."

Paul shoots him a sympathetic-yet-knowing look as he opens his backpack and unfurls the inflatable kayak. While inflating it with a hand pump, Paul considers, not for the first time, following Ethan through the portal should they locate it. He hates himself for gaming this move out for several reasons: because he knows it can't really be possible—there can't be any time portal; because he deplores deceiving people, especially his friends; and because of the risk he'd be taking if it magically worked. Profile pictures of three or four prospective online dates he's got align in his mind like action figures. He hates how much these pointless exercises in human courtship are affecting his thinking. He doesn't want his life to be dictated by dates, doesn't want to look forward to small talk and spending what little hard-earned money he has on dressing it up in formality. But he's also got to listen to his body, which is demanding he engage the opposite sex. He knows it's the healthy thing to do, much healthier than what he's been doing almost nonstop since moving out of the dorms. How he got through a year of room sharing freshman year he doesn't dare fathom. He has at least one vivid memory of masturbating in the closet. Even if he didn't mind spending his time mastering the art of flirtation, this foray into the apps feels too much like a modern marker of adulthood after which one is increasingly beholden to the demands of society; increasingly removed from the visceral, tactile experience of youth. He senses the comforts of his carefree college life slipping away, a life in which he can walk leisurely to class and play detective to his heart's content and not worry about healthcare. A life in which chronic masturbation is still a somewhat reasonable lifestyle, not entirely sheathed in pathos.

"You coming?" Ethan calls back from the water's edge, where he's preparing to mount the raft. Paul nods, finishes packing his bag, and tosses the kayak into the raft. A minute later, they're paddling into the horizon, chasing the sun even though it's already set.

"I'm glad I agreed to this," Paul says.

"Why?" Ethan asks as he casually rows, unable to make Paul do all the work. "You seemed pretty exasperated about the whole thing."

"Well, I was worried," Paul responds. "And, you know, it's crazy. But now that we're out here, it's great. It's great to get away for a minute."

CHAPTER SEVENTEEN
THE DAMNED DAM

April 8, 2023
Dear Leroy,
    First of all, apologies for the long delay in responding. These days everything takes longer. And you know me, I can be slow to process and what you wrote required a bit of processing :). You must be sick of these smiley faces in writing—do students use them all the time? I'm amazed by how much writing style and syntax have changed since my time as a student reporter. I imagine the 1969-70 El Gauchos would seem quite archaic compared to whatever they're publishing these days. Like everything else, language evolves. Still, it would be nice if my niece would include some punctuation, even just a comma or two, in her text messages. Are all older people equally put off by this or just those that were formerly copy editors?
    To be honest, your letter made me quite sad. In the moment, in that van, I possessed an uncharacteristically hardened resolve to move on with my life—on to what, who knows. Looking back now, I view it with more typical-Denise mixed feelings. Seeing things from your perspective makes it all that much harder to justify, which I suppose is not unexpected. I never imagined you would throw that priceless ring into the lake, though. I feel horribly about that. Do you really think it might still be down there?
    I want to tell you I had some righteous reason for departing so abruptly, and to provide some reasonable explanation, as if one could

exist, but I can't. I wasn't ready to be engaged, that's about as close as I can get, although saying that sounds silly now considering I got married only a couple years later. Although I can see in hindsight that I still wasn't ready then. Anyway, in your 20s, a few years seems like a long time. I believe I intended to have a sit-down talk with you about "things" when we returned from the trip, but I sensed you had an itchy trigger finger with that ring, and I could see that Lake Powell was as good a place as any to get down on one knee. I indeed knew that you were quite romantic, or at least aspired to be in your more susceptible moments.

As for your question about the van and who was in it, I'll admit I can hardly believe the truth myself. Increasingly the past blurs together for me, and I question my recollections, which flow like stormwater through my mind, flooding in from every which way and laden with flotsam. But in this case, I'm certain—Edward Abbey was in that van. Yes, that Edward Abbey, the wild, mischievous chronicler of the West during those years when large-scale development descended and environmentalists found in the hulking bridges, wide roads, and rerouted rivers a manifest adversary, and flesh-and-blood foes in those pulling the levers. He wasn't quite so well-known then, but his star was certainly rising. As you may recall (unless your memory is even worse than mine), I was intimately familiar with his book Desert Solitaire from my coverage of the tragic death of that Faculty Club caretaker, Dover something (I doubt you're sharp enough to remember his full name—I just looked it up and left a hint for you in this parenthetical).

Anyway, I hate to imagine what Abbey's reaction would be to the way I live now. He would turn and sprint in the other direction if he ever bore witness to my oversized, air-conditioned house with a lawn (at least only partial) requiring year-round watering in one of the most inhospitable parts of the country, so hot and dry that most of the residents decamp for half the year. But before running, he'd launch an immense tirade at me, and I would deserve it. You know what? I might even appreciate it. It's been so long since someone's treated me with the intensity that he did. That degree of passion, regardless of the intent, might be good for me. It might help snap me out of these funks I get in, even if his outbursts were equal parts intoxicating and overbearing. He was never pleased with himself, and even more rarely so with others.

So are you shocked? I don't know what you could've expected. There's not much more to it; you know how liberated and impulsive things were then. I met Ed the day before we took off in his van—I'd never met anyone so charismatic, with so much, I guess, lifeforce (the old anthropology professor Bill Allen maybe could be described in a similar way, but he didn't have that something extra that made him sexually irresistible as well.) Anyway, I initially encountered Ed on a walk around the campsite while you were out on a supply run. He was alone and very affable. I assumed his wife or whomever he was with was out on a hike. But he told me that he was on a solo trip to check in on Lake Powell, or as he called it, "the imprisoned river by the damned dam." He had a notebook out and he mentioned something about research. He eventually informed me of who he was. I told him I loved his book about living and working in Arches, and that it'd fallen into my lap during a trying moment. I remember he appeared pleased by that. I think trying moments were his favorite kind. Before I knew it, I'd told him about my premonition of your intention to propose and the doubts I harbored. He said he'd been married three times, so maybe I shouldn't listen to him, he was no expert—but then again, maybe he was. He said he thought I should break it off clean. And so, when I saw him packing up the next day (it's possible I went searching for him without admitting it to myself) and he offered me a ride, well, I made one of the rashest decisions of my life.

I soon realized that I'd bitten off more than I could chew. Ed was bursting at the seams with energy and was just as likely to erupt in anger at any moment as he was to shower me with love. I even started to miss your level-headedness and precautious approach to life (I fear maybe some of these qualities I so cherished in you have withered away over the years?). I might as well say it though, the sex was some of the best of my life. I've often thought, based on that experience, that a couple weeks on the road with someone is just the right amount of time and the perfect setting for a love affair. Other than eating by a campfire and watching the stars, I don't remember too much aside from the love making (and the rants, of course). Even when you're young, you recognize there won't be many intervals of such untarnished living; life only offers up so many of these opportunities. You also know they can't very well last. If they did, well, I guess civilization would be scarcely recognizable compared to what it is now. Ed also made a point of stating the transitory nature of our affair, both, I guess, to make sure to appreciate it in the moment and so I didn't get the wrong idea.

After ten days or so he dropped me in Vegas. From there I hitched a ride back to L.A. and took the train up to Goleta. Upon my return, I remember going by your house and not seeing your car. When you weren't there the next day, I started to grasp that you weren't coming back. I was vulnerable then and had you been around I might've dropped to my knees in apology. But I knew you planned to move out shortly after the trip—that was partly why you needed to propose. And the rest, as they say, is history.

Well, this recounting is indeed exhausting. I hope you didn't find it too painful. And in a way I do feel better. Maybe this is therapeutic for both of us ;). It's the couples therapy we always needed. Although I'm not sure that existed very much back then. Now, from what I can tell, it's more common than even divorce.

A parting thought: Despite the heavy subject matter, is this becoming fun or is it just my imagination?

With love,
Denise

• • •

April 18, 2023
Dear Denise,

It was a great relief to receive your response, even if the contents left me near flabbergasted. I laughed aloud while reading, which is something I rarely ever do (I read a lot of dry academic material, and usually when I exclaim it's due to frustration with the sub-par writing or faulty research). I expected to experience renewed anger and hurt upon learning your side of the story, but I can't seem to suppress a smile, which is all the more surprising considering the high level of frustration I easily summon for almost everything else in my life. You ditched me for a fling with the author of The Monkey Wrench Gang? Haha. I have that book on a shelf, I think my son acquired it for a course once (and probably discarded it after reading a few pages to go back to video games, knowing him). I perused it after reading your email. Talk about writing style evolving. There's a very Doonesbury-ish aspect to the whole concoction. And, I must admit as long as we're trying to be open with each other, I find the casual sexism and crude humor refreshing. No publisher would greenlight a book like that nowadays. They'd be terrified of being canceled! Even if the characters are more-or-less caricatures, they still provide for quite a romp. It's clear Abbey had a vibrant mind though, brimming with ideas of all sorts, many of them far-fetched, even if he wasn't exactly a master of prose. And I can relate to his outrage over the environmental degradation the dam will cause; it's a clear parable of man's abuse of nature, of our failure to steward the land in any responsible way. It hits you right where it counts, or at least it should if you've got half a brain. If he wrote the book now, however, his editors would force him to devote half of it to climate change, making it boring and unreadable. Maybe he could work in some alien invasions or resuscitated plagues, which are equally as likely to decimate the planet as global warming. I recently saw that plant life is booming, so there shouldn't be any issue with the carbon cycle. Thinking of Abbey reminded me how much I used to enjoy popular fiction and made me wonder why I turned away from it. Maybe some deeply buried resentment around my failure to become a writer, or failure to even really try.

While it may be too late to make good on my writerly aspirations (unless you count these emails as literary works ;) there's still time to delve back into reading. It's one of the few activities I know I really enjoy—and one of the few that being an over-the-hill geezer doesn't detract from. I was even inspired to stop by a bookstore—yes, they still exist, at least a few—in downtown Santa Barbara the other day. My *enthusiasm was quickly extinguished though by the overwhelming prevalence of woke books. It seemed everything I picked up from the new fiction table was about a minority figure struggling for recognition, or the challenges of being gay or trans, or some riff on a world experiencing catastrophic environmental upheaval. There were also, strangely, a lot of books featuring octopuses, not sure what to make of that. Maybe next time I go, platypuses will be in vogue. Even the science fiction I perused had wokeness baked in, you know, some different-looking outsider long suppressed by those in power goes on to…finds community…does good. I don't know, I don't want to sound too embittered, but it's hard for me to believe those are the best new books around. I skimmed through a few; the writing was nothing special and the plotlines predictable and either slow moving or overcomplicated. In the end, I found an acceptable spy novel by a British author and I also purchased the new Stephen King book. What are you reading these days? Perhaps you have some better suggestions for contemporary authors? They must be out there. Maybe you use one of those apps that match you with books through some fancy algorithm. I find that distasteful, like online dating but even more ridiculous, plus I don't want anymore apps on my phone. I thought about asking the bookstore attendant, but the young man was covered in tattoos, highly off-putting. I checked his staff picks' selection though, something by a Sally Rooney. I read a few pages but that's all I could tolerate. The writing was decent but the subject matter completely asinine.*

 I'll have to rediscover the fiction that I like. I don't think I want to reread much of what I used to read. I still have The Electric Kool-Aid Acid Test after all these years, which I greatly admired for its literary merit and powerful insight. Now I can't even bring myself to pull it from the shelf; I know I would find it abstruse and highly obnoxious. But noticing it the other day reminded me of another memory we share, this one less controversial but just as climactic. Do you recall the first time we made love? Not the first time we had sex—which, aside from the obvious significance was forgettable—but made love. At least that's what you called it. At the time I didn't understand the difference, but I have come to appreciate it more now. It coincided, not coincidentally, with the first and only time I did acid. Now you must know what I'm talking about.

It was late August 1969; I remember because the Manson murders were still fresh on everyone's mind, not that we called them that at the time. Like many others, I was convinced the gruesome killings were connected to the anti-establishment movement, something to do with hating the pigs as we were led to believe. Anyway, I worried that I might have a bad trip due to all the negative vibes going around but you convinced me that was silly. We both stayed in Isla Vista that summer, taking courses and getting more involved with the anti-war protests (mostly you). I remember several bake sales with your roommate to raise money for this or that fund. Anyway, fall semester was about to start and we felt like cutting loose. I don't remember where you got the acid, but I recall the two innocent-looking tablets and the soft afternoon light in your living room as we swallowed them. I think you suggested we head outside before the effects fully kicked in. Traversing the few blocks to the beach seemed to take eons, but we eventually made it. I don't think I said much over the next hour, my head was literally in the clouds and my mind entirely preoccupied with sensation. Sort of like a baby, I guess. But eventually I came back to Earth. I specifically recall feeling the sand in my clothes, damp and coarse. That's when I made the totally reasonable decision to toss them aside and dash into the water naked. You followed suit (with no suit), and we embraced in the waves, smiling and laughing in the encroaching dusk. The sky resembled a flat canvas, the blue gradients drawn across it slashed open and bleeding color. I tapped into some primitive energy then and nearly entered you right there in the water. But you had the presence of mind to keep things playful. So, we played for who knows how long before emerging from the ocean. I felt the unfathomable depths of time at that moment, like I was connected to whatever creature first crawled out of the ocean to take up residence on the land. Which I suppose I am.

Your roommate was out of town that night, so we had your place to ourselves. I think before falling into the couch, we first stripped down to our underwear (having just gotten dressed on the beach), ate some kind *of pastry leftover from a fundraiser, and drank a couple glasses of water as we must've been quite dehydrated. When you pulled me close to you, I felt we united in some metaphysical way. Never before and never since have I merged with another body during intercourse like that. I sensed your every ripple, felt your every goosebump. I heard every whimper and anticipated every moan. I was a love-making machine—I must've been close to what Abbey was capable of, no? I think you may have used that phrase later on, love-making machine, and we joked about it for a while afterwards because it was so far off the mark. When you're that age though, you can still slip easily into some character that you're not, and I inhabited the character of a love-making machine for that heightened interval. The mental hardening (and physical softening) of age makes it so much more difficult to lose yourself to this sort of whim, at least that's what I find. And yes, I'm sure the acid had something to do with it (no I do not want to do acid again, I'm almost certain I'd have a bad trip this time). On that day, the two of us were more than just the sum of our parts.*

I've perhaps gotten a bit carried away. It's been a while since I revisited that experience. Maybe you remember it differently, but I know you were happy then and there with me. I know we were happy. I know I was happy.

If you don't find it in you to respond to this email for weeks or months even, I will try my best not to despair. But why would you not? It's free therapy.

Yours,
Leroy
P.S. This is a little bit fun, yes.

CHAPTER EIGHTEEN
NO CLUE

"Holy shit, holy shit, holy shit," Paul repeats like it's his new mantra as they approach the shore. "This is definitely different. The houses are so much farther back from the coast. Insane how fast these cliffs erode."

"Yeah, that's one difference," Ethan says, still a bit peeved at Paul for following him through the portal but also thankful for his familiar presence. "Welcome to 1969."

The raft scrapes the sand. Under the faint light of the crescent moon, the two of them drag it to the edge of the bluffs.

"It's so much darker too," Paul says. "I don't think I've ever seen so many stars around here."

"I guess so, less light pollution."

"So what do we do now?"

Ethan squints into the night at the slim stretch of beach leading to an undeveloped parcel of land. "We should try to get some sleep."

"How the hell am I supposed to sleep after that?"

"Are you not exhausted from the trip? I'm ready to collapse."

Paul pauses to consider. "I guess once the adrenaline runs out, I might crash."

"Let's find a place to rest down there." Ethan points towards the craggy edge of the bluffs near the far end of Isla Vista. "And maybe we can find a spot to stash the raft."

As they walk, Ethan expresses his concern over the diminished size of the portal. "I think it's closing up. It used to be much brighter."

"Maybe we should both only stay a few days then."

Ethan shrugs. "Maybe."

The purr of the ocean lulls their energy-sapped bodies to sleep. Less than five hours later, Paul awakens with the first morning light. He goes to the shoreline to rinse his face in the crisp ocean water. Ethan joins him, and they return to the grassy patch of terrain shielded from the shore by earthen boulders and from town by the bend of the coastline. They stretch like cats after a nap and soak up the rosy dawn sky strewn with linty clouds.

"Maybe tonight we can find some mattresses to bring down here," Ethan says as he readjusts once again to get comfortable. But Paul's lost in thought and doesn't register his words. A few seconds later he speaks.

"You know, there's so much we could do here with our knowledge of the future, it's mind-blowing."

"Yeah, like what?"

"I don't know. We could invent something or invest in something. We could go to Woodstock or watch the moon landing or prevent the Manson murders." Paul picks up the fanny pack and pulls out the Ziplock bag of coins. "If we invested this smartly, which we shouldn't have trouble doing, I'm sure we could make a lot of moolah."

Ethan's expression is skeptical. "Isn't that just like fifteen dollars?"

Paul scrutinizes the bag. "Closer to 20, but I see your point."

"I have a better idea," Ethan says, brushing himself off. "Why don't we invest it in some breakfast. Aren't you only staying for a few days anyway?"

"Fine." Paul counts out some of the change. "I'm still not totally convinced this isn't all just a vivid dream, anyway. Do you think the coffee is good here? I'm worried it's going to be that bitter, weak stuff. You know the instant kind. Maxwell House or something."

"Maybe we can find an espresso place."

"Oh, yes, now you're thinking."

After concealing the raft in some dense underbrush growing along the steep remnants of a minor landslide, they scamper up a rudimentary path through the bluffs and embark towards central I.V. Near campus, they locate a small cafe that meets Paul's approval, at least under such extenuating circumstances. Sitting outside on a square patio, they observe students filing to campus for morning classes.

"Man, I forgot to wear my 1969 clothes," Ethan says. "I feel so self-conscious about how we look."

"Yeah, although at least we're not wearing anything too synthetic and futuristic," Paul responds as he tears at a small hole in the knee of his jeans. "If anyone asks, we can just say we're Canadian."

"Aye," Ethan says. "I like that."

"I love the hairdos and the clothes," Paul says. "I'm not sure if it's just the newness, but everyone seems more attractive."

Ethan nods. "Yeah, there's some super babes around."

"The guys too, though," Paul says, slurping the final drops of his double espresso. "And nobody's fat."

Ethan has an *El Gaucho* on his lap. He points to a black box in the top left corner.

"OK great, here's the notice for the memorial service for Dover at noon, which I saw in the archived version of this paper." He flaps the paper in his hands. "It looked so ancient online but it's so fresh now. I can smell the ink."

"So you want to go to that?" Paul asks, reaching into his pocket and then abruptly removing his hand. "I can't stop grabbing for my phone, this is absurd. For once, I was just trying to check the time, not…"

"Not what?" Ethan asks.

"Oh, you know. Check my dating profile."

"Hah. I keep forgetting you're doing that. Probably because it seems so unlike you."

"Yeah, Yeah," Paul says, happy to leave it at that.

Ethan pulls up his sleeve and proudly displays a black plastic watch. "At least I remembered my trusty cheap timekeeper, and unlike the phones, it still works over here. We've got almost two hours to kill until the memorial, which of course I want to go to."

"What should we do until then?"

"Check out the Faculty Club?"

The Faculty Club is a Mediterranean-inspired structure with the curb appeal of a condominium complex. But in the back there's a pool overlooking the lagoon. Approaching it from the north side of campus, opposite the lagoon, Paul and Ethan see no evidence of damage from the recent attack. Expecting to find the facility heavily patrolled and cordoned off, they are pleasantly surprised that it is instead abandoned. The main entrance is cordoned off with yellow tape, however, so they walk around the side of the building towards the lagoon-facing patio and pool. Rounding the corner, the explosion's impact is immediately apparent. The walls facing the patio are stained black and the sliding glass doors leading into the dining hall and adjacent windows are shattered. The entire perimeter is marked off with yellow tape, but Paul and Ethan sidestep it after a quick looksee to make sure the coast is clear.

Ethan goes ahead of Paul, entering the building through a jagged-edged opening in one of the doors.

"Where are you going?" Paul asks.

"I just want to check something. I'll be right back. You keep watch here."

Paul nods and turns his focus to scanning the area around the blast. A few minutes later, Ethan returns with a book in his hand. Paul gestures to him to hand it over.

"*Desert Solitaire*? You know we have plenty of these in 2023," he says, rifling through it.

"Dover was reading it when I was here," Ethan responds. "I think it helped him make sense of the oil spill, to understand our role in it."

"You mean how humans see fucking up the environment as just a necessary externality of progress."

"Something like that. Anyway, he made a lot of notes in the margins. I doubt it means much to anyone else so I thought I might hold onto it."

Paul slows his page-turning and reads more closely. "Looks like he really wanted to visit the desert."

"Yeah, he told me that reading about Arches National Park made him realize how little of the West he'd seen, and how much it had to offer. He said it seemed like another planet."

"Arches is quite spectacular," Paul says. "And it is kind of like another planet…one that's overrun with human tourists. I bet it was a lot more solitaire back then, though. I mean, now."

Paul shoots Ethan a glance. "You're not thinking about making a trip to Arches now, are you? We don't have enough money for that, or time."

"No, no. I just thought since Dover discussed this book with me, he might not mind me taking it as a keepsake, you know, now that…" Ethan's expression is grim, and he turns away from the maimed section of the Faculty Club. "OK, let's get out of here now."

He starts walking, but Paul grabs his arm. "Hold up a second."

Ethan watches Paul approach the edge of the patio and extract a small, dark chunk of something from a ribbon of ivy lining the perimeter. He inspects it closely before showing it to Ethan.

"You know what this is?" He asks.

"Umm…a piece of cardboard."

"Yes," Paul says. "And judging by the state it's in, I'm guessing it was part of the explosive package." The cardboard is scalded at both ends, torn almost all the way through, and covered in ash.

"OK, so now you've got a souvenir too," Ethan says.

"Well, I think it could be more than that." Paul holds the thumb-sized piece by the edge. "There's some tape on it, and under the tape there's a few hairs."

"Yeah, so?"

"Well, if we can get this back to 2023, we might be able to get a DNA test on it and that could lead to identifying the bomber, assuming he's in the criminal system."

Ethan looks interested. "They never solved the case?"

"Nope, I looked it up," Paul says. "But it's not too late. I mean, even back in the future, it's still not too late."

Before Ethan can respond, he sees a campus police officer in a hard hat and clunky boots step into the blasted-out frame of one of the Faculty Club's sliding doors.

"This area is off limits," the officer calls down to the two alarmed trespassers. "Please stay put."

The officer turns to alert his partner to the situation. Ethan and Paul exchange a glance before racing down the hill towards the lagoon.

• • •

Leroy emerges onto his house's narrow covered porch and stares across the yard. He hasn't seen Lonnie since the day of the bombing. And he only saw Russell briefly a few days ago, looking even more strung out than usual. From what he's read, the police still don't have any solid leads, but you never know. Nonetheless, the more time that elapses, the less likely the crime gets solved. He sips his instant coffee and swishes the warm, acidic liquid around his mouth before gulping it down.

In the week since the bombing, he's had to admit that his suspicion of the neighbors is based on little solid evidence. His conviction that there's a secretive nefariousness about the two misfits, and that they've been up to no good, hasn't diminished, but that's far from enough to press charges, and he's not convinced it's enough to even call the precinct about, although they're probably desperate for any and all leads. He's especially hung up by the few occasions that Russell went out of his way to strike up a conversation with him. Russell typically scowled, smiled too flagrantly, or showed too many teeth as if a bit rabid. But during these interactions he'd almost come off as normal, or at least sociable. Still, Leroy never felt very comfortable around him or

Lonnie. Even during their friendly debate over The Beatles' best album—his, A Hard Day's Night, vs. Russell's self-titled—he'd been wound up enough to spring back when a dorm friend poked him on the shoulder to say hi. Denise at least agrees there's something devilish in their demeanors but supposes they're just up to their eyeballs in drugs and conspiracy theories.

But now the house is vacant and has been for several days. Leroy knows they frequently traveled to remote desert locations or up the coast towards the Bay. They liked to discuss these drug-addled excursions when in the company of others, regardless of the number of disapproving looks it garnered them in return. They did a lot of gun toting in the desert and a lot of womanizing near the Bay. At least Russell did. He's not sure Lonnie got in on much of the action. He seemed more like a lackey, one who was often left behind.

And yet, there's one encounter from a month or two ago that he just can't shake. He was pulling weeds by the pressure-treated wood fence running along both their backyards, which is green with algae near the bottom and starting to warp, when he overheard Russell discussing some kind of building project. At first Leroy thought he was talking about reconstructing a stereo or some other electronic, but then he heard the words pipe and chemical explosion. Leroy inched closer to the garage to see if he could better make out what they were saying, but the conversation soon turned political, as was common with those two, and Russell launched into a diatribe about government-sponsored murders in Latin America.

Suddenly the side door of the garage flung open and Russell, looking brawnier than ever, stared down at him through red-rimmed eyes. Leroy lowered his head and proceeded to unearth weeds, but he could feel Russell's venomous focus boring into him.

"Mind getting the weeds along the garage?" Russell said eventually, a slight retreating shift in his weight. "We've been too busy to take care of the yard lately."

Leroy nodded cautiously as Russell slammed the door in his face. Before long, The Beatles' self-titled album blared onto the stereo and not another snippet of conversation reached his ears. He made sure to weed their yard at least as thoroughly as his own.

He related this incident to Denise, but she thought he was blowing things out of proportion. Now, as he watches her walk briskly down the street deploying the full extent of her long stride to arrive at his house, he thinks she's right. In any case, he wants to agree with her because he loves to see her smile. She greets him with a peck on the cheek.

"Sorry I'm late," she says, her chest heaving and sweat glinting under her sandy bangs. "We'd better get going to the memorial service."

Leroy nods, his eyes flickering from Denise's over to the neighbor's house. Both yards are overdue for some additional weeding.

"Oh, come on," Denise says. "You don't still think those guys had something to do with the Faculty Club?"

"Don't you think it's a little weird they've been M.I.A. since the explosion?"

"Not particularly," Denise says with a wave of her hand. "They're here today-gone tomorrow types, from what I can tell." Leroy is briefly distracted by her long, slender fingers. "Anyway, you have seen them—just only for a minute, right?"

"Yes, that's true, but ..."

"That's enough for now, Leroy." Leroy melts at the sound of his name from her mouth, the way she hits "lee" like a snare drum and winds up the "oy." "They're probably on some hippie farm having an orgy."

"An orgy, really?" Leroy hadn't considered that.

"No, no," Denise says with a laugh of disgust. "Well, maybe Russell. I'm not sure the other one could handle even one woman."

"So you've thought about the other one, then, being with a woman?"

"I said that's enough."

Denise takes Leroy's hand and yanks him gently down the porch's three steps, allotting him just enough time to deposit his near-empty coffee mug on a round, glass-topped table covered in a paper-thin layer of dust and pollen. As they walk towards campus, fingers intertwined,

Leroy decides he'd better just table his suspicions, at this point they're only causing him trouble. The cops will surely track down the perpetrator before too long. At least they have something to do now other than breaking up peaceful protests and writing out tickets for any number of minor offenses.

The crowd for Dover's memorial service spills out of the Lotte Lehmann Concert Hall, a three-story building rung with cement balconies and plastered in red-pebbled panels. The president of the Faculty Club, the chancellor of the school, and a representative of the Church are slated to speak. Most students have little interest in suffering through their bromides and long asides—too much like attending class—and are content to mill around outside keeping vigil. No longer holding hands, Denise and Leroy take a seat on one of the long steps leading up to the concert hall. Becca spots them from across the main thoroughfare and heads over with Steven at her heels.

"We know so little about who this guy was, what was important to him, it's embarrassing," Becca says in lieu of a greeting, her curly hair bobbing. "Yet here we are, gathered in his memory."

Denise nods. "Yeah, poor guy."

"I would've liked to include more about him in our reporting, but his family weren't eager to talk and there's just not much else to go by."

"Well, it's about much more than this Dover fellow, though, isn't it?" Steven asserts. He's dressed formally enough to attend a memorial service, unlike most everyone else. "We're also here to show solidarity against these activists who think violence is an acceptable form of expression."

"Yes, yes, of course," Becca says with a weariness like she's reluctantly reengaging an ongoing debate. "Although I'm not sure I'd call whoever's responsible for this an activist. If they're trying to be one, they're way off the mark." She pauses, her round face scanning the crowd, which is several hundred strong. "Anyway, I think after something as traumatic as a campus bombing, it's good we're coming together and generating some positive energy. There's just so much to bring you down these days."

"And while we're all gathered here," Becca continues, indicating with her outspread arms that she's including everyone in attendance, "Steven's going to see if he can uncover any fresh anecdotes about Dover, right?"

"Oh, yeah right," Steven says, delicately running his fingers through his coiffed hair as he looks around for potential subjects. "I'll guess I'll see you back in the office later then."

"I'm actually meeting a friend on State Street after this, someone up from L.A.," Becca says. "But the deputy editor's anticipating the copy."

"Oh, OK," Steven says, unable to fully mask his disappointment. "Well, have a swell time."

"OK, I'll have a swell time," Becca says with a slight eye roll, but Steven doesn't notice. He's distracted by a commotion involving several campus police officers charging at full steam down the lagoon path towards the sprawling gathering.

"What the hell?" Steven says, and soon Leroy and Denise are on their feet too, watching the three officers lunge up a narrow concrete stairway and disappear behind the concert hall.

"They'll be coming around the other side," Denise says, and the four of them begin pushing their way through the crowd. As they round the building, there's an eruption of screams. The police officers are surging towards the students, their batons waving.

"My God," Becca says. She's standing on a low concrete wall dividing the promenade. "What if there's another bomb."

"Oh gosh, you're right," Steven all but shrieks. "Let's get out of here."

"Hold on," Denise says perched next to Becca. She gestures for Leroy to join them. Leroy slips as he steps onto the two-foot-high wall, which is just over a foot wide. Becca grabs his hand and Denise pulls him up from the arm as the retreating crowd collapses around them. Balancing between the two young women, Leroy focuses in the direction of the approaching trio of officers. Denise is pointing towards the front of the crowd, which has dissolved into utter chaos.

"Isn't that Ethan?" she asks. Leroy squints, identifying a young man in a hoodie and jeans sprinting towards the ragged front line of people. Before he can respond, Denise calls Ethan's name several times. Ethan looks up, his eyes full of fear. He adjusts course towards Denise and Leroy and arrives at the short wall completely out of breath.

"Denise, Leroy, so glad to see you," he says between deep inhales. "You've got to hide me from those officers."

Denise looks to Becca, who frowns and shakes her head, indicating she's not going to intervene. The cops are halfway through the crowd, which is antagonizing them with jeers and a smattering of pencils, notebooks, and a handful of undergarments.

"Steven, give Ethan your jacket," Denise says sharply. Steven frowns, clearly not pleased at the prospect of losing his cherished sartorial item.

"Now, Steven," Becca says, pulling at the sleeve of the jacket. In a flash, it's off his shoulders and in Ethan's hands. Ethan rips off his hoodie and pulls on the jacket. The arms are too short and his wrists are exposed, but as long as he doesn't try to button it, it fits well enough. Having slowed down, the cops are scanning faces and pulling aside the occasional student for closer inspection.

"Let's get into the building," Becca says. "They won't want to disrupt the service."

Denise grabs Ethan's hand and leads the way, followed by Becca, and a befuddled Leroy and Steven. They're cutting across foot traffic when a tall kid with lank hair and acne scars collides with Ethan and causes him to stumble onto the pavement. Ethan collects himself on one knee while the others stand by nervously. Just as he's preparing to stand, a police officer shouts, "You, in the blue hoodie, don't move."

Denise presses her hand on Ethan's back just below his neck. He keeps his head down as the four pairs of legs encircle him, their calves rubbing up against his folded body. From the corner of his eye, he sees Becca push Steven slightly forward and whisper, "Just answer their questions, it'll be fine." Steven gingerly steps out of the comfort of the circle and Becca reaches across the gap he's created and yanks Leroy towards her. Denise, Becca, and Leroy form a wall separating Ethan from the officer. Denise taps Ethan's shoulder with her heel and, with a hand behind her back, points towards the side entrance to the concert hall, which is only about ten yards away. Ethan raises his backside like he's a track runner waiting for the starting gun. Glancing back, he sees a couple of guys jogging towards the auditorium. He hops up beside them as they pass and follows them undetected into the memorial service.

The campus cop approaching Steven is below average height and his intelligence is probably a little low too, Becca thinks. His uniform is too loose, and his boots could use a buffing. He's not much older than them, and when he speaks, Becca flinches at the spittle he casts in their direction. To his credit, he's observant enough to gather that Steven, standing like he's been called to attention by a drill sergeant, isn't his man.

"Where'd you get that sweatshirt?" the officer asks. Steven observes the unzipped garment as if noticing it for the first time. His pause is unnaturally long. Just before the officer is about to follow up, Steven remarks, "It was a gift."

"A gift from who?"

"Excuse me, officer…" Becca calls out from behind. The officer shifts his attention from Steven to Becca and responds, "Officer Schwab."

"Thank you," Becca says with an ingratiating smile. "Well, Officer Schwab. I know for a fact that Steven's ex-girlfriend gave him that sweater and he probably doesn't want to bring that up in front of me, which I greatly appreciate."

Becca steps away from Denise and Leroy and approaches Steven's side. "I don't know what all this commotion is about, but we were heading into the memorial service and would really like to join the gathering before the minister speaks, if you don't mind."

Officer Schwab observes Becca from behind his aviators with pursed lips before responding. "Alright young lady, you and your friends go ahead in." He gestures with a short, underhanded flick of his wrist towards the concert hall before turning away abruptly. The other two police officers are advancing along the far edge of the gathering, seemingly without much success either. The unrest is dying down. Becca takes Steven's hand, and they join Denise and Leroy heading to the side entrance to the concert hall. Denise mouths something to Becca as their eyes meet. Leroy's not sure what she says, he's distracted by their bright expressions, but he thinks it might be, "So rad." As the doors close behind them, Becca releases Steven's hand, which grips hers firmly for another second before responding in kind. Inside, they proceed down a bright corridor lined with whispering students.

"There's a minister speaking that you want to see?" Steven asks Becca.

"No Steven," Becca says. "I made that up to help get you out of that pickle."

"Oh right." Steven shoves his hands into his pants pockets. "Thanks."

Becca turns to Denise. "What on Earth is going on here? Who is that guy?"

Denise doesn't respond. She's scanning the hallway for Ethan, who she expects to be waiting for them. But he's nowhere to be found.

"Maybe he went into the memorial service?" Leroy posits.

"Yeah," Denise says. "I suppose that would be the safest spot."

Becca pokes Denise's arm and Denise finally gives her attention. "So, I am extremely curious about this," Becca says. "But I really do need to make my way downtown. Let's talk later?"

"Oh yes, of course," Denise says. "It's nothing, anyway. Leroy and I met Ethan a couple months ago, briefly, and then didn't see him again until now. That's really all I know."

"Alright," Becca says skeptically.

Steven plants himself in front of the two ladies. "So should I get back to filling in color for the Dover story?"

"No," Becca says.

Steven is dismayed. "No?"

"Did you not just experience the same police-induced mayhem that I did?" Becca asks. "I'd rather know what's going on with that."

"You're exactly right," Steven says.

"I know I am," Becca says. "And, I don't know, maybe Denise will have a few minutes to see if anyone has anything to say about Dover?" Becca raises an eyebrow at Denise.

"Sure, yeah," Denise says. "I'll try to get a couple quotes."

"Thanks so much. If you don't get anything, we'll just borrow from the speeches."

Through the main auditorium entrance they hear the muffled voice of the chancellor. Becca gives a little wave and turns to go. When Steven doesn't follow her, she pulls his shirt. "All the action is this way."

Her tug on the hoodie reminds Steven that he's still wearing Ethan's garment and a look of disgust flashes across his face. He yanks his arms out of the sleeves and hands the sweatshirt to Denise like it's a dead cat.

"Please return this to your friend and retrieve my blazer," he says, not waiting for a response before trotting off after Becca. Readjusting the hoodie in her arms, Denise feels something in its interior zipper pocket. Something thin, rectangular, and bendable, like a book. She slips the item from the pocket and rests it on her forearm.

"*Desert Solitaire* by Edward Abbey," she reads aloud as Leroy looks over her shoulder. She flips open the cover. There's a yellow post-it note on the first page: *If found, return to Dover O. Sharp, UCSB Faculty Club.*

Denise looks up and shares an awed look with Leroy. "What is this book doing in Ethan's jacket?" Leroy asks.

Denise is already flipping through the pages. "There's notes throughout the margins in that same handwriting," she says. "This is remarkable."

"I don't understand why Ethan would have this," Leroy says.

"Well, I guess we'll just have to ask him."

Denise reaches into the pocket to see if she missed anything, finding only a frayed piece of burnt cardboard with a shred of tape on it. She shoves it back in.

CHAPTER NINETEEN
WHEN THE BLOW COMES

"Yo, I'm up here." Paul grins at Ethan from the bluffs. "Got tired of all the gnats down there. I was starting to worry you got caught."

Ethan shields his eyes and waves unenthusiastically at Paul from the spot where they stashed the raft. He backtracks to the staircase leading up from the beach and follows a gently curving packed-dirt footpath towards Paul.

Paul snaps a quick embrace around Ethan when he arrives. "Man, that was crazy. My adrenaline was pumping even harder than when I almost got in that knife fight. I didn't realize how badly I wanted to stay away from the cops in this era. Did you see the one guy waving his baton? That could've been really bad."

"Yeah," Ethan says. "I'm lucky Denise called my name. Otherwise, I'm not sure I would've gotten away, even in that crowd."

Ethan's face is red, his lips cracked, his eyes a little mad, and he's walking with a slight limp. For once, Paul thinks, he actually appears unhealthy.

"So that's what happened," Paul says, pulling at the hem of Ethan's jacket. "I guess this had something to do with it?"

"Yeah, I swapped shirts with this guy she was with. He was trying to hold onto it too, prick."

"So then, you don't have the book or the cardboard anymore?"

Ethan shakes his head and takes a seat on a nearby bench overlooking the ocean. Paul joins him.

"What's the point of solving a crime 50 years later anyway, right?" Paul says. "The guy is probably dead by now."

The quiet scene presents a poignant counterpoint to the whirlwind chase, the frightful surge it shot through them finally sputtering out. Paul feels grateful to have evaded capture and to not be shackled to 1969. He figures Ethan is processing a similar emotion. A cluster of California Towhees chitter away in the lower branches of a nearby sycamore.

"Isn't it amazing how much this path changed location over 50 years—or, I guess, how much the earth around it shifted?" Paul says after a minute. "Like, back home, it's right next to the edge."

Paul points to the cliffside, about 25 yards away.

"I just can't get over the amount of erosion going on here. I'm never going on one of those Del Playa balconies overlooking the ocean again."

Ethan nods but doesn't appear to share the same fascination with the erosion.

"Where did those cops even come from?" Ethan asks, still looking out to sea.

"I don't know," Paul says. "I guess they were making the rounds. We hung around too long."

The sun, midway through its descent, warms their cheeks from its perch above the ocean's horizon. A salty breeze nips around the cliffs, but the ocean is tranquil. The waves can't be much taller than two feet. Paul reaches for his phone again, curses himself.

"What do you mean we hung around too long?" Ethan asks.

"I mean we knew we were someplace we shouldn't be."

"Yeah, but like, how do we know where we should be?"

Paul glances sidelong at Ethan and stands up.

"Is that like a rhetorical question?"

Ethan shrugs. Paul paces back and forth between the cliff edge and the bench a few times.

"I think we should go back tonight," he says. "I don't think I'll be able to calm down here, after the day we've had. This is like some video game where unexpected things keep popping up, some of them trying to kill you."

Ethan's attention is somewhere far off as he watches the miniature waves tumble over themselves and dissipate into the ocean. The portal's not tugging at him anymore. Instead, his feet feel glued to the ground, like the magnetic force has shifted from the horizon to the Earth's crust.

"I don't think I'm going back," he says.

"What? You want to hang around and track down your hoodie?" Paul asks, taking a deep breath. "I guess we could do that. Maybe we could even find it by tonight if you know where these people live."

"No," Ethan says. "I'm not going back for a while."

"A while? What's a while? You said yourself the time travel thingy is closing up."

"Well, maybe it will open again."

"That's not a bet I would take. In fact, that's a very bad bet."

"Life's a bad bet," Ethan says. "Your mom's a bad bet."

"Your sister's a bad bet," Paul says, stomping off down the footpath, but not before registering a tinge of pain in Ethan's expression. He turns back after fifty yards.

"OK," he says. "Sorry about that. Your sister actually seems kind of badass for what it's worth."

He scratches his scalp before continuing. "What about your family? And your identity? And money? And, you know, the space-time continuum? Like what if you're still here in 30 years when you're supposed to be born?"

Now it's Ethan's turn to get up and walk in a circle. He stops midway and observes a distant grove of eucalyptus trees, their creamy trunks almost appetizing. There's a yucca plant nearby, several feet taller than him. He runs his fingers down its daggered leaves and presses on their sharp end points.

"I just, I don't feel like I have cancer here," he says after a minute. "At least not yet."

"This is totally nuts," Paul says. "You were totally fine with never coming back until you read about Dover."

"Yeah," Ethan says. "I can't explain it. It's just, doesn't this world seem better than ours?"

In a way, Paul understands what Ethan's getting at. He hasn't felt like masturbating since their arrival but doesn't believe the hiatus can last. He thinks that's part of what's stressing him out, the uncertainty of how long he can go. The uncanniness of ejaculating 2023 semen into 1969 disturbs him, as if it might impregnate the planet and give it some 21st-century mutation where everything is hotter, drier, meltier, angrier, techier, more grotesque. Epigenetically, he wonders how this whole experience is going to affect him. If it might slash away at his DNA somehow. He doesn't trust the portal and wants to get the reverse trip over with ASAP.

"What about your sister, though?" he asks. "And your mom and dad. Even if you do make it back, they'll assume the worst after a while."

Ethan thinks of his dad. His aging, dying father. What his sister said about him beginning some perilous, irreversible descent; in his heart he knows it's the truth. For some reason, it's harder for him to bear his parents' mortality than his own. More difficult to live through. And impossible to joke about.

"That's beyond…" Ethan waits for more words to come. "My purview?"

Paul punches the palm of his hand with his fist and makes a pained expression that Ethan's never seen before. He derives a smidgeon of satisfaction knowing he's upset Paul so much, as if he's watching his own funeral procession go by.

"Dude, you are not making any sense!" Paul all but screams.

"Well, my mind is made up."

"Numbskull."

Ethan starts walking towards Isla Vista. That's when the blow comes. As his vision blurs and rotates sideways, he catches sight of a young couple walking down the footpath. They pause to observe an enormous kaleidoscope of monarch butterflies, more than he's ever seen clustered together in the future. He smiles briefly before his head hits the ground and he sees Paul standing above him cradling his right fist in his left hand.

"What are friends for," Paul says with a shake of his head. And then the world goes dark.

CHAPTER TWENTY
OM SHANTI

Lonnie reads about Dover's memorial service in the paper while seated at one of two chairs in the efficiency apartment he recently rented in Goleta. Even though he's less than two miles from Russell's place—his old place—he might as well be a continent away. The single-story rectangular dwelling is located behind the property's main house and separated by a xeriscaped yard in need of some TLC. An array of potted plants, having overgrown their chambers, are perpetually parched, their roots protruding from the dry soil like partially excavated bones, and the rock garden spills over its earthen boundary onto the stone walkway. The sun-scorched stucco wall surrounding the yard provides a degree of privacy from the neighbors sorely lacking in Isla Vista. At least Lonnie tries to convince himself of this in his more lonesome moments; moments during which he might even welcome an exchange with someone as unamicable as Leroy. The main house is also occupied by students. Not your typical disorganized, always late, incapable-of-feeding-themselves undergrads, but three graduate students who, from what Lonnie's observed so far, adhere to strict schedules and dress and act like full-grown adults. He gets the sense they want little to do with him, which is a sense he finely homed throughout his youth as a kid who never fit in, never clicked with a clique. For all the problems he has with Russell, at least he deemed him worthy of sharing his feelings with, even if those feelings were often seeped in vitriol.

Walking along the sidewalk—something else much of I.V. sorely lacks—Lonnie sees people of all ages inhabiting the nicely spaced residences lining the block, even children. Ostensibly, he's gone from being a student in a campus ghetto to a respectable member of middle-class suburbia, at least on a month-to-month basis. But on the inside, under his skin, he feels nothing like the tranquil surroundings, although they do act as a salve to soothe his pain, if only temporarily. His innerworkings mash together like tectonic plates fighting to usurp one another. He squares his shoulders and raises his chin when he's out in the neighborhood, hoping to mask the hollow ache that never really goes away and is currently inflamed.

A substantial part of donning this mask entails actively avoiding thinking about Dover, about what he did to Dover. The alternative is crippling, and he's already spent several days in bed suffering through it like a medieval bout of plague, full of hallucinogenic visuals and odorous sweats. Even with his newly reengaged meditation practice, which he'd originally adopted early freshman year as a coping mechanism for the dorms—for a roommate who outright detested him, for a cafeteria full of unsympathetic peers—it can be hard to meet the day with anything but darkness.

The two-week-old paper he's reading, containing the story about Dover's memorial service, was left behind by the former tenant who moved out on short notice for a job in San Luis Obispo. It's been sitting on the windowsill since Lonnie's arrival and only now, with nothing to occupy him as he shovels oatmeal into his mouth, does he pull it down and take a look. He just finished his morning meditation and he's feeling, for once, perhaps for the first time since the incident, almost well enough to coexist with his peaceful surroundings; with the world around him, which if not on his side, is perhaps at least indifferent to him today. Without straight-out admitting it, he's testing himself to determine if he's self-possessed enough to read about the memorial without spiraling into a funk. He's expecting something dry and banal, quotes from speeches, and there's a bit of that, but much of the article is about a book titled *Desert Solitaire* that Dover was apparently enamored with. He's not quite clear on what the book is about—it sounds more like a journal—and he knows almost nothing of the Southwestern terrain beyond the Phoenix metropolitan area, but a quote that Dover apparently highlighted, and that's included in the article, resonates with him:

"A man could be a lover and defender of the wilderness without ever in his lifetime leaving the boundaries of asphalt, powerlines, and right-angled surfaces. We need wilderness whether or not we ever set foot in it. We need a refuge even though we may never need to set foot in it. We need the possibility of escape as surely as we need hope; without it the life of the cities would drive all men into crime or drugs or psychoanalysis."

What appeals to him is the part about needing the possibility of escape. In the days after the Faculty Club explosion, he longed for escape. Even as he held the vague conception of peace, or peacefulness, in his mind upon hearing Leroy's girlfriend—if that's what she was—mention it, the undercurrents of his thoughts carried him towards crime, drugs, or, less likely but possibly, psychoanalysis. Not that he exactly knows what psychoanalysis is and he's sure it costs more money than he has. What has saved him, for now and possibly for good he hopes, from the pull of this debilitating riptide, is a torn and crumpled piece of paper—a flier—that blew into his face after being caught in a gust of wind. He nearly tossed the invaluable sheet aside, but the grainy image of a serene Indian man sitting cross-legged caught his eye, and he gives thanks during each meditation that it did. He often evokes the fateful moment during these meditation sessions: Seated on a bench in a park just north of State Street in Santa Barbara, where he camped for a few days after leaving Isla Vista, he was in the midst of deciding, for the umpteenth time, whether to skip town or return to school. On the far side of the park a circle of hippies beat their bongos. They would've welcomed him with open arms and rolled joints, and some of them weren't half-bad looking. But he was immobilized by indecision, waiting for the shock to wear off from Dover's death, or waiting for something shocking to snap him from his despairing state. And then, the timely blast of wind arrived.

Initially, he wasn't sure he would return to campus for more than the introductory session on Transcendental Meditation promoted on the flier. Freshman year, he'd had no specific meditative practice, just cultivating calm and liberating thoughts, but he needed something more immersive now, and that seemed to be what the flier offered. After attending the two-hour meeting in the UCen's lounge, his thoughts opened like a roly-poly bug exposing its vulnerable underbelly to the world after a period of fitful, fearful clenching. The lagoon, as viewed through the UCen's floor-to-ceiling windows, was so pristine and lovely—if he could only disassociate his bitter encounter with Dover there from it, which he hopes he can with the aid of meditation. And college life could be peaceful, as long as he steers clear of Russell and other bad influences like him, of which there's no shortage. And while he's not so determined to finish university, whenever he so much as peeks behind the curtain of his future, he sees that getting a degree in sociology isn't something he'll regret, but dropping out he very well might. And he already has enough regrets about his choices.

It irks him that Russell would approve of his adoption of Transcendental Meditation—he doesn't want anything to do with Russell, his abuse, his violent aims, or his negativity. Not long ago, The Beatles traveled to India to practice TM, as those in the know call it, under Maharishi Mahesh Yogi. And Russell approves of anything The Beatles do. Although, Lonnie's aware, The Beatles and the yogi subsequently had a falling out. And so, he's now renounced The Beatles along with Russell, and has decided they must've somehow wronged the yogi, who he's convinced will guide him to a spiritual awakening, leaving him contented and at peace.

Lonnie rises from the table and walks the few steps to the cramped corner bathroom, which barely accommodates a narrow shower, a sink, and a toilet. Observing himself in the mirror, he's pleased to find that he doesn't look tired. The bags under his eyes, which had become almost a feature of his face, are gradually fading. His hair, meanwhile, is longer than it's ever been, almost down his neck, and he hasn't shaved in a week. He approves of his appearance. He looks like someone who might meditate seriously.

He glances at his watch. It's time to catch the express bus to campus. He smooths his hair back behind his ears and winks at himself in the mirror. Is he really feeling good enough to wink at himself? He's not sure but he doesn't regret it. What's the harm in a wink? He rushes down the street, around the corner, and three blocks further to Hollister Ave. Waiting at the bus stop, he tucks in his striped flannel shirt, which is a size too big but otherwise not a bad shirt, although the elbows are quite worn, he notices. He'll have to find a way to increase his income soon. He needs new clothes, and his rent is higher now. His parents occasionally help him out but it's far from enough to get by. That's another reason he didn't drop out; he doesn't want to lose the supplemental cash provided by his folks.

The yellow-roofed, baby blue-streaked bus grinds to a halt. Lonnie lunges up the three large steps and flashes his student ID at the driver. There's at least one person on every bench, so he'll have to double up. He firmly grips a metal pole suspended from the underside of the roof as the bus accelerates forward. His eye catches on someone seated in the row just beyond the bus's midpoint where there's a step up. It's the girl from outside Russell's house who said the thing about remaining peaceful. He takes a deep breath and proceeds forward just as the bus screeches to a halt at a stoplight. He nearly tumbles backward before catching himself on a seatback. When he looks up, the girl is looking back at him. He smiles at her, but she doesn't move a muscle. She's looking through him. He shuts his eyes and focuses on his yogi, his guru MM, and channels his inner peace. Maharishi Mahesh would want him to sit by this girl, this much he is certain of. It is fated. She will see him, the new him. He steps alongside her bench and lowers himself into it, facing forward with a firm, rooted posture that he hopes makes him appear elevated, in mind and body, and also grounded. The bus is chugging along, they'll arrive at campus in a few minutes. At the next light, Lonnie clears his throat and speaks.

"I'm Lonnie."

Denise lifts her gaze from her reading material and observes him. She's wearing a lightweight cotton V-neck sweater and the light from the window pools around her partially exposed collarbones, rippling across her skin and making it appear almost liquid.

"I think we, um, crossed paths, in Isla Vista the other week," Lonnie continues, battling hard to keep his focus inward. Being in such proximity to Denise is messing with his equilibrium. "You were with Leroy, outside his house."

"Oh, really?" Denise says. "I don't recall."

"That's not so surprising, it was only a brief encounter. But I want to thank you for what you said."

"To thank me?" Denise folds her hands in her lap, now genuinely interested. The loose, linty strands of her sweater rise with static, and she rubs her sleeve passively.

"For what you said, yes. You said that peace is the answer—or something along those lines—and at that moment, that's what I needed to hear."

Denise is confused and taken aback. Maybe she misjudged Lonnie, whom she now recognizes. She turns to face him. He's small in stature and appears highly strung, but his coffee-colored eyes are wide and eager, and his mouth is oddly cute.

"Well, that is surprising to hear," Denise says. "I do remember that now. I certainly didn't think my words would stick with you, but I'm glad they have."

"You helped kickstart a process that got me out of that toxic place," Lonnie says. "I'm now living in Goleta."

Denise nods approvingly, her eyes reassuring.

Lonnie's heels are tapping the floor of the bus, and he's gripping his knees.

"Far out," he says, and he's about to repeat the phrase when the book in her lap catches his eye. He tilts his head to read the cover.

"Wow, is that *Desert Solitaire*? I was just reading about that book in the school paper. Did you know that the guy who…" But he can't finish his sentence. He doesn't want to remember that he's the person who did what he did. He needs the mask to stay on. He shakes his head and looks forward through the bus's windshield, where campus is coming into view.

"Oh," Denise says, thinking maybe Lonnie has something stuck in his throat. "Did you read that article about Dover?"

Lonnie nods. "It was really good, you know, especially compared to most of the crap in that paper."

Denise breaks into a smile. "Well, I guess now it's my turn to thank you."

"Why is that?"

"Because I wrote it."

Lonnie blushes. He's not used to complimenting girls when he's not trying to get in their pants. His momentary crisis is passing and he's regaining his meditative composure. The bus is pulling into the campus terminal, a large roundabout. Denise holds the seat in front of her and stands as other riders shuffle toward the exit and emerge into the kind of splendid southern California morning that acts as a goldrush for the senses, drawing millions of Americans to relocate to the state.

Once outside the bus, Denise faces Lonnie, the sun at her back. "Anyway," she says. "Thanks for letting me know how my words affected you."

Uncharacteristically, she holds up her middle and pointer fingers and displays the peace sign.

"Peace," she says, surprised by herself as the moment unfolds.

"Peace," Lonnie replies. And before Denise can turn away, he gives her a wink.

CHAPTER TWENTY-ONE
LEGALIZE REALITY

September 29, 2023
Dear Leroy,

    I can't believe it's been five months since our last correspondence. Again, I have no excuse, this is simply how I operate these days. For long periods, time slips past me without making itself known. Occasionally I grasp for it but of course it eludes me. And I'm not just talking about aging. Anyway, it always happens that eventually one day, after a seemingly interminable downcycle, I wake up feeling refreshed, like my battery's finally been charged, and I treat myself to everything I want in the ensuing days—expensive coffees, manicures, movies (usually a matinee), new hardcover books, a trip to Joshua Tree—because I know the desire will wane. Mostly I'm fine though so don't get worried. I'm in good health, and that's saying a lot. And I don't want this to be all about me and my woes because today is a special day for you :). You didn't think I'd forget your birthday, did you?

    I almost avoided emailing you on your actual birthday because, I don't know, it seemed inappropriate. I haven't said happy birthday to you since Nixon was in office. Thinking about Nixon and how ancient all that seems now made me rethink my hesitancy, and I decided you'd be tickled that I remembered after all these years—even if you just saw the email arrive but waited to open it. I often do that with messages I've been anticipating (not that there are so many of those), sort of like a gift waiting to be unwrapped. I like to reflect on how the person giving the gift or sending the email thought about me for a few minutes while they worked on it. Once you tear open the gift, or click the email, you lose that connection to the person. The moment passes, as all moments do. In its wake, there's just another item in your life to categorize and file away. Although after five months, you may have lost all hope that I'd respond and be annoyed at seeing my message after so long. It's a risk I'll have to take.

So happy birthday! In lieu of an actual gift (maybe next year?) I'm attaching a photo I took of an old picture I found in an El Gaucho issue from 1969.[VI] It features you walking under a shaded corridor near the newspaper office, shafts of sun slicing through the almost Mayan-inspired columns (how strange the architecture sensibility was back then). You're facing the other way, so the viewer only sees your back, and you're not identified in the caption. In fact, all the caption says is, "Legalize Reality..." Just like that with both words capitalized and an ellipsis. And the best part is it's not connected to any of the surrounding stories. Isn't that hilarious? I can't help but shake my head in wonder at some of the things we published back then. For the most part, though, the paper was well run, thanks to Becca (you must remember Becca, I always thought she intimidated you a bit). I often found myself in awe of her ability to get so much out of us. We were really just a bunch of kids playing at being journalists. Going through the papers now, I see how Becca also created space for the pure weirdness that pervaded everything in those days and gave the publication its own voice. It almost jumps off the page in our coverage of the many momentous events of the day. There's the standard lede-nut graph-interview-context stories of course, but also impassioned editorials, quirky commentaries, poetic interludes, goofy profiles, and much more. Even the advertisements are fascinating. I mean, would a jeweler place an ad for wedding rings in a student newspaper these days? I hardly doubt it. And then there's an ad for a camera imploring parents to get a shot of their son, "before he goes from fraternity to paternity." There's also boatloads of movie, makeup, meditation, grocery, record, and stereo ads, but it's these blatant appeals to impending adulthood that catch my eye because of how much that element of college has changed. Adolescence is much longer now than it was in our day, which in many ways is a positive—what's the rush to settle down—but also contains *within it a kernel of, I'm not sure exactly what, something like despair. Despair at the state of the world, and dreading taking one's place in it. We had a lot of problems with authority and societal norms and prejudices in our day, but we invested everything we had in building community and putting down roots. I'm not sure that's the case anymore. We live in a culture not of building bonds, but of breaking them. Breaking them from the molecular level right on up to the structure of society. Oh dear, I'm getting carried away. Rereading this, I think, 'this could be lifted right off the pages of those old El Gauchos.' Couldn't it? Have things changed all that much? I've never been able to really see the forest for the trees. I get caught up looking at all the trees.*

Legalize Reality...

Anyway, back to the photo—there you are, one tree of so many. Do you remember the moment that it was taken? It's nothing special. As far as I can recall, we were hanging around the newspaper offices in the fall of 1969, not too long after school came back into session, when one of the new staff photographers asked if you wouldn't mind posing for a few photos to take advantage of the playful light. I could tell you were less than keen, but you went with it, to please me I imagine. I seem to recall this took place shortly after the LSD experience you so vividly recounted in your prior email (and I think you got it just about right, so don't worry about any divergence in memory there). I'm perhaps imagining it, but I sense a bit of a "walls closing in" framing in the photo, and maybe this photographer—who I honestly don't remember at all beyond that he was friendly and male—had it in mind to capture that lonely and disturbing period, when the identity of Sharon Tate's murderer remained unknown (personally, I always believed Roman Polanski to be tied up in it all somehow, and I still do). And yet, I have no idea how that connects with Legalize Reality, or if it even does. For all I know it's a reference to an album title of one of the many bands I casually listened to in those days. Music really was the soundtrack to life for us.

Whatever underlying message it does or does not contain, I thought you'd appreciate the photo; that maybe it would bring a smile to your— as I imagine it—worry-worn face. I'm just now realizing it might remind you of those family photos that were recently stolen, and I assure you I had no intention of drawing that connection. The truth is, I've been spending a lot of my spare time, of which there is a lot (especially during the summer when the sun scorches the Earth here) going through the old issues of El Gaucho and The Daily Nexus (the name change occurred at the beginning of 1970—you can have your preference, but one is much more PC). They function as scrapbooks for me, long-neglected scrapbooks. It's somewhat remarkable that I saved a copy of almost every paper while I worked there. I had a hunch that one day I'd want to look back through them. And I guess I was right.

If there's a theme to the newspapers from 1969 it's a student body agitating for change. And not simply relating to the oil spill or campus safety (after the bomb at the Faculty Club), but radical ideas revolving around war, civil rights, women's rights, drugs, and, above all else, authority. Again, I can't put my finger on why back then all this activism seemed so much more urgent and righteous than it does now. I support today's youth in their struggles for equality and equity (two different things, I've learned) but it seems so different now, somehow it rings hollow. Like everyone knows the system is fucked for good, excuse my language. While at the same time we have come a long way and I recognize that progress doesn't come easy. But is progress actually being made? Sometimes it seems like we're backtracking, perhaps all the way back to another civil war. Based on what you've hinted at in your emails, I'm sure your views on this are much more extreme than mine. You seem to have truly made the transition from youthful liberal to aging conservative, which I hope to avoid. It's hard though, giving the youth credit when you're no longer one of them. And then there's the way our generation set them up for failure, laid the groundwork for catastrophe, but that's a can of worms I don't want to get into and I'm sure you don't want to hear about.

I'd be curious to know how someone like Bill Allen views the current zeitgeist. Remember I spent so long following him around with the intention of writing a profile and then never did? He was such a major figure on campus for that short period up until the bank burning. I've recalled now, going through these papers, how his firing ignited the protest movement on campus. And that's why, I think, I never got around to finishing that profile; it became too intimidating an undertaking. He went from being a beloved anthropology professor who turned classes about South American Indians into dialogues about Vietnam to a highly controversial figure fired for what even the most tuned-out student knew to be dubious reasons.

Here's a few paragraphs from a November 6 story announcing his likely firing:

Sources with the anthropology department have stated that the reasons for Allen's dismissal are not those given by the tenured faculty.

Claude Warren, former assistant professor in anthropology, contends that tenured members of the department, in discussing Allen, said "It's a good thing he's (Allen) a non-tenured radical so we can get rid of him."

Feeling among Allen's undergraduate supporters is that he is losing his job because he works closely with causes the students find important and because he is willing to express his anti-authoritarian views in public.

Things really escalated a week later when students demanded a public hearing on the reasons for Allen's firing. Several of the other untenured professors openly supported these hearings.[VII]

I don't know, I'm pretty isolated out here in the desert, but my sense is that this kind of activism doesn't exist on campuses anymore. Instead of supporting professors for speaking out, students castigate them for saying the wrong things. It's almost like the notion of free speech has been flipped on its head. It feels silly to say these things to you, as you're still smack dab in the middle of all this. It must be very different than it was back then to be an anthropology professor. Do you still find common cause with and derive inspiration from your students? I hope so. (I'm also attaching a copy of the public hearing article in case you're interested).

I've enjoyed writing this email, it's helped me gather my thoughts. Unfortunately, I don't quite trust myself to improve in punctuality in this email correspondence. There's some intractable barrier to logging in and putting the words down that I find almost insurmountable, even when I'm not caught up in one of my battles to get out of bed. So, the conclusion that I've arrived at is that maybe we should arrange to meet in person. How's that for a birthday surprise? What do you think?

With Love,
Denise

• • •

Students Demand Public Hearing[VIII]
El Gaucho, November 12, 1969

Focusing generally on the tenure system and specifically on the firing of Professor Bill Allen, groups of anthropology students yesterday confronted Anthropology Department Chairman David Brokensha, tenured faculty member Charles Erasmus and one untenured-faculty member, demanding an open hearing on the issue.

In an effort to determine how power is delegated within the department and to ascertain the motives behind Allen's firing, one group of students entered Professor Geoffrey Gaherty's anthropology 5 class in Campbell Hall and demanded that the issues be discussed.

One member of the class, who is a senior anthropology major, initiated the discussion by asking Gaherty what exactly is happening with Allen and why the department has fired him. Gaherty, surprised at the question, asked the students how many still wanted to hear his lecture on physical anthropology, and when only two or three raised their hands he proceeded to discuss the issues as brought before him.

When asked how department politics work and how concerned students can go about getting the facts, Gaherty replied, "I don't know...I can't get them and I'm a member of the faculty. I've heard a different story from every tenured faculty member."

Both Gaherty and Allen are entrenched in the lower echelons of power in the anthropology department. Since they are untenured, they have no voice in the hiring and firing of professors. When asked if he was prepared to take a stand on the Bill Allen issue, Gaherty said, "I've already committed myself."

When Allen was fired, Gaherty and two other faculty members, Professors Mavalwala and Warren, who are no longer on this campus, wrote a letter to the Chancellor asking for an "alternative view." Gaherty received back a Xerox copy of the Chancellor's letter which stated that their opinion was not desired at the time. Gaherty said that he doesn't think that the reasons for the firing of Allen are valid and that he would participate in an open hearing on the matter, but added that it is doubtful the department will allow it.

A student then asked how students can affect tenured faculty members, and Gaherty answered that undergraduates have to organize in order to present an independent voice. Approximately 50 students then walked outside and discussed what should be done. They reported back to the class that they would meet again at 1:45 p.m. in the North Hall quad to ask Brokensha for an open hearing on the Allen case. At 2 p.m. approximately 30 students entered Brokensha's office and presented a demand for an open hearing on the Allen affair.

The written demand asked that specific charges against Allen's competency be brought out and supported and that Allen be given a chance to refute the charges. Brokensha responded that if the decision to hold an open hearing came down to him as chairman, he would resign that position. He refused to make any personal opinions on the case and concluded by telling the students that a final decision on Allen's case would be made by next Wednesday, Nov. 19.

After leaving Brokensha's office, the group of determined students decided after some discussion to present the demand to Charles Erasmus, who was holding a class at that time. The group filed quietly into Erasmus' class and, at a transitional point in the professor's lecture, asked him to address himself to the problem of the tenure system and Allen's ouster.

Erasmus at first declined to comment on Allen's specific case but said he would discuss tenure in general. He said, "I think the tenure system stinks." He added that he would favor a system in which all faculty members were given five-year contracts which would then be subject to review. Further, Erasmus commented, "I have been opposed to the tenure system throughout all of my professional career." When asked why he had done nothing personally to change this setup, Erasmus responded, "I don't think anything can be done."

Moving to the Allen case, Erasmus was convinced to discuss the idea of a hearing. After seeing a copy of the demand, he stated, "I can't speak for the department on this matter." When further pressed for some sort of personal commitment, Erasmus evoked laughs from most of his class members by saying, "I'm not an individual, I'm a member of a group."

All three of these meetings with anthropology faculty were marked by low-key presentations of opinions and clear attempts to open channels of communications between anthropology faculty members and students which, in the opinions expressed by students yesterday, have been closed in the past.

• • •

Dear Denise,

You sure kept me waiting for a response, and many days that bothered me, I'll admit, no matter how hard I tried to push it out of my head and tell myself it's not personal. But in the end, you wrote back, and it brightened my birthday, so I'll forgive and forget—mostly forget ;). With each passing year it gets harder to find anything exciting about getting older, and your email, which I read immediately, gave me something to look forward to in the coming year: seeing you. You also saved me from spending the bulk of the day ruminating over the other big thing I'm anticipating in the next year, my approaching retirement. That's right, I finally gave in; I'll quit teaching at the end of the semester. The decision brought relief but it's also a tough pill to swallow, so I was glad to have this unexpected proposal to distract me.

How did I know the time was right, besides feeling like a dinosaur? I daresay our revived communication played a part. I don't quite know how to explain it, but even before we reconnected, I had this sense that you were somehow in my orbit again, and that you—or your memory—would play a role in recalibrating the trajectory of my life. You see, for a long time I treated my own history as a sort of ancient civilization that *had been wiped away and replaced by this new, supposedly more advanced, version of myself. I didn't want to think about that old society and refused to acknowledge it even when confronted by it face to face (for instance, after my divorce). But it never fully went away, obviously—was never annihilated—and over time it mounted a guerilla comeback, eventually catching me off guard by deploying your image as a secret weapon. Now, the old and the new are attempting to cohabitate in harmony. Anyway, that's a somewhat confused analogy (which I suppose is something I'm known for) of how I feel. And, just to bring this thought full circle, the former me has been pleading with me to retire, not in so many words exactly...it's as if I can feel it in my bones.*

I'm also just sick of academia. Your reference to Bill Allen reinforced this aversion, which has been causing me increased discomfort for years like a cancerous tumor. But, also, as I believe you too experienced, made me long for those seemingly more potent and virtuous days. I'm sorry to inform you that faculty politics have not improved much over the ensuing half century. Not too surprisingly, I've not always been on the right(eous) side of the debate. At a certain point in life, at least in mine, avoiding dramatic changes assumed preeminence over all other aims—often at the expense of fairness in the case of faculty dealings. I started viewing change as an enemy rather than an opportunity, because, I think, in a way every big change in life becomes a reminder of the ultimate one coming at life's very end. Is that too fatalistic? Perhaps, but there's truth in it.

As for Bill Allen, I was acquainted with him personally and was a huge admirer. Although, if a fresh-faced PhD entered the department now and began using lectures as a soapbox to spread political ideology, well, that would almost be normal (as long as the ideology was liberal). Still, I would detest the little shit. But, as we've already established, I was a very different person back then, in possession of a very different perspective, and I fully supported Bill and his approach to education. So much so that I was one of the students mentioned in that article you attached to your email (I guess you forgot this juicy detail). I vividly remember marching into Gaherty's class in Campbell Hall and hijacking his lecture. The cavernous room was so charged with potential energy upon our arrival, it easily could have erupted into chaos had Gaherty not so diplomatically dealt with our intrusion. In fact, the lasting impression I took from that day was not the progress towards our demands—an open hearing for Bill, which I wholeheartedly supported—but the directness and frankness with which Gaherty, and later Charles Erasmus, treated the students. They made us feel heard, which is what we needed. (My cynical side wants to add the aside that young people love feeling heard, until they become old enough to realize no one's really listening.) Regardless, I wish I'd kept that example closer to mind over the years when dealing with unsatisfied or problematic students who just required a little more attention. But even if I had, I so often act at odds with my intentions that it may not have mattered much. My student ratings still probably would have been disconcertingly low, at least to someone who cared, which I haven't in a long time.

And now I care about those ratings even less because I'm retiring. Don't get the wrong idea though, I still plan to work, putting all my efforts into a book summarizing the dozens of important contributions I've made to the field of anthropology. In fact, if I can find the time to adequately tease out the themes and focus on the writing, I think I could have a best-seller on my hands. I'm not saying I'll be the next Stephen Jay Gould, but I do think I can put together something that anyone with even a cursory interest in anthropology would find intriguing.

While I'd like to commence this project as soon as possible, with a goal of completing a draft by next fall, I can foresee that I'll be exhausted by the end of the semester. On top of the regular class load, and the decrease in TAs at my disposal (cuts, cuts, always cuts), there's a crippling amount of paperwork and untold bureaucratic nightmares to endure before the university will deign to release me from its chokehold. Just thinking about all that's involved makes me start to hyperventilate. The more technology advances, the harder it is to get things done. And all this hype about A.I. taking over is a load of bull, let me tell you. Everything will just become even more unnecessarily automated and counterintuitive, meanwhile privacy will erode even further. The kids running Silicon Valley have no idea what they're doing.

The upshot being that a trip out to the desert (unless you really desire to return to Santa Barbara? But I would prefer to get away) would be most welcome. After my last email to you months ago, I considered proposing an in-person meeting in the near future, but the notion weakened as the wait for a response prolonged. In fact, I'm in the early stages of planning a trip East to visit my son over the holidays, but his in-laws will also be in town, and I'm somewhat dreading such a long overlap. They are fine, unremarkable people, but I can't keep my mouth shut when confronted with their world view, which, let's say, aligns with Bernie Sanders. It's not so much the arguing I mind, I tend to relish it to be honest, but the way my son always feels the need to intervene and moderate everything so nobody's feelings are hurt. That turns my stomach.

Anyway, I'll have a chance to see him in the spring and without having to fly so far, which, aside from being painfully inconvenient, is also very expensive during the holidays. So I've decided to reschedule. With that cleared up, I should be free within a few days after finals in mid-December to make the drive into Palm Desert or somewhere else convenient for you. But first, you'll have to respond sooner than usual in order to secure plans.

Best,
Leroy

CHAPTER TWENTY-TWO
DON'T BE A PUSSY

Only after moving to L.A. did Samantha remember how much she detests driving. Driving gets under her skin like few other things—its indignities, its aggravations, its dangers, its demands. But not all driving is created equal, and today, for the third consecutive month, she's driving out to the desert to meet with a board member. And the part of this drive that comes after Riverside, when suburbia subsides, congestion eases, and the landscape opens up along I-10, this part of the drive is halfway decent. Initially miffed to have to babysit a gay, middle-aged board member who made his fortune before the dotcom bust and is now meting it out to various environmental causes, Samantha's come to appreciate these daylong breaks from routine, from staring at a screen.

    She likes that his office is far from any office park. Instead, it sits on a half-acre of well-maintained but not overly manicured land. She likes that his two wiener dogs are always around, ready to hop up and down like animated Oscar Mayers at the slightest provocation. She likes that he always provides a fresh, healthy lunch, and that he lets her go around 3:30 p.m. to avoid traffic on the return trip, as if that were a thing. She likes that they talk about work, but also about other things—TV shows, tech startups, urban sprawl—and that sometimes they go into the main house and have a coffee with his husband.

She's a few minutes late leaving her house this morning due to the added demand of packing an overnight bag. With Christmas around the corner, she's finally accrued some vacation time and booked two nights in Joshua Tree, about 45 minutes north of Palm Springs, where the board member lives, at one of those Instagrammable hotels with an outdoor shower. She planned the trip with a high school friend also living in L.A., but the friend bailed a week ago after getting cast in a pilot for some YouTube show about living in L.A. Samantha was disappointed, but also glad the room had a no cancellation policy, because she knows she'll still enjoy herself. As she's packing, she notices she's including the accoutrements for an evening in a bar followed by a night in a bed. She had a one-night stand in New York once, but that had been during one of her lower moments, during a week of rain and tears. This will be different, it will be a vote of confidence in herself, a means of getting what she needs as a young, professional, independent woman in L.A. A way to bring an eventful year to a close. Or not. She might just end up drunk in bed watching cable. That would be OK, too. The important thing is that whatever happens will be OK. She can't stop having high ambitions, she's always been achievement-oriented, but she's coming around to lowering her expectations. Somewhere in the middle of high hopes and low expectations is the sweet spot she's looking for, the equilibrium she needs in life to keep her running steady.

She makes it to Riverside without hitting bumper-to-bumper traffic and that's got to be an auspicious sign for the trip. She arrives on time and double-clicks the door lock on her 2018 Toyota Corolla with a grin on her face. The morning proceeds smoothly. The board member's latest fixation is on how captured carbon dioxide is transported between production site—industrial facility, power plant—and underground reservoir. Points A and B can sometimes be hundreds of miles apart. The board member doesn't like pipelines, doesn't want the solution to the problem to involve building more of them. Or at least tons more of them. Samantha, conforming to her role as research assistant allaying board member doubts, tells him there's ways to get around this problem. Ways to pull the carbon directly from the air and bury it, sort of like an offset. The man frowns at the use of the word offset. He doesn't believe in offsets. Samantha can't blame him. She knows how hard it is to verify that anything is actually doing anything for anything. They're verging into negative territory, into a discussion that loses steam, that steam condensing into a murky puddle in which they can see their mirror images, images that remind them of their near impotence in the face of the problem.

The man, whose thinning blond hair is closely kept, stands up. He could be playing golf later, Samantha thinks, based on his khaki shorts, synthetic polo, colorful quarter-length socks. She notices a golf bag in the corner. He is playing golf. Her opinion of him wavers. Golf courses in the desert are the epitome of human cancer upon a landscape. She remembers from school that there are enough golf courses in the U.S. to more than cover Delaware. The board member sees her observing the bag.

"Yeah, I've got a golf game this afternoon," he says. "I'm not a big fan, but my husband enjoys it, and he wants to bring his nephew along today."

Samantha nods. That's better than nothing, better than enjoying golf. The man waves a tanned forearm, indicating that they head across the stone path to the main house for lunch. Taco trays are laid out on the kitchen's marble counter, which is bathed in the natural light provided by three skylights.

"Think we got enough?" says a voice from across the long, open room, which includes a dining area and a couple couches facing a bay window. It's the board member's husband, a shorter, hirsute, balding, even tanner figure in similar attire. He's tailed by a young man with disheveled hair, a loose t-shirt, and the slightly baked demeanor of someone who spends all their time with other students.

"Oh hi, Samantha!" says the husband enthusiastically. "This is my nephew Paul, he's visiting from UC-Santa Barbara. Winter break just started for them." The man looks back at Paul, whose face has come alive with surprise. "You're a junior, right?"

Paul nods, then tears his eyes away from Samantha.

"You go to UCSB?" she says. "My brother goes there."

"Oh yeah," Paul says, feigning innocence. "What's his name?"

"Ethan."

"Ethan Trousock?"

"You know him?"

Paul gulps, feels a lump in his throat. "Oh yeah, we're pretty good friends."

"Wait," Samantha says. "You're Paul! Like his buddy Paul. That's so funny. I can see it now, you guys even sound similar."

"Yeah," Paul says. "We get that a lot."

Paul recognized Samantha from the photos he'd seen, but in person she's much more transfixing. He immediately respects her and wants her to like him. There's the obvious sexual attraction but also something open and inviting about her. And her lively eyes remind him of something out of Jane Austen.

After several more comments on the smallness of the world, the four of them fill their plates with taco fixings and sit at the white oak table. The dachshunds circle their ankles like yippy little sharks. The conversation pings around the table between bites of grilled chicken, fried tilapia, beans, cheese, salsa, and tortilla.

"Unfortunately, I don't think Paul can come out with us this afternoon," says the husband. "He's got to catch the train back, and there's not a good late option."

"Really?" says the board member. "You mean your visit is already coming to an end?"

"Yeah," Paul says after finishing a mouthful. "It's like a six-hour trip. Maybe next time I'll rent a car. Anyway, I don't know the first thing about golf."

"You're taking the train back to Santa Barbara?" Samantha cuts in. "Is that even possible?"

"It is," Paul says. "But it's a pretty big pain in the ass."

"Coming from New York, it's amazing how bad the trains are here," Samantha says. "I've been in L.A. since summer and haven't used the metro yet. You know what, I can give you a ride back, at least to L.A., and maybe all the way to Santa Barbara. Maybe I'll surprise Ethan a few days early. I'm planning to pick him up on the way home anyway."

Paul takes a prolonged sip of Topo Chico before responding. "Well, that would be great. I mean, if it's not, like, a problem for you."

"Ethan's still there right? I don't think he went home yet."

"I don't think so."

But even as Samantha asks about Ethan, an alternative agenda is forming in her head. She's glad she didn't mention her trip to Joshua Tree to the board member, otherwise she'd have to explain the abrupt revision in plans.

"So, should we all hit the links, then?" asks the husband with a rub of his tummy.

Paul looks questioningly at Samantha.

"It sounds fun," she says. "But if it's OK with Paul, I'd prefer to leave early to try to beat traffic."

An hour later, Paul is buckling himself into the front passenger seat of the Corolla. Samantha's appearance in the kitchen jarred him out of the pleasant stupor he'd spent the last three days in while being wined and dined by his wealthy uncle, who he hasn't visited since the summer after high school graduation, and even then, his parents were with him and he wasn't yet 21. Back then he slept in the cramped guestroom off the hallway. This time he got the spare king-size bed and a jacuzzi tub all to himself. He refrained from watching porn, but still masturbated several times. He was preparing himself for the long trip back to Santa Barbara, where he'd hang out for the weekend before flying home to Santa Rosa. He's grateful for the ride, but nervous about making conversation. He intends to suggest they can call Ethan once on the road. That should eat up fifteen minutes or so.

Samantha doesn't know exactly what she's going to say until she starts the car, which forces her into action.

"So, here's an alternate proposal," she says, putting the car in reverse and looking through the rear-view mirror. Making eye contact with herself, she hesitates, but then proceeds. "I was actually planning to spend two nights in Joshua Tree after this. The hotel's already booked and nonrefundable. It's got two beds. My friend canceled at the last minute. You want to come? Then after that I can take you back."

"Ummmm..." Paul is too stunned to respond. Samantha flips the car around in the spacious driveway. They pause, facing the curvy road that leads down to the state highway.

"You in a hurry to get back?" she asks. Paul shakes his head. "Then don't be a pussy about it."

"Hah," Paul laughs.

"What? Sorry," Samantha says. "I guess that was maybe too much."

"No, no," Paul says. He's starting to relax, remembering that he likes spontaneous adventure, or at least that he should. "It's just that, I tell myself that sometimes."

"You tell yourself not to be a pussy?"

"Yeah."

"How's that working out for you?"

CHAPTER TWENTY-THREE
BEFORE CLIMATE CHANGE KILLS ALL THE JOSHUA TREES

Leroy arrives in Palm Desert a night early, having graded the final paper of his 40-year teaching career two days before. He doesn't want to show up at Denise's disheveled with bloodshot eyes and sweaty armpits after more than four hours of driving, and anyway they planned to meet early in the day. In the desert, it's best to do everything early in the day, even in mid-December. After checking into a well-rated chain hotel, he takes himself out for a steak dinner. Slipping into an old road trip habit, he tucks his phone away and reads the local paper as he relaxes in the squeaky booth sipping a glass of wine and awaiting his meal. There's a long article on the future of the Salton Sea, located about an hour's drive south. Formed from Colorado River water siphoned off to 20th-Century California farmers in the Imperial Valley, after a brief heyday as a resort town in the 1970s, the briny sea is now an eyesore and a headache. It's been in decline for decades and is known for mass fish die-offs and an overall post-apocalyptic ambiance. The smiley vacationers are long gone, leaving behind a dusty, salt-encrusted ghost town, Salton City, as well as some dustier, even more encrusted satellite outposts. They should just shut the whole area down and make it a wildlife preserve so it becomes the government's problem, Leroy thinks, or give it to some Indian tribe desperate enough for land to accept it.

The article suggests the solution to the sea's woes may be to build a tunnel or canal to the Gulf of California 70 miles away and allow ocean water to flow via gravity towards the inland sea, which is 200 feet below sea level. This seems crazy to Leroy, but then he reads that the seabed is rich in lithium and is potentially a vital source of the critical mineral. The governor has even gone so far to refer to the region as the "Saudi Arabia of lithium." With that much money at stake, they'll surely find a way to make better use of the place. The waiter is approaching with his meal. He pushes the paper aside. He doesn't like to read the news while he's eating; it leaves a bitter taste in his mouth.

He mulls over the recent past while chewing through his medium-well steak. His departure from the university felt subdued, anticlimactic, and surreal, like someone was following him around with an eraser. But he's not sure how it could've been different. A big going away party would've only exacerbated things. If he'd wanted that, he should've retired a decade ago. He orders another glass of wine along with a slice of pecan pie, calories he justifies as a belated retirement celebration. He rests both hands on his belly as he awaits the dessert. Even though he'd like to shed the extra weight stored within it, he gently caresses his stomach with something resembling admiration.

His insides are becoming unsettled though, as if he's just consumed a plate of nerve endings. Tomorrow he will see the woman he adored so strongly and whom he missed for so long. This thought, and its potential significance—although he can't quite pin down what that significance is—keeps bubbling up. He finishes his second glass of wine and shuts his eyes. He wonders how much of the past will still be present when they meet in the morning.

Palm Desert, about a half-hour southwest of Palm Springs, is mostly desert and palms. It could be mistaken for a beautiful place but the barren mountains surrounding it give away that the there's two conceptions of beauty at play, that of the natural world and the contrasting man-made version, and while they exist in tandem, the juxtaposition is unnatural on the eye, and not to Leroy's liking. Leroy takes in this incongruous scene the next morning as he exits his hotel room onto a second-floor outdoor corridor and into a penetrating morning light, which feels more hot than bright. He packs the car, cranks the AC, and plugs the nearest drive-thru Starbucks into his GPS after checking out. Wide, gridded roads extend under the cloudless sky, making Leroy feel like he's navigating purgatory.

About a third of the way through his coffee, he turns down a residential street and the female GPS navigator tells him that his destination will be on the right. He proceeds cautiously, counting down the addresses until Denise's house comes into view. The neighborhood is a tad rundown, the landscaping not as immaculate as some of the surrounding communities, many of which abut golf courses as if they were a critical resource. The yellow paint on the one-story house could use a touch up, but the two tall palm trees in the front yard look as good as new. He parks alongside the curb and gets out, his eye lingering on the perky palm trees, which remind him of his sometimes mantra to perk up. He removes his sunglasses but it's just too damn bright, so he puts them back on and approaches the door. When he's a few feet away, it opens. The woman framed in the doorway is unmistakably Denise. Her hair is streaked with gray, and her face lined with age, but her buoyant smile hasn't sagged one bit. His mental image of her updates during the few seconds they stare at each other through watery eyes.

"Leroy, my goodness, you're really here." Her voice is a little scratchier but still possesses the gentle timbre he remembers it having.

He smiles clumsily.

"What's left of me at least," he says.

Denise scoffs. "Oh, don't be silly. We both look good for our ages."

Leroy emits a deep cackle then suppresses another as if it were a hiccup. They remain several feet apart. Something about a hug doesn't suit the moment, nor could it capture it.

Denise glances over her shoulder into the house. "Let me go grab my bag and we'll get out of here."

"You don't want to invite me in?" Leroy asks.

"No, it's more that…" Denise pauses. "I guess I don't really want to. I want this to be a totally separate experience from what goes on in there." She gestures inside and some remote recess of Leroy's mind flickers to life at the way she flips her thumb back.

"Can you understand that?" she asks.

Leroy nods. "Sure, I suppose so." But there's resistance in his voice and his tone is unconvincing. Denise ignores it. Part of her allure has always been knowing when to ignore things.

"Great, then I'll meet you at your car in a minute," she says. "I think you're going to like Joshua Tree. Did you check out the hotel I found? It might be a little trendy for us seniors, but I couldn't resist the photos my friend—my friend's daughter really—posted of it on her Facebook."

Leroy watches Denise shut the door with a lightness in his chest, like decades have been lifted off it. He suspects she's hiding something from him, but at their age who isn't?

CHAPTER TWENTY-FOUR
NEW CONSCIOUSNESS

"What do you say we get out of this cave for a bit?" Becca says, convening the final all-staff editorial meeting of the year. The two dozen student reporters, editors, copy editors, and photographers file out of the cluttered office into the cool, overcast afternoon. They amble 30 yards before resettling on a wide cement flight of stairs leading up to the University Center.

"I don't know about you all, but this year fried me," Becca says to murmurs of approval. She tries to make eye contact with everyone; everyone except Steven that is, who's seated directly in front of her on the third step up. His gaze perfectly meets hers when she looks straight ahead, a direction she is now consciously avoiding.

"I didn't feel like I was editing a school newspaper and you all probably didn't feel like you were working for one. The stories we covered were gnarly. But they were damn important and I'm thankful for the work each of you contributed. Together, we got through it. My prediction is that next year will be even tougher and we'll have to work even harder to keep up with the news. One thing we can be certain of—one thing this past year can leave no doubt about—is that we don't know what's coming. The best we can do is try to be prepared. With this in mind, I want to clarify a few beats going into the new year."

Becca catches Denise's eye and gives her a nod before proceeding.

"Denise did a great job covering the oil spill, and I've asked her to keep focused on the environment. She's been attending meetings of the new Get Oil Out group—GOO for short—and is fast becoming an expert in energy policy. Denise, please, no more oil spills."

Denise cracks a smile. "I'll see what I can do."

Becca continues her updates, but Denise's thoughts drift back to an encounter on the bus the previous day on her way back from a GOO meeting in downtown Santa Barbara. As she reviewed her notes from the meeting, which centered around protesting a new oil platform in the Santa Barbara channel, Lonnie appeared at her side. Two weeks had passed since their initial meeting. She invited him to sit down, and he asked her what she was working on. When she mentioned Get Oil Out, he said he was considering getting involved with them as well.

"That's surprising," she said. "It's mostly for, like, environmental diehards. I didn't take you for one of those."

"To me it's all one thing," he said, his hungry eyes feeding off hers. "If we can't be at peace with our surroundings, with the Earth, then we can't be at peace. In my meditation this morning, an inky blob kept seeping into my mind's eye, and I thought, 'that's the oil spill.' You know, like it's still there just out of sight waiting to swallow us up again. Like everyone else in this town, I'm suffering from the collective trauma we lived through. It's gonna take a lot of concentrated meditation to work through that."

"I think I see what you mean," Denise said. Lonnie closed his eyes and took a chest-expanding inhale.

"By the way," he said, eyes reopening. "I'm glad I ran into you again. I wanted to ask you about something. I just enrolled in a course called New Consciousness where you learn to heighten your awareness and experience each moment, you know, to its fullest. I thought you might be interested in joining with me. It's not a big time suck or anything, just once a week."

"Why do you think a course like that would be good for me?" Denise asked, her tone a bit put off.

Lonnie leaned across the seat, concern carved into his face. "Oh, nothing negative. I just sense some repression underneath your beautiful smile—we're all repressed, right—and I thought we could both grow into better versions of ourselves through something like this. You dig?"

"Yeah," Denise more sighed than spoke with a glance out the window. "Maybe you are onto something. What exactly goes on in this class?"

"It's just people tuning in, getting in touch with their joys and their needs and desires. Everyone works together, as one, you know, not like out here." Lonnie gestured up and down the bus as it pulled onto campus. "Where it's fend for yourself."

"Alright, well, I'll think about it."

Lonnie nodded knowingly and scribbled Denise a note with the class info and his phone number on it, handing it to her as the bus pulled into the campus traffic circle.

"And now, we return to the cave for pizza."

Becca's pronouncement stirs Denise from her daydreaming. She stands up, dusts off the back of her skirt, and notices Steven standing next to her.

"Congrats on your new assignment," he says, drawing a hand back over his head and realigning any stray hairs. "Our first environment reporter."

"Thanks," Denise responds.

"Aren't you excited?"

"I am, but also overwhelmed."

"How do you mean?"

"I don't know exactly. It's like, the environment is everything. And then when you start thinking about all the ways we are harming it, it can sort of swallow you up."

"Hmm…" Steven says, the same hand now caressing his chin. "I guess I wasn't thinking of it like that, but maybe you're right. Most environmental coverage does focus on stuff like pollution, and that could become draining. But in a way that's the nature of news. I mean, the crime beat doesn't provide much relief either. People just can't turn away from a car wreck, you know."

"Only with the environment, it's not a car wreck, it's a million-car pileup," Denise says. "Like how I felt when I first encountered the oil spill—hopeless and small and insignificant—I just think that might keep happening."

"OK," Steven says, eyeing the dim office and festive conversation within. "I'm sure in the long run, the environment—nature—will be fine. Humans are great at addressing problems once they know what they are, and we're just getting a handle on how we're impacting the environment." He takes a step towards the office. "I hope these feelings won't get in the way of your reporting. I mean, the oil spill upset everyone around here pretty bad, but that was a once-in-a-lifetime thing. Like you said, it was a million-car pileup."

"I hope you're right," Denise says. "Anyway, I'll be fine. It'll be fine."

Denise follows Steven into the office and takes a piece of pizza back to her desk. She's surprised to find a short article about the New Consciousness course Lonnie invited her to in the paper. After finishing her slice, she wishes Becca a Merry Christmas and slips towards the exit. As she's leaving, Becca grabs her arm and gives her a paper plate with two slices of pizza on it.

"For Leroy, or whoever," she says. "We way over-ordered. Apparently, freshman no longer eat like pigs. You OK, by the way? You seem a little distracted."

Denise assures Becca she's fine and Becca sees her off with a tender look.

Denise parks her bike along Leroy's porch and removes the folded, grease-caked paper plate containing the pizza slices from her bag. She observes the house across the yard, half expecting to see Lonnie emerge. The door squeaks behind her and she turns as Leroy comes out. He's squinting to adjust to the light, his hair is tousled, and he's got the strained look of someone who's been studying for hours.

"What are you doing here?" he asks before realizing he's being rude and stepping out to give Denise a hug. As he embraces her, he sees the pizza. "Oh, you've come to eat pizza in my face when all I have is cereal."

Denise holds the greasy plate out for him. "It's for you. I already ate at the newspaper end-of-year thing."

"Ah, in that case, thanks. How was it?" Leroy takes a slice and chomps off the bottom third of it.

"It was alright." Denise looks back across the yard at Lonnie's old place. "Becca thinks next year will be even more exhausting than this year."

"She does?" Leroy says with his mouth full. "Well, she's usually right, right?"

"Yeah."

"Although this year was pretty brutal."

"Yeah."

Leroy devours the slice in a few more bites and puts the other one on the side table.

"Thanks for bringing that over. I'm in the middle of cramming for my final tomorrow, so I should get back to it."

"Oh sure," Denise says, reaching into her bag. "Just one quick thing. A friend invited me to take this New Consciousness class next semester." She hands him the newspaper folded over to the article about the course. "At first I thought it wasn't for me—I mean, it's pretty unconventional, to say the least—but maybe it could be good to try something different. You know how stressed I've been and I think it might help me decompress a little."

Leroy takes the paper from her and begins to read aloud.

"...The opportunity to come together and explore the uniqueness of each participant...Emphasis on experiencing an event rather than seeking an explanation from it."

Less than halfway through the short article he ceases reading and hands the paper back to Denise.

"This doesn't sound like you at all," he says. "Like zilch. We're not at university to sit around in something called encounter groups talking about our feelings."

"I know, I know, but I thought maybe I might benefit from being in the moment a little more," Denise says hesitantly. "Maybe I could tune into some other, I don't know, wavelengths."

"Tune into some other wavelengths," Leroy repeats bemusedly. "OK, it's your deal. I just feel like you've already got so much going on."

"That's part of the problem. It can feel like too much."

Leroy leans his arms on the porch banister. "Who's this friend anyway?"

Denise clams up. She should've anticipated the question.

"Well, he's more of an acquaintance," she says, suddenly unsure of how to position her body.

"He? Who is this guy?"

"Um, I don't think you know him. I met him on the bus."

"Some guy you met on the bus invites you to expand your consciousness and you're actually entertaining the idea?"

"There's nothing wrong with meeting someone on the bus," Denise says. "It's nice to meet new people, maybe you should try it sometime."

"Oh, I see, now I'm the one with the problem," Leroy says. "Listen, I don't have time for this right now. I need to focus on my final, which is about an actual topic of study, not some hippie mind-meld or whatever."

"Fine," Denise says, gripping her bag tightly across her midsection.

Leroy jerks open the screen door to his house. It looks like he might slam it, but his posture softens.

"Thanks again for the pizza," he says, turning and picking up the remaining piece. "We'll work this out later, I don't want to get too sore."

"OK," Denise says. "I'm sure we will. It'll be fine."

Strangely, she wants Leroy to wink at her. But he doesn't. He smiles lips-sealed and lets the screen door flap shut behind him.

Standing motionless, she wonders why she lied to him about not knowing Lonnie. Only one explanation makes sense.

CHAPTER TWENTY-FIVE
INTIMATE

The semester is over, but Ethan hasn't gone home. He strolls around Isla Vista in a daze, often wandering onto campus and around the lagoon, which, devoid of people during the long holiday break, feels hazy and dreamlike, especially before the morning fog lifts. His dreams of 1969 are becoming more vivid, too. Sometimes on the lagoon he forgets what year it is. He watches waves of students pack up their bags and head back to towns scattered across the state, towns they still consider home. His parents ask when he's coming and offer to drive down and give him a ride. He tells them he's dating someone and they're both hanging around. He says he'll come when Samantha picks him up.

He listens closely to his dad during their brief chats, alerted to anything unusual, anything that might be interpreted as forgetful or out of character. He's got some kind of rash along his groin, and he thinks one of the moles on his arm might be doing weird things, changing color and size. Telling signs of skin cancer. His knee clicks sometimes, and he wonders if it could be an early indicator of arthritis. He knows his dad must be dealing with even more aches and pains than he is, batting away more signs of mortality. He can't imagine being old, but he also can't stop imagining it.

He passed all his classes but just barely, and he's yet to sign up for next semester's courseload. He attempts to think about his future, but it's even more opaque than the morning mist. Instead, he thinks about the past, the one he had the opportunity to briefly inhabit, the one that felt so fresh and newborn. Some part of him remains on the other side of the portal, transmitting flashes of that world in vivid spurts and caustic sputters. He's been getting more headaches than he remembers. He wonders if maybe they're migraines.

He revisits the *El Gaucho* archives and reads ahead from where he left off, thinking that might lend some structure to his thoughts, illuminate some clearer connection between his waking life and his dreaming one, between the past and the present. He reads about the riots and the burning of the Bank of America that took place in late February 1970. He walks by the Bank of America in Isla Vista, which is just an ATM, eying it as if it might spit out something other than cash or accept something other than his debit card.

One aimless afternoon, as he's sitting on his duplex's patio watching the placid ocean and listening to music, the only other roommate not yet departed for break napping on the lumpy, fraying couch inside, his phone rings.

Ethan pauses the music and answers.

"Samantha?"

"Ethan, guess what."

Ethan hears ambient noise in the background, like the rush of traffic, and Samantha's voice is more distant than usual.

"Are you on speaker phone?"

"I am," she says, her voice louder now. "I'm driving. And Paul's in the passenger seat."

Paul leans close to the phone. "Hey Ethan."

"Hey man. But how did…" Ethan's glad he's not standing because his knees would've buckled underneath him. For a second he's certain there's another time-slip involved. That Samantha and Paul are somewhere in the future, calling him, perhaps calling to him.

"Yeah, I know, right," Samantha interjects. She explains the circumstances that led them to be driving along a parched incline bordering Joshua Tree National Park enroute to the eponymous town.

Ethan attempts to engage in the lighthearted conversation suitable for multiparty phone calls, but his feelings are hurt and he can't muster much enthusiasm. He knows no one's at fault, but he senses he's missing out on something important. He's been left out in the cold by this unexpected coincidence, this convergence of his lives, and he can't seem to banter.

Samantha, well attuned to her brother's moods, lets the discussion wind down. She tells him she'll pick him up at the end of the week on her way to mom and dad's. Her arrival in Isla Vista, which seemed just around the corner a few minutes ago when Ethan was indifferent to the passage of time, now feels eons away. Ethan tells them to have fun and they say they'll see him soon and it's somehow the most awkward, disassociating exchange with two of the people he's closest to. Hanging up, the sensation that he's traveled to the future lingers, and he doesn't like what he experienced there, not one bit. He much preferred when all he could discern was a nebulous landscape of lives playing out. Now he feels the acute pain of losing intimacy with friends and family, of the way time wears away at relationships much like it does the human body. Of the way time and space keep pulling the center of the universe apart.

CHAPTER TWENTY-SIX
THE EARTH IS UNDULATING, LIKE THE SEA

There's a twenty-minute wait for a table when Paul and Samantha arrive at the restaurant, an upscale Mexican spot layered with sharp edges and adorned with succulents. Joshua Tree is a Main Street town that's outgrown itself in the era of Airbnbs and glamping. The one-block stretch between The Sacred Sands hotel, where they're staying, and the restaurant is crowded enough to be in Vegas. After checking into the hotel, Paul propped himself up on a bulbous teal toss pillow on the outdoor patio daybed and intermittently worked on a crossword, scanned dating apps, and contemplated if he was going to masturbate in the bathroom later. Samantha took a shower and joined him outside in a sleeveless sun dress, sitting in one of the wicker chairs and putting her legs up on another. After fifteen minutes of tanning, she reluctantly retrieved her computer and responded to a flurry of work emails. They didn't say much until the shadows started to grow long and she suggested going to dinner.

Paul orders drinks at the bar and reconvenes with Samantha on a bench outside the restaurant's front entryway. They sip their beverages and absorb the bustling scene. Couples sit facing each other, some engaged in animated conversation and others dead quiet. Families occupy the larger tables, and several raucous parties appear to be exclusively teenagers. An older couple three benches down catches Paul's eye, mostly because they're old. But then he recognizes the man.

Paul delicately pokes Samantha on the shoulder. She's downed her dark 'n' stormy while he's hardly made a dent in his. She looks up from her phone.

"That's one of my anthropology professors over there," he says, indicating with his head. Samantha sizes up the senior, whose Eddie Bauer shirt is tucked into starchy jeans.

"Do you want to say hi?"

"Do *you* want to say hi?"

Samantha shoots Paul a half-condescending look. "Sure, I mean, unless he's a real ass or something. Otherwise, why not?"

A glimmer comes into Samantha's eye and she's about to say something, but Paul pre-empts her.

"Don't even say it. I thought you wouldn't want to say hi. He's not well liked, you know, among the student body, but we kind of get along."

As Samantha downs the last of her drink Paul takes another look at the woman, realizing it must be Denise. They're only an hour from Palm Desert. Why else would Prof. Bourman be waiting for a table at a hip restaurant on the fringes of civilization? Samantha nudges Paul and they make their way along the restaurant's blackwashed brick exterior to a bench abutting the patio.

"Professor Bourman?" Paul says as they near.

Leroy turns his head from Denise and gradually recognizes the interrupter.

"Paul, my gosh, what are you doing here? You from around here?"

"Well, no, but…we're just, me and um, this is Samantha…"

Samantha reaches across Paul and offers her hand to Leroy. "We're just on a little vacation, before heading home for the holidays."

Samantha recently turned 24, but she looks a generation removed from most UCSB students. Her hair is tied back and she's wearing a jean jacket over her dress. Leroy fails to respond so Denise fills the void.

"Us too," she says, extending her hand for Samantha to shake. "I mean we're also on a little vacation. My name's Denise." She rubs Leroy's arm. "And call him Leroy. Dropping that professor bit is part of what we're celebrating."

Paul finds Denise's presence both unassuming and inviting.

"You're the Denise that lives in Palm Desert?" he asks.

There's a moment of confusion while Leroy remembers the sequence of events from the preceding year that put him on such familiar terms with Paul.

"Oh right," Leroy says. "Denise, this is the young man who tracked down your email for me, and also who got his hands on that scrap of paper I mentioned in my correspondence."

Samantha's hands go to her hips. "Um, what?"

Paul takes a swig of his drink and assures Samantha that he'll fill her in later. Then, turning back to Leroy and Denise, he asks, "So this is the first time you're seeing each other in like 50 years?"

"Closer to 53, and yes," Denise says. "Leroy just picked me up this morning."

"Wow," Paul says. "And you were a couple in college, right?"

Denise and Leroy exchange a glance.

"Did I really tell you all this, Paul?" Leroy says. "But yeah, you could say that."

Samantha inscribes an imaginary circle with her arm around Paul, Leroy, and Denise.

"Well, I'm surprisingly intrigued by all of this."

"It does seem like we have a lot to discuss," Denise says. "Would you want to join us for dinner? Like I said, on top of seeing each other again, we're also celebrating Leroy's retirement."

Paul thinks of the kind of comment he'd like to make to Ethan about Leroy finally departing academia. Instead, he says, "So we finally got to be too much for you."

Leroy grins apprehensively, as if worried Paul might say something more.

"I learned a lot in your class, it's kind of too bad, I hoped to take another," Paul adds. "I'm sure you're looking forward to retirement, though."

Leroy is about to bring up his book project when he notices Paul's glass is shaking, the ice cubes frenziedly clinking. Then Paul's entire body is in gumby-like motion. And then everybody's off kilter and off balance. People flee the restaurant as if they've just seen a ghost, their screams mingling with the sound of shattering dishware. The Earth is undulating, like the sea. His drink in one hand, Paul feels something warm take up residence in his other. It's Samantha. She pulls him towards the bench, and they squat down and grab onto it. Paul sees Leroy tumble backwards and Denise crawl towards him. Samantha looks on worriedly as Paul struggles past Denise, gracefully falls next to Leroy, and cups his head in his arms. The shaking is relentless. The professor appears to have lost consciousness. Samantha and Denise half hug each other, each with an arm around the bench. They remain like this for the most excruciating seconds of their lives. The sound of car alarms and collapsing shelves and kids' screams are deafening.

Finally, the ground settles. There's commotion but less chaos. The roof covering the restaurant's patio has folded in on itself and taken out a few tables, but no one appears to be hurt. Leroy, unalert but breathing evenly, is in good hands, as Paul passed his EMT training the summer before college with an eye on fighting wildfires. Denise cautiously leaves the bench, sits next to Leroy, and helps Paul place his head on her lap.

"I don't think he's bleeding," Paul says, getting up. "I'm hopeful he'll come to soon."

Samantha puts a hand on Paul's back and says, "Way to act fast." She looks around, taking in the shaken panorama. It reminds her of David Hockney's Pearblossom Highway, the famous photo collage depicting a desert road north of Los Angeles. Some mix of her own jostled mind and the upheaval in front of her eyes lends the scene that same mosaicked essence, that same uncanny perspective. As Paul and

Denise attend to Leroy, she keeps talking, in part to keep any distress at bay.

"You know, my first thought, when I realized it was an earthquake, was fracking," she says. "How messed up is that? When a natural disaster strikes, my mind goes straight to man-made."

Denise looks up with recognition. "Makes sense to me."

"Yeah, but, that was way too big," Samantha says. "And I don't think there's much fracking around here anyway."

The moment stretches out and Denise commences a deep-breathing exercise while stroking Leroy's head. Her eyes are closed like she's meditating. Suddenly, they open.

"He's awake," she says.

They gather around Leroy. His dilated pupils roam within the whites of his eyes. He attempts to sit up but grimaces and brings a hand to his temple. Paul tells him to stay still.

"I was there at the lake," Leroy says.

"What lake?" Denise asks.

"Lake Powell, where you left me way back when. Edward Abbey was there with me."

Denise's mouth opens and closes, but no sound comes out.

"He pointed towards the reservoir and said, 'The water is low, maybe you can rescue the ring.'"

"OK," Denise says. "OK, maybe."

"Wow," Samantha interjects. "So many questions. For instance, what ring?" But a prolonged wail of sirens drowns her out.

"Where are you staying?" Paul asks Leroy once they've passed.

Leroy points down the road. Jagged asphalt lines rift the pavement, and a layer of sandy dirt covers most vehicles.

"Just down the block at The Sacred Sands," he says. As the sun sets, it becomes apparent that the power is out all along the street.

"Hey, us too," Paul says.

Leroy pushes himself to his feet with a groan. "I don't know about you all, but I think we should head back to the hotel. I need some water."

Three Sacred Sands employees rush towards them and inquire about their well-being as they stagger into the lobby, which looks like it's been ransacked by toddlers. But otherwise, the hotel, a new building, appears undamaged. The hotel manager, a thin man in his 30s with a flop of hair hanging over his side buzz, invites them to take what they want from the pantry.

They stock up on snacks—junk carbs, but also healthy bars, bananas, apples, a six-pack of yogurt, and a variety of juices and sodas. Paul puts a bottle of Jameson under his arm, grabs a two-liter ginger ale, and rescues some ice from the freezer before it melts. They arrive at Leroy and Denise's room first, filing in and unloading the cargo on a round table in the corner. A glass sliding door covers the entire far wall of the room. Denise opens the curtain and twilight filters in saturating everything in a cool, flattering light. Paul passes around a bag of Chex Mix, reaching up from his seat on the floor to hand it to Denise on the bed, who passes it to Leroy in the desk chair, who offers some to Samantha on the loveseat. Then Paul starts in on the whiskey gingers, supplying everyone their own in a clear plastic cup.

"You know, I haven't been camping in over a decade," Denise says between sips of her whiskey ginger. "This makes me miss it."

"Yeah, camping is great," Paul says. "Should we move out under the stars?"

Leroy shifts his weight in the chair, where he'd been slumped, milking his drink and assessing himself for any lasting damage from the fall. "Yes, that's a good idea, for safety purposes too."

They relocate to the outdoor patio, which is slightly larger than the room.

"Holy moly, the stars are amazing," Denise comments. They all look up. In the desert winter, twilight is truncated, and darkness and coolness descend quickly once the sun abandons its post. The power remains out.

"Instead of stars, I'm just thinking about light pollution, or the absence of it I guess," Samantha says. "Again, fixated on the human element, rather than the natural wonder."

"I can't get over how scary that was," Denise says. "I'm somewhat of a fraidy cat, but I haven't been that freaked out in a while."

"I haven't been that scared since the wildfire evacuation last summer outside of Sequoia National Park," Paul says. "That was much worse; one minute we're setting up camp as part of this weeklong mini-course, the next we're fleeing for our lives. I could feel the heat searing into my back and the smoke burned my eyes. Made me realize I wasn't cut out for fighting fires. For anything that puts you in that kind of danger."

Paul takes a drink and notices everyone still paying close attention to him. "It made me feel like there wasn't much I could do, you know, against something that big, like an ocean of fire. It gave me a weird sensation of being stranded in my own body."

"I remember that," Leroy says, reclining heavily in one of the wicker chairs. "Fouled the air along the coast for a week. Couldn't turn off the damn alerts on my phone telling me to close the windows and stay indoors."

"That's one nice thing about this desert," Denise says. "Not enough vegetation for something like that."

Paul refills the drinks and passes around more snacks. Stars populate the sky in ever greater numbers until they resemble luminous cities on a nighttime map; cities birthing brightly into existence one after another; cities with electricity and power and lots of it.

"You were asking about the ring earlier, in Leroy's vision," Denise says to Samantha. "Well, I only recently learned that Leroy threw his beautiful, turquoise-studded heirloom ring into Lake Powell after I abandoned him there during our first, and last, camping trip. You see, he wanted to propose to me, which I had a premonition of. At the time, though, I wasn't sure I loved Leroy—I wasn't even sure if I wanted to get married."

Denise pauses.

"I knew I cared for him a lot, and that he could make a good life partner—I was pretty sure of that much. But there was another current running through me, growing stronger by the day and stirring everything up within me. I felt like I needed to live more somehow—who knows what that meant—before settling down. And when the opportunity arose to hop on in a van with Edward Abbey, it was like I had no control over the decision. I had to take it. Even if it meant breaking the heart of the person closest to me."

"In the dream Edward Abbey said the ring might be retrievable?" Paul asks. "Could that be for real?"

"Perhaps," Leroy says. "It's funny because I was recently reading about how the water level in the lake is lower than it's been since, well, since I tossed the ring down there. Makes me wonder if that's somehow wormed its way into my subconsciousness. I do distinctly remember, after I tossed it, it landing on a sandy outcrop well back from the water. So, it's possible, I guess."

Samantha is meandering around the perimeter of the patio, her hand rubbing the rough edge of the stucco wall. "Edward Abbey is the *Monkey Wrench Gang* guy, right?

"Yep," Denise says, finishing off a handful of corn nuts. "The foul-mouthed desert rat who wrote some of the most influential environmental prose of the second half of the twentieth century. Who was also an amazing lover."

Samantha laughs giddily. "I'm glad we ran into you two. And you too, Paul. If I'd been here alone, this trip might've been memorable for the wrong reasons."

Paul raises his glass towards Samantha and an electricity generator saws into the night.

CHAPTER TWENTY-SEVEN
MOUTHFEEL

El Gaucho, **Cover Page, January 22, 1970:**[IX]

(a thought-feeling)

It's been said so much, you're sick of hearing it.

The rape of the oceans is an oily reality.

(Think of it. The oil still vomits its vile toxin, one year later.)

The Black Panthers are being exterminated.

(Think of it. 25 have been murdered by pigs—yes, pigs—we must say it—in the past year.)

10,000, who knows, maybe 20,000 young men are in jail for refusing to become licensed murderers. (Think of it. In jail!)

Reagan says education is a capital investment and tuition a necessity. (?)

Agnew says peace marchers are rotten apples, to be discarded.

Mitchell says the radicals must be isolated.

The Justice Department says desegregation shouldn't move too fast.

Vietnam for Uncle Sam.

Get the Gooks!

And God Bless the Silent Majority.

Industrial slime is an ecological crime.

The Man has gas, guns and a face mask.

It's just the same old radical rhetoric. Stale, simplistic and sarcastic.

But true.

It's in the news every day. We can't escape it!

We should not escape it. We must confront it.

We must come together. Right now.

Come together, in our understanding

The words mean little, but the feelings say most.

The actions say all.

We must come together, in our obligation to say NO MORE, in our obligation to remain sane.

Welcome to the Age of Aquarius. We will all drown in this sea of fascism, unless we learn to swim.

Unless we learn to swim. Unless we learn to swim. Unless we learn to swim.

Swimming: 1. To propel oneself through water, or whatever. 2. To oppose the current; to speak out; to come together and get together and organize. 3. To do whatever is necessary to keep from drowning. To do whatever is necessary to stop murder—murder of black people who are brave enough to say NO MORE. FREEDOM NOW. Murder of the earth, the waters, the trees, who say NO MORE, OR HUMANITY WILL BE NO MORE.

To do whatever is necessary to live.

To LIVE! To LOVE! To be FREE!

Remember January 28.

Love, Life, Freedom. Fascism, Pigs, Repression

Rhetoric. Reality. Which is which?

Reality IS.

Death, spiritual or physical, IS.

Unless we learn to swim. Unless we learn to swim.

January 28. January 28.

An Unacceptable Response[x]
El Gaucho Editorial, Monday, January 26, 1970

"The strength of the University of California, as in the case of all great universities, lies in the quality of its faculty. The faculty and especially the departments play a key role in maintaining this quality."

This in essence, is what lies at the bottom of the growing controversy over the firing of Bill Allen: the Administration insists that the faculty are the only members of the academic community who can determine hiring and firing of instructors.

In his statement to the signers of the Allen petition, Vice-Chancellor Buchanan repeats the same tired procedures that the faculty have gone through in reaching their decision. But he disregards the core of the students' demand.

He disregards the feeling held by those 7,776 students that they, too, have a right in determining what is quality in a professor and what isn't. Buchanan says "...to obtain reliable evidence and candid evaluations from qualified authorities, it is essential that review procedures be confidential."

The implication can only be that faculty departments are less than candid in communicating to students their reasons for hiring and firing. In this case, they are not only less than candid, they are totally secretive.

The Administration says that students are invited to participate in determining policy "at all levels of campus activities..." They say that students' opportunities "have never been brighter." This smacks of hypocrisy since, in the area that counts, you gotta listen to the Massa.

We believe that the Administration has made a very poor case for refusing an open hearing on the Allen firing. This belief is supported by the fact that over half the students at UCSB have come together in a demand for reasons. In this "marketplace of ideas" the refusal to give reasons for actions is inexcusable.

The Administration's handling of this affair has demonstrated that they have moved from the point of rational discourse to one of executive fiat.

Students, at this point, have exhausted all the legitimate channels that are open to them. Since the Administration has done nothing to include students in the decision-making that really matters it is not surprising that the students are not satisfied with the decision made by those at the top. This peremptory response will not do.

• • •

Lonnie is in the back by the baking rack cutting donuts from a long cylinder of dough when he hears the door chime. It's 10 p.m. and he's more than halfway through his shift at Campus Donut, Isla Vista's only 24-hour establishment, where he's been working for a month. He raises his hands up to his baker's hat, which is dusted with flour, and is about to remove it when he changes his mind. At first, he found the hat ridiculous and would take it off whenever someone came in, but it's growing on him. Also, the manager, a fifth-year senior who hides beers under the counter, told him his tips would get docked if he got caught with it off.

Lonnie's coworker recently clocked out and he's on his own until midnight, when the graveyard shift begins. At which point Mike, a 30-something guy who's deaf in one ear, takes over and Lonnie will bike home to Goleta and pass out after 20 minutes of meditation. It's a Tuesday night and it should be slow, although a recent write-up in the school paper has increased traffic. Even though it gave the food quality and decor one star each, it praised the low prices. Lonnie wipes his hands on his apron as he approaches the counter and asks, "What can I getcha?" even before raising his eyes to the customer.

"I'll take the Lonnie special," replies a voice Lonnie's dreaded hearing for months. "Which is what? A disappearing donut?"

Lonnie's hands clench his apron. Russell's eyes are bloodshot, but not in that hazy stoned way. His expression is borderline menacing, as if he might leap over the counter at any second. He emits a guttural laugh. "Or maybe it's just a really short donut."

Lonnie detests comments about his height, and he nearly pivots towards the prep station and its array of knives. But he catches himself, silently thanks yogi MM for the reassuring presence of his meditative calm, and forces down a gulp of the room's sugary air.

"Russell," he says, offering a slight nod. "Good to see you. Figured I'd run into you eventually."

"What you should've figured on is running far away from here," Russell says. "After the bullshit mess you left behind."

Russell glances over his shoulder to make sure no one's approaching the neon-lit storefront before leaning over the counter. "And don't think I don't know what happened to my little explosives project."

"Alright, alright," Lonnie says, a bead of sweat appearing from underneath the white-banded rim of his hat. "Take a chill pill. I know what I did was way uncool, and I owe you. Big time."

Russell nods emphatically, his fingers heavily tapping the counter.

"How about this?" Lonnie says. "Free donuts for as long as I work here. For starters, at least."

Russell lets out a crazed laugh.

"Just for starters," Lonnie repeats. His toes curl in his shoes, as if they could retract.

"Oh, fuck it," Russell says, heaving himself back from the counter. "I don't have time for this. I'm working on something new. Something that won't get compromised because of my poor vetting. Something that will make your little solo effort look like a dress rehearsal."

Lonnie nods uncomfortably. "Well, that's good. I never meant to…I mean, I wasn't trying to sabotage…"

"Save it, pipsqueak," Russell says. "Just give me a dozen donuts. For starters."

Lonnie quickly fills a white paper bag as he watches Russell extract a coke from the cooler, his grip like a stranglehold around it.

"Nice decor in here, by the way," Russell says as he turns towards the door. "At least for a shit hole."

"Yeah," Lonnie says. "The owner loves The Beatles."

"I'd say he has good taste," Russell says from just inside the doorframe. "But then again, he hired you."

Lonnie fixes his facial features in neutral positions and nods.

"And don't forget, now I know where to find you," Russell all but snarls before venturing into the night.

The door squeaks closed and the chime hanging from the handle fills the room with lighthearted jingles before fading into silence. Lonnie remains still, his breathing heavy and unsteady. His heart is pumping in overdrive, bailing him out as if he might drown internally. He considers escaping out the back door and not slowing down until Los Angeles, or maybe Tijuana. The bailing slows until there's nothing left at all and his heart aches with emptiness. He goes to the phone on the wall and dials the number that's always at his fingertips lately. Denise answers after four rings.

"Hi Denise, it's Lonnie."

"Lonnie, my goodness. What's going on? You know it's almost eleven o'clock."

"Yeah, sorry to call so late. It's just, something just went down at work and I need help re-centering. If you're still up, I thought maybe we could run through a couple of exercises from class."

"Right now?" Denise asks. "Are you hurt?"

"I'm not hurt, but I'm worried I might get hurt. If you know what I mean."

"Uh huh, OK, well, jeez…my roommate is participating in some overnight baking marathon so…so I guess it's OK if you come by, if it's really an emergency."

"Thank you for your gracious kindness, Denise," Lonnie says. "You are saving me, majorly."

"And Lonnie," Denise says. "Can you bring me a donut?"

Lonnie knows his coworker is next door at a bar, and he convinces him to cover the rest of his shift by offering to double his pay. Ten minutes later, he's at Denise's. She lets him in, directs him to the couch, and goes to the kitchen to make tea and get a plate for the doughnuts. She's wearing gray sweatpants and a button-down flannel pajama top. Lonnie wonders if that's what she sleeps in or if she changed into something more modest in anticipation of his visit. He's never seen a woman in pajamas before, at least one not related to him. Denise places two mugs of steaming herbal tea on the coffee table and sits in an aging upholstered chair next to the couch.

"So," she says, reaching for the tea and blowing on it. "You do look pretty rattled. Do you want to talk about what happened or do you want to calm consciousnesses first?"

Denise brushes a strand of hair from her face with the back of her hand. Lonnie watches her hand before settling on her eyes, which are soft and sleepy and as inviting as a cool pillow.

"I think...I don't think talking is the method we need now," he says. "How about back-to-back breathing?"

Denise takes another sip of her tea and stares out the window for a moment, even though all Lonnie sees outside is darkness. "OK," she says. "Should we sit on the floor then?"

Lonnie nods and slips off the couch onto the mock-oriental carpet that's been passed down through several generations of roommates. Denise does the same and they shuffle around so they're leaning into each other's backs. Lonnie takes a deep inhale, Denise releases a deep exhale; Denise takes a deep inhale, Lonnie releases a deep exhale; and so on, breaking after a dozen rounds.

"I'm feeling calmer," Lonnie says after completing the last exhale. "Should we do some face-to-face breathing too?"

"If it's helpful for you, then sure," Denise says. Lonnie can't see her face, but he senses some reservation in her response.

"Just like in class," Lonnie says. "When we breathe in sync, I feel so grounded. That's what I need now. You dig?"

They pivot and face each other on the carpet, legs folded, knees just about touching, hands palm-down on their knees. With eyes closed, they repeat the same breathing pattern as before. Midway through,

Denise feels a fingertip gently descend on one of her own. Then another, and another. The same thing occurs on the other hand. Her breathing grows heavier but remains steady. When she opens her eyes at the conclusion of the repetitions, Lonnie is already looking at her. His fingers are smoother than she'd imagined, as if they'd acquired the donut dough's texture after so much kneading. Without speaking, Lonnie leans forward. Denise's back remains stiff at first, but then she makes a decision. Lonnie tries to read her expression as he's falling towards it, but it's masked. Which is funny, because for once, for the blink of an eye, the duration of an exhale, his isn't. Then their lips are sealed.

They kiss for several minutes, getting to know the contours of each other's lips, the warmth of each other's breath. When Lonnie leans all the way forward, lowering them both to the carpet without allowing their mouths to part, Denise pushes up onto her side with her elbow.

"I don't know, Lonnie," she says, flushed. "It seems like you're feeling alright now."

Lonnie initially rises to meet her, but with her comment he tumbles onto his back. She's disarmed him with humor.

"Yeah, I guess I am," he says. "I sure didn't expect that to happen, but then the energy was just there. So groovy."

"I suppose it was," Denise says, pulling down Lonnie's shirt so it covers his stomach. "But I'm not comfortable with going any further, right now. For starters…"

Lonnie cuts her off before she can ruin the moment. "I know, I know. I came here so you could help bring me back from the excruciating encounter I just had, which you did and for which I am eternally grateful. I feel blessed, by an angel. The physical stuff can wait."

The word 'wait' lingers in the air like a question mark.

Denise gets back into the chair and sips her tea. "I'd like to know more about what happened, but I think all the newspaper stuff this week is finally catching up with me. I'm exhausted and not thinking very clearly."

"What do you mean?" Lonnie asks, reaching for his tea from the carpet.

"Well, it's the one-year anniversary of the oil spill, and I'm leading the coverage. I've been pulling together several opinion pieces, while also trying to prepare for the day-of events, and then there's stuff going on with the actual ocean drilling, which they want to keep doing."

Lonnie nods, recalling the oil spill anniversary for the first time since their meeting on the bus.

"And on top of that, I feel like I'm still mourning all the damage, all the dead birds and the ruined coastline," Denise says. "It's like the oil is stuck inside me, glommed up, you know?"

"You want to meditate through it?" Lonnie asks, hopping onto his knees. "I can guide us."

"No, no," Denise says. "I'm not functional enough right now."

Lonnie leans back onto his butt.

"Plus," Denise says. "There's all this stuff going on around Bill Allen again, who I used to want to write about before I was drowning in environmental coverage. The authorities still refuse to hold any open hearings on his retirement and it's pissing everyone off. Becca says she hasn't seen the student body this riled up before. It's got everyone at the paper, I don't know, somewhat on edge but also kind of excited. First, they gather all these signatures and now there might be a rally."

"Well," Lonnie says. "I know little of this Allen character, or what he represents, but students need to make their voices heard somehow and a peaceful protest might be the answer. I just hope it's not hijacked by any of those loonies who want to escalate everything, cause you know the cops are ready to pounce."

"You think they're that eager to intervene?" Denise asks.

Lonnie nods several times and Denise discerns a firmness in his demeanor that she hasn't noted before. The change in topic has altered Lonnie's mood, he looks distracted, like he just connected some dots and the picture they formed isn't to his liking. He gets up and straightens his corduroy pants.

"Well, I guess I've kept you up long enough." He looks like he's about to approach Denise for a kiss, but instead he winks. "I'll see you around then, honey," he says, heading out the door.

Denise rises and waves goodbye through the screen door. She can't understand why she's drawn to this odd little man, and she's given up trying.

CHAPTER TWENTY-EIGHT
APPEAR WHEN SUMMONED

Ethan is in the library perusing a book about how many of the UC Santa Barbara student activists of the late 1960s and early 70s abandoned their youthful idealism as they matured into adulthood. He finds it both inspiring and dispiriting. Inspiring because at least they were passionate about societal change at some point, and they did make some waves. Dispiriting because they ultimately conformed to societal norms without too much objection. Even more dispiriting is how pursuing these lofty aims typically left them at a disadvantage to their peers when it came to professional success later in life, having lost ground to them during formative years. Ethan envies the moral imperatives so front and center in that era. He knows there's still a thriving, if splintered, political activism movement, but he feels alienated from it, having perceived no obvious entry point to inserting himself into the dialogue, not that he's tried very hard. He didn't realize he had a desire to get involved in anything resembling activism until he traveled back to 1969, where all he had to do was walk around campus to feel part of something greater. Even if it required the toxic fallout of an environmental disaster to catalyze the swell of engagement, there was still something intoxicating in the air back then. Now, he finds campus isolating and isolated, the air thin, insipid, and likely full of carcinogens. For a while he thought he was over it—over the way being part of something bigger made him feel more alive—but he's not.

Especially now that he knows the main confrontation is fast approaching; at least fast approaching 53 years ago in the alternate timeline where he expends much of his imagination. Feeling more confused than ever about the present, he buries himself in the past.

He reads a passage specifically about the Isla Vista riots of 1970 that gives him pause:

Virtually everyone in the crowd was young and white...These were California's "golden youth," undeniably middle class, from predominantly conservative families...Until now, UCSB had been known as the "play school" of the California university system, and Isla Vista was seen as its lively playground. The sun and surf were thought to more than compensate for the crowded, relatively expensive, and often rundown apartment buildings, the absence of community government, and the paucity of basic public services..."[XI]

He lifts his hand from the book and lets it shut, raising his head to observe the sun and the surf from the eighth-floor window of the library. Something meaningful is buzzing around his mind like a fly, but he can't quite get hold of it so instead he swats it away.

His phone flashes. Paul wants to know what he's up to this evening. Paul used to represent the impenetrable core of his comfort zone. Hanging out with him was, almost by definition, time well spent. But ever since Paul went through the earthquake with Leroy and Denise, not to mention Samantha, he's been getting on Ethan's nerves. Ethan doesn't like the way Paul wants him to feel about Leroy and Denise's rekindled relationship. He doesn't like to think about the old, decrepit versions of Leroy and Denise at all. They taint his memories, and he's worried they'll infiltrate his dreams if he spends any time with them. They're like the uninspiring aged versions of the youthful rebels in the book he's skimming. He's thus far managed to segregate Prof. Bourman from 1969 Leroy in his mind, but it's a precarious endeavor. And then there's the way Paul returned from Joshua Tree with such admiration for his sister, something Ethan feels too but has never considered expressing outright, especially not so unabashedly. At least they didn't hook up. Ethan knows Paul to be a bad liar, a guilty liar, and he hasn't let slip any indication that he might be covering up something even more intimate than what they went through. Samantha spoke similarly highly of Paul during their time together over the winter break, which grated at Ethan but not as severely. Impressing his older sister is always welcomed, and so rarely has she taken a liking to any of his friends.

These emotions stew within him, boiling down not into a nourishing concoction, but evaporating entirely, leaving behind a stupid little puddle. He feels like an idiot. Which makes him wonder, will he ever be any less of an idiot? Is he destined to always grab at ideas like flies, only to end up swatting them.

What're you thinking? he responds to Paul, more sick and tired of his own thoughts than of hearing Paul's.

Maybe a smoke at the beach?

Sure, why not.

Ethan hasn't smoked in several weeks and realizes that may be contributing to his elevated stress and atypically short fuse. Smoking can be disorienting, sure, but sometimes it rewires the brain in just the right way to charge through to new mental territory. To arrive at a formerly shrouded thought, now glistening with freshness and ripe with utility.

At Paul's, they head out to the balcony, beers in hand.

"There's something I wanted to run by you," Paul says, leaning forward. He waves a hand in front of Ethan's face. "Are you paying attention?"

"Yeah, man." Ethan says, redirecting his attention from an actual fly buzzing around his head.

"Good, so, when I was talking to Denise recently, I asked her about going to Lake Powell to try to retrieve Leroy's old wedding ring. Remember I told you that whole story about how she ditched him there and he tossed it over the canyon rim?"

Ethan nods.

"You'd think she'd be, if not excited, at least supportive of this idea. I mean, Leroy literally had a vision about it. And I'm not asking her to do anything, I'll go by myself—or with you, if you'll agree to come, I guess. Anyway, she's adamantly against it. And when I ask her why, she doesn't elaborate much."

"What does she say?"

"She says it's hopeless and that it could be dangerous. When I tell her it's not hopeless and it won't be dangerous, she says something vague, like, 'they might not be ready to confront what the ring represents.' I mean, it's not like finding the ring would force her hand in marriage, which is the only concern I can understand. It just doesn't sound like her, and that's how I know she's bullshitting. I asked her if she's hiding something from me, and from Leroy, and she basically admitted it by saying she's not ready to talk about it yet."

"What do you think it is?"

"I have no idea, but my hunch is that it's something from way back when, you know, around the time we visited or when they broke up. I'm not sure how to get her to discuss it. I mean, how bad can it be? Especially if it's ancient history like that. And I want to try to retrieve that ring. I've already lined up a good metal detector and a whole climbing rig."

"Interesting..." Ethan says. "Hard to imagine Denise being so secretive."

"It's not that hard if you've met the present-day version," Paul says, finishing his beer. "So what do you think?"

"I think you're right," Ethan says. "You've got good intuition."

"Thanks man," Paul says, all smiley. "So, should we head out?"

The wind is whipping down the coast when they arrive at the beach. Ethan pulls up the hood of his fleece and Paul takes his beanie out of his pocket and pulls it down over his ears. The whites of the cresting waves are angrier than usual, foaming at the mouth and crashing hard.

"Well, I guess it is winter," Paul says as they look for a crevice in the bluffs to provide shelter for a lighter. "And people say we don't really have seasons here."

Ethan trips over a stone half immersed in the sand, landing hard on one knee and his palms.

"Shit man," Paul says. "Be careful."

Brushing himself off, Ethan joins Paul against the damp cliffside. They can see the underside of a banister attached to a patio above them. A stereo in a nearby duplex plays something that sounds like Drake. Paul hands Ethan a cone joint, which Ethan admires, partially for its craftsmanship, and partially because he knows Paul appreciates the acknowledgement.

"It should smoke nicely," Paul says, watching Ethan rotate the joint between his fingers. After a half-dozen false starts the lighter flame finally sparks to life. Ethan inhales deep into his diaphragm, not holding back on the first hit as he often does. He hands Paul the joint and emits a resounding cough in the direction of the ocean. For a moment, he thinks he sees a light somewhere far out on the surface. He rubs his eyes and it's gone. But there's something off about the night, like it's been laundered and left out to dry.

"I feel a little like I'm tripping," Ethan says after his second hit.

"Yeah, this stuff is pretty potent," Paul says, his voice constricted due to the inhale of smoke contained within his lungs. He exhales and resumes talking. "I was telling Denise she should maybe try smoking to relax. But she said she's scared of how strong marijuana is these days. And she's right, there's like, ten times more THC in weed now."

"Did Denise used to smoke?"

"She did, but not with Leroy. She said he was never really into it."

"Woah, was that lighting?" Ethan abruptly asks, pointing out towards the horizon. Paul turns and observes. "I don't think so man, the sky is pretty clear. You sure you're OK?"

"Yeah," Ethan says. "I might be a little dehydrated."

"We can stop and pick up a Gatorade on the way back. I'm craving some chips or something, anyway."

They listen to the roar of the waves.

"Sometimes I wish we could've gotten that hair sample back here," Paul says. "How cool would it be to solve a decades-old case like that? I mean, it still would've been a long shot. I'd need to find someone to run the DNA for me, although I think I've got that covered, and then hope that the bomber has a criminal record. But still, filling in history like that—setting the record straight. Something very satisfying about that, I imagine."

Ethan nods. "I guess so."

The cold wind easily penetrates their thin layers and before long they head back to the wooden staircase leading up to Del Playa Drive. Paul watches Ethan grip the wooden railing with both hands as he gingerly ascends.

"It's nice that no one cares how messed up you are in this town," Paul says as he takes Ethan's arm and aids him up the last few steps. As they proceed towards the road along a dirt path lined with duplexes on either side, Paul's phone dings.

"Ok then," he says, looking up from the screen. "Greggy desperately wants me on his beer pong team since last time we kicked ass."

"You go on ahead," Ethan says, desiring to be alone now that the opportunity has presented itself. "I know I seem out of it, but I'm fine."

"Might be a good opportunity to pick up some new business, too," Paul says to himself as much as Ethan. "You sure you don't want to come?"

Ethan shakes his head emphatically no.

"I'm getting a bit of déjà vu, here," Paul says. "But you're not stupid enough to take the raft out on water that choppy, right?"

"I'm done with that ocean stuff. The portal's gone anyway."

Paul nods and departs without any further resistance. Ethan heads into the nearby park in the middle of I.V. to relieve himself, resting his hand on several trees as he walks and absorbing their damp, sandpapery texture. He feels like he's on some elaborate set, but not a movie set this time. A play. And as if he's writing the play as it unfolds, he realizes where the next scene takes place. His link to the past is no longer the oil spill, but the bank burning, and he's being tugged in the direction of the Bank of America ATM. After peeing, he exits the park, stage left. The wind is so strong on the street that he shields his eyes against the swirling dust and debris with his hand. He walks up the block like this, his field of vision restricted to a few feet ahead. He watches his legs go back and forth, one foot in front of the other, reveling at the coordination required for each step, as if learning to walk again. But then he loses track of his body, and it becomes part of the stage. He observes his body stop in front of the Bank of America ATM and turn to face it. His hand drops from above his brow and both arms go limp at his side. Instead of the ATM there's a soft blue light. It beckons him forward. He enters into it, one foot in front of the other.

CHAPTER TWENTY-NINE
MAN-MADE MIRAGE

"Are you certain you didn't become a therapist?" Leroy asks between sips of coffee from his near-overflowing to-go cup. "Sometimes when I talk to you, I get the sense I'm in therapy. Even more so than during our email correspondence."

Denise dips her teabag once more before placing it next to her cup on a napkin. "I think that's just called having a normal, open-ended discussion. Therapy is different, trust me—I've been through my share of it." They both smile, but with restraint. "But seriously, you said you felt like you had to get in touch with me for your life to move forward. I mean, you should be in therapy just for that. And here I am, providing you, if not therapy, therapeutic conversation, free of charge, yet again."

"Well, I paid for that tea," Leroy says. "And my hotel expenses are starting to add up."

"Oh…" Denise pauses and observes the large strip-mall parking lot surrounding the coffee shop patio. Only in the desert can a parking lot appear attractive, like another species adapted to the harsh landscape. Like a man-made mirage. "You can head back to Santa Barbara if you want, I've already said that."

"But I don't want to." Coffee drips from the rim of Leroy's cup onto his lap, but he takes no notice. "And I understand why you don't want me to stay with you. At least, I understood. I mean, I haven't even been in your house yet."

"I know, I know, I'm working through it with my therapist."

"You are?"

"No, Leroy. I told you, I haven't been to therapy since my therapist retired three years ago."

"Oh, right. So then what are we waiting for again?"

"We're not waiting for anything. At our age that's not a very advisable strategy. I'm just taking this—us—at the speed that I feel comfortable with. I'm incapable of anything else."

Leroy exhales a long sigh.

"Let me ask you this, Leroy. Do you know what you want? It seems to me like maybe you never quite learned to do anything but take the simplest route into or out of a situation or relationship. To just, I don't know, glance over your shoulder and head for the finish line. A form of opportunism that allows you to avoid too much self-reflection. Some, enough to satisfy some need to question yourself, but not too much."

"Wow, I guess the conversation is no longer therapeutic." Leroy crosses his arms in exaggerated consideration. "I acknowledge there's some truth to that. Life is kind of a race, and I don't like to waste too much time second-guessing myself. I don't think simplest is the right word though. But what are you getting at?"

Leroy wipes ineffectively at the coffee stain near his crotch with a damp napkin as he waits for Denise to reply.

"I mean," Denise says, "What if we were just meeting for the first time? Wouldn't you proceed with a little more caution? I'm honestly asking, I don't know. But this isn't some fairytale scenario where two people separated by circumstances for decades reunite and immediately fall madly in love again."

"Who said anything about immediately? It's been almost two months since we met up, and there were the emails before that. For me, that's long enough. Like you said, time is of the essence. And we aren't strangers. We knew each other before, intimately. You can't just write that off." Leroy leans forward with his hands on his knees. His eyes shut and he looks pained. Then he speaks. "Denise, I love you."

Denise appears bemused. "So this is when you say it? A very male move, to drop the L-word for the first time in the middle of a discussion about your level of emotional maturity."

"It felt appropriate."

"So I suppose now you're expecting some reciprocation?"

Leroy shrugs his shoulders and wipes at the stain on his pants again.

"OK, so I love you too," Denise says. "But here's the thing, I can't trust my love. At least not yet."

"What do you mean?"

"I mean…" Denise hesitates. "I mean, after we broke up, I followed my heart and, well, it got me into a lot of trouble."

"But Denise, that was eons ago."

"Sure, and so was our romance. But here we are still chasing after it."

"Oh, come on, Denise. We're different people now, different enough anyway. I loved you then and I love you now, both versions. You've got to learn to trust yourself by this age."

"I don't know, I'm not sure I've changed enough to place any additional trust in myself. I mean, shouldn't it worry me that I can fall in love with the same person 50 years later? Like, is there some moment in the past where my personality froze, and it hasn't evolved since? After all I've been through, I'd like to see some results. Some progress, although I admit it's hard to say what that would mean."

Leroy doesn't immediately respond. The sound of cars rushing by on the six-lane boulevard across the parking lot washes over them.

"I think," Leroy says, "that the important thing is that we want to be with each other now. And I wish that—since there is obviously something more holding you back—that you would tell me what it is."

"I'll think about it," Denise says. "It's very hard for me. I don't only have trouble trusting myself, the same goes for other people."

"Well, I can't blame you there. People, for the most part, are not very trustworthy. Especially those of a political persuasion, and anyone under 30."

That evening, Denise is bringing groceries in from her car when a dented green Chevy Suburban pulls up along the curb. She knows who's behind the wheel even before the tinted driver's side window descends. She places the grocery bags on the front stoop and observes a face she hasn't seen in over three years come into view. The man, whose every feature she knows intimately, is thinner and his skin is sagging around his chin more than before. But he looks good for someone their age, especially since he recently got out of prison. A smile ripples across his round, leathery face.

"I thought you might stop by at some point," Denise says. "Did you receive the money I sent you?"

The man leans his head out the window and glances up and down the street, which is empty and bathed in the warm pastel tones of the setting desert sun. "That's the best greeting you can offer?"

"No," Denise says. "But it's the greeting you get."

The man chuckles but remains in the car. Denise walks over, her hands in the pockets of her summer dress.

"Looking good," the man says. "Too good for Leroy, who looks like he's about to keel over."

"Lonnie," Denise exclaims, her arms rising from her pockets. "I can't believe you've been following me."

"I miss you," Lonnie says, his eyebrows now raised. "I still love you, you know."

Denise blows through her clenched lips in disgust. "You and Leroy both," she says under her breath.

"Huh?" Lonnie asks.

"Never mind. Don't make me remind you of all the reasons we can't be together anymore."

Lonnie stares ahead through the windshield of the oversized vehicle, his fingers tapping the steering wheel. Denise thinks he looks even smaller than usual trying to fill the capacious driver's seat. Then she wonders if maybe he's shrunk with age.

"Fine, fine," Lonnie says. "You still got my stuff in there?" He nods towards the house.

"Unfortunately, yes."

He nods again. Denise catches a whiff of stale cigarette smoke. It threatens to evoke decades of her past in one convoluted, chaotic image. She inhales deeply, nonetheless, appreciating the redolent odor.

"You know, my meditation center is still open, along with the yoga studio," Lonnie says.

"Yeah, I know. Tara is running it."

"I can't believe she turns me in and then…" Lonnie pauses. "Wait a second, you don't go there, do you?" Their eyes meet. Denise recognizes something in Lonnie's expression both foreign and familiar.

"To tell you the truth—what a novel concept—I do go occasionally. Tara lets me in for free."

"Bitch."

Denise grinds her heel into the ground. "What are you doing here, Lonnie? You want me to send you your stuff, I'm happy to. You want me to get a restraining order, I'm also happy to do that."

Lonnie extends his arm out the window, palm up. His beady pupils rest entreatingly in his cavernous eye sockets. "No need to say things like that, honey. I'll stay out of your hair. I'll admit though, I was more than a little upset to see you with Leroy. I feel somewhat personally endangered by it if you know what I mean. All the old memories that must be getting dredged up. In my opinion, it's best to leave that stuff buried. We'll be underground with it soon enough."

"I do know what you mean, Lonnie, and don't worry. I missed my chance to do anything about that. It's just something I have to live with. Something we both do."

"Mmmhmm," Lonnie says. "It's nice to talk to someone I know, even if that someone's even more sick and tired of me than everyone else. So, I'll just tell you something crazy and then leave before I really overstay my welcome. You know, I once, not long before I met you, traveled to the future, to just around now—I think last year, 2023. Through this little illuminated hole in the ocean. Me and Russell jumped through it. When we looked Leroy up and found he was still on campus, it gave Russell an idea. He wanted us to threaten Leroy, young

Leroy, because he suspected he knew something of our plans. Russell's plans really, to meet violence with violence is how he thought about it. We got some good ammo to use if the moment ever arose. But of course, as you know, it didn't. Anyway, maybe Leroy told you he got robbed not too long ago? Well, that was me and Russell, and all we took were some stupid family photos. But they would've been quite shocking to Leroy back then. That's assuming we're still on that timeline, but who the fuck knows."

Denise looks at Lonnie like he's losing his marbles. To her dismay, though, she can't entirely disregard his outlandish story, even though she knows him to be a near-pathological liar. It resonates with the mysterious exchanges she's had with the past lately, and with what Leroy's told her about his own. Time is dynamic, mercurial, indifferent. Time flows, but maybe there's a way to swim upstream, occasionally. It's the kind of conspiracy theory that appeals to her new age mentality.

"And why, might I ask, did you never tell me this before?"

Lonnie furrows his brow. "Honestly, I didn't think about it much. I probably preferred it that way. Seeing Leroy is what summoned it back to me. And what I remember most is how completely terrifying I found the future then. Everyone with a screen in their hand and the enormous cars and trucks motoring by at wild speeds, and even the people seemed, I don't know, monstrous, and not just in size. Being around them made me feel ill at ease. I felt like ancient history. Like time had sped up. And now that I've lived long enough to be here now, in the present, guess what? I was right."

"You were right about what?"

"I was right about the future. It is terrifying, and time has sped up—and not just because that happens when you age."

Denise nods apprehensively. "Things weren't so la-di-da back then as you'll recall, but I won't argue that it's a scary time now. Like we're at the precipice of something bad, rather than the start of something good, which is how I used to feel back then. Does this have to do with prison? Not the time travel, but how you feel about the present. Was it that hard for you?"

"Actually, most days I didn't mind it much. It was like I'd been preparing to be incarcerated my whole life, all that meditation and yoga. Like maybe I always knew I'd need it someday."

"Well, you needed it out here too. But maybe you lost track of that."

"I won't argue that it's harder being out here now, harder than it ever was before. The criminal system, man, it just messes with people. Nothing good comes out of it."

"Sure, Lonnie," Denise says. "I don't imagine you're very far off there."

Lonnie faces forward and puts the key in the ignition. "But you've heard enough of my BS opinions for a lifetime. I'll do my best to leave you alone—you've earned that at least." He pulls the visor down to block the sun's slanting rays. "One last thing, though. Have you told Leroy about me yet?"

Denise looks down, kicks at some pebbles, turns away. "I have not."

"You should get around to that before too long, don't you think? Or maybe I should take care of it for you."

Denise's agitated response is drowned out by the revving of the Suburban's engine. As he departs, Lonnie gives her an inscrutable look, punctuated by a wink.

Leroy won't miss much about the hotel, but he will miss the pool and the workout room and the sauna. He's never spent much time in gyms, but he's never stayed by himself for over a week in a desert hotel, either. On the first day, he left the hotel grounds after his continental breakfast intending to walk for an hour to get his steps in, but he quickly encountered an overgrown hedge blocking the narrow sidewalk. In his frustration, he stepped into the street, which was already steaming with heat, only to be nearly run over by a truck. The road was lined with big box stores and gated communities and hotels. It was bleak. And he'd forgotten a water bottle. So he trudged back to the hotel and after a period of sulking in his room reluctantly visited the gym.

Each day since, he's returned for a speed walk on the treadmill, or a rotation on the rowing machine, or even a battle with the Stairmaster, followed by an improvised weights regimen, a dip in the pool, and a few minutes of blissful recovery in the sauna. It's where he retreated yesterday after his baffling discussion with Denise at the strip mall coffee shop, at the conclusion of which they decided to spend some time apart. Returning from that unpleasant and disappointing parting, he'd stomped across the parking lot cursing her under his breath. Amazingly, almost profoundly, he'd felt good after the workout, his body and mind at ease, the sauna a godsend. He even managed to get down 1,200 words of his book before dinner. The thought crossed his mind that if things didn't work out with Denise, maybe he'd move to the desert anyway. It's significantly cheaper than Santa Barbara, and while he loves the ocean, a pool is much more practical for his needs. Maybe he could even afford his own sauna.

By the next morning, when a fussy green Suburban pulls into the hotel parking lot just underneath his second-floor room, his mood has soured again. He misses Denise and he's also bitter about what she's putting him through. Maybe they were only destined for a fling. Maybe his love for Denise is the kind that you set free for lack of better alternatives. The stress is giving him stomach problems and he's been in and out of the bathroom since 5 a.m. And the desert is just too hot and inhospitable. Could he even tolerate moving out here to be with Denise? Santa Barbara is like heaven compared to this baking slab of asphalt and the alien flora surviving off borrowed water. He's standing along the outdoor corridor gauging his stomach's travel-readiness when a short man, easily of retirement age, emerges from the Suburban. But rather than walk towards another room, he glances up at Leroy. Then, he waves. He's smiling. Dark sunglasses shield his eyes.

Leroy looks to his left and right. Nobody else around. Certain the man's attention is on him, he speaks. "Sorry, are you waving at me? Do I know you?"

"Well," Lonnie says, standing almost directly below Leroy with his neck craned upwards. "It's been a long time, but I think you'll remember me."

"OK," Leroy says, relief and confusion in his voice. "I'm having trouble placing you. Could you just tell me how we know each other?"

Lonnie looks around. "Is there somewhere we could sit for a minute?" As he speaks, he sees a small, shrub-encircled patio with a couple tables near the front lobby. "How about over there?"

Leroy nods and descends the outdoor staircase. Lonnie rests his feet on a table. The rising sun slices the patio in half.

"We used to be neighbors," Lonnie says once Leroy's seated.

"We did…well, I guess, I haven't moved in almost thirty years. You're from Santa Barbara?"

"In Isla Vista, my house was next to yours."

Lonnie removes his sunglasses and lets his gaze rest on Leroy's face. He smiles when, after a few seconds, Leroy jumps back in his chair.

"You're…You're Lonnie."

Lonnie nods, clearly relishing the surprise.

"But what are you doing here? And how did you know I was here?"

"Well, I've lived around here—just a couple miles away—for many years."

"That's strange, so has…" Leroy cuts himself short.

"Yes, I know," Lonnie says. "So has Denise. As it turns out, we shared a house, and a bed, up until recently."

Leroy stands up and leans on the back of the steel patio chair. "What are you saying? Are you saying that you were together all that time?"

"Yep, we were married. Got married in Vegas in the mid-70s. Honeymooned in Big Sur."

"I cannot believe this," Leroy shouts. "I knew something was wrong with her. I knew she cheated on me with you a few times back then. But this…this is unfathomable."

"In fact," Lonnie says, holding up a weathered hand with a loose-fitting ring on the middle finger. "We're still married."

"You're still married?"

"Yes, although." Lonnie puts his hands back on his lap. "To be fair, she no longer wants anything to do with me. I don't want you to get the wrong idea about her. She may be confused, and we both know she's got her own way of going about things, but she does mean well."

"Oh, well thank you very much for that reassurance," Leroy says. "But we've been seeing each other for two months and she hasn't…" He throws up his hands. "Why the hell am I telling you any of this? And by the way, how do I know you're not lying? I'm starting to recall why I used to find you so repulsive."

Lonnie replaces his sunglasses as the angle of the sun approaches his line of vision. "Oh, I think you know I'm not lying. But feel free to ask her."

"No, no…I think I'd better just get out of this shithole now." Leroy starts to leave but turns back after a few steps. "I don't know what's gone on between you two, but you'd better leave Denise alone if that's what she wants."

"Oh OK, sure. I guess you'll be keeping an eye on me from your cute little light-blue house in the foothills of Santa Barbara. Unless you're planning on moving into this hotel."

"How do you know what my house…you know, never mind," Leroy says. "And yes, maybe I will be watching you."

"Take care of yourself," Lonnie says to Leroy's back. "You look about twenty years older than me, and I just got out of prison."

CHAPTER THIRTY
THE FIRST DRAFT OF HISTORY

Peace, Togetherness: it was a beautiful victory[XII]
El Gaucho Editorial, Sunday, Feb. 1, 1970

Many students described Friday afternoon's happenings as "beautiful." There was a fantastic jubilation in the crowd at the end of the day, probably difficult to understand for persons not present.

Students who participated seemed to feel that they had won a victory for all students. And indeed they had.

Despite the presence of 300 very nervous police, and 4,000 defensive students, there were only a few violent incidents, and all were initiated by police. Despite the absence of any well-defined leadership, students were able to come together and stay together.

For 24 hours Friday, we truly were brothers to each other.

We watched out for each other's welfare and took on responsibility as it became necessary. Some of us donned white armbands and took care of our injured brothers. Some of us ran up close to the police lines to make sure that no one provoked them. All of us held back the anger we felt after being jabbed in the ribs, or after seeing a brother brutalized.

We really did keep cool, and that was our power. Many of the police seemed stunned at the peacefulness of the crowd. It was probably difficult for some of them to remain in that robot-like state when we smiled at them, and sang, and danced.

Cynics will say that most of us were there as spectators. There is no way of knowing how many of us were "demonstrators," but we know there were thousands of us. Those who did not regard themselves as participants soon became our brothers, as they, too, looked out for their brothers' welfare.

Our greatest victory, then, was in our togetherness, in our love and peacefulness. But there were other victories.

In terms of our struggle for an open hearing, and student participation in hiring and firing, we showed, by our numbers and our commitment, that the issues are important enough to us that we are willing to face the possibility of arrest and/or injury.

We showed that the University has no reason to fear that we will mar its public image, since we are determined to be non-violent and not to provoke the police.

We showed that it is not the police we are interested in fighting, but the Administration. Many of us are more determined than ever to continue pressuring the Administration's stubborn, uncompromising stance.

We are tired of hearing from administrators that the situation is out of their control, since they supposedly receive orders from Sacramento and Berkeley. We cannot respect men whose primary motive is the retention of their jobs. We cannot respect men who refuse to talk to us because of alleged orders from UC President Hitch.

We know that the University will someday be forced to change...

• • •

Lonnie is covered in sweat and sugar. He's been working overtime since Friday when the protests ignited. The student body is hungry for more than an administrative rebuke; it also craves carbs. So it's been all hands on donuts at Campus Donut. When Lonnie does get a break, he's too wiped out to do anything but bike home in a zombified state and collapse onto the unruly pile of dirty sheets sprawled across his bed, his head landing on one of two lumpy pillows if he's lucky. Initially, he held out hope that he'd have a chance to catch up with Denise over the weekend and, piling even more hope on top of that, that they'd pick up where they left off—entangled on the rug. But as the hands of the clock on the wall of Campus Donut circled again and again, time simply ran out on his ambitions. And judging by the frenzy of activity beyond the intimate confines of the overheated donut shop, Denise is likely just as busy and exhausted as him anyway.

He's heard snippets of conversation about what's going on out there, breathlessly exchanged between excited groups of students as they await their box of piping hot donuts, so fresh that when they grab them their fingers bore right through the dough. He's gathered that the rally on Friday escalated into a standoff between police and students, resulting in a handful of violent outbursts and close to 20 arrests. A few more protests followed over the weekend, one taking place just across the street in the one-square-block Perfect Park, or Dog Shit Park as it's known colloquially.

Lonnie glances at the clock during a brief lull after a cohort of wild-eyed and body-odored students depart with three-dozen donuts. His shift ends at 1 p.m. He remembers it's Tuesday and he'll see Denise at the New Consciousness class that evening. He plans to go home and take a nap in the interval; at least he does before overhearing the conversation between the next two customers, a pair of shaggy blond guys who look like brothers and Brothers. One of them isn't wearing a shirt; against the rules of Campus Donut, but Lonnie can't bring himself to enforce the policy, justifying his decision as a temporary, protest-time allowance.

"You just came from the Faculty Club?" the shirted one asks.

"Yeah man," replies the shirtless one, who's got the smooth, tanned musculature of a surfer. "It was far out. We hung around the administrative building until someone decided we should march over to the Faculty Club. Then, they like, barricaded the road with furniture from the club and everyone went inside. We had it to ourselves, man."

Lonnie hasn't been back to the club since delivering the bomb. He wonders if the place has been repaired. If his crime has been erased. He wishes he didn't wonder, but he does.

"And people went in the pool?"

"Hell yeah. We also ate the food and drank some of the booze. So rad."

"That's wild. Is it still raging?"

"For sure. Then there's supposed to be some more speakers over by the admin building later."

"When are they going to figure out that we're not giving in on this, man. They must be feeling so screwed."

"I hope so."

Lonnie interrupts the exchange to hand over the donuts. He looks at the clock again, feeling revived and even more eager for his shift to end.

Taking the last remaining donut from the bag Steven brought to the protests that morning, Becca licks her fingers, relishing their sticky sweetness, as she observes the mayhem encompassing the Faculty Club.

"So why exactly are they—we—occupying the Faculty Club?" Steven asks from her side. His unflappable demeanor has taken a few dings over the long weekend, but he's still the most put-together person in sight, especially since the cops and any university personnel are conspicuously absent.

"I suppose it's a show of power," Becca says. "Staying power. And there's certainly something symbolic about conquering the place where faculty members are meant to gather exclusively. But I do worry it could spiral."

Becca suppresses a yawn and takes a large bite from the donut.

"So do you want to go in?" Steven asks.

"I don't think so. Denise is over there, and so is the new photo guy. If anything, I'd like to take a nap on that couch they're using to barricade the entryway."

"Did you get enough sleep last night?"

Becca observes Steven as she takes another sizeable bite from the donut, demolishing everything but a small chunk pinched between her fingers. Steven has stayed late with her the last three nights putting the paper to bed. Last night, he woke her up in her chair and offered to walk her home. It was after midnight and, inexplicably, she nearly kissed him as they locked up the office. But she didn't, and she doesn't plan on it. Although she has, in spare moments stolen between the stresses and strains of the job lately, found her eyes resting on the contours of his body and appreciating the snug fit of his clothes.

"Enough sleep, yes, but not enough to feel energized," she says after chewing through the slightly stale dough. "Thanks again for not leaving me in the office to rot."

Steven smiles, a little too ingratiatingly for Becca's taste.

"You know," Becca says. "Maybe there is something to say about the way the Faculty Club went from a crime scene to another sort of scene of, if not crime, vandalism, in less than a year. That might be an angle for a crime reporter to take here. Reflect a little on the role the Faculty Club is playing in this revolt. The many faces, or facades, of the Faculty Club. See if anyone has anything interesting to say about that."

The smile evaporates from Steven's face. "So you want me to venture into that mess?"

"That mess is made up of your peers. Go see what they're up to exactly. Denise is getting color, maybe you can gather some string for an editorial. I've got to head back to the office to check my messages."

Steven pleads with his eyes before nodding. "I'll see you back at the office then."

Becca waves over her shoulder as she walks away. Steven waits to see if she'll glance back, but she doesn't. He watches her ass sway in her jean shorts, as if it'll tell him something more than it already has.

Denise is having trouble maintaining her journalistic integrity. The pastries along the Faculty Club's breakfast counter look so appetizing, especially considering all she's eaten today is a slice of zucchini bread from a day-old loaf her roommate left on the counter. She watches as a shirtless guy scoops up three of them, Danishes she thinks, with one hand. She glares at his bare back in disapproval, even as she admires its form, which is almost aquatic. He hands one of the pastries to a familiar-looking girl. Maybe someone from her dorm, but maybe not. The more time Denise spends immersed in these throngs of protesters, the more everyone looks familiar. Yet rarely does she run into anyone she knows. It makes her uncomfortable, feeling that she's just another familiar person to everyone else. Just another college student with whom to share a few formative years of life before the whole experience sheds away like so much dead skin, so many dead cells. It adds a peripheral melancholy, melancholy once-removed, to the already emotionally draining hullabaloo.

Her attention returns to the pastries. If she takes a pastry, then she's allowing herself to become part of the mob. If she doesn't, then she can at least hold onto the notion that she's an objective reporter, a chronicler of unfolding events, a writer of the first draft of history, and not a participant in it. To her surprise, she arrives at a clearcut decision. She walks across the room somewhat sheepishly and snatches up one of the dwindling number of pastries.

She leans against the wall chewing each bite thoroughly, as if still working through the ramifications of her decision, which when taken to its limit, implies that she's not cut out to be a journalist in the long run. She swallows this conclusion almost as effortlessly as she does the creamy pastry interior. Something's got to give, and maybe this it is. She doesn't have the energy or emotional wherewithal to fight her instincts right now anyway.

Temporarily mollified, she recalls the last time she came by the Faculty Club; to double-check a descriptive detail in a story about the explosion that killed Dover. The cheese Danish stops tasting so good, an untoward aftertaste infusing the saliva pooling in the back of her mouth. It's a bit like desecrating the caretaker's grave, what's going on now. She looks around for signs others are harboring similar apprehensions, but no one appears the least bit remorseful about what's going on. The general mood is triumphant.

From the corner of her eye, she recognizes an unmistakable profile—that of Steven. While his dry-cleaned attire and hoity-toity manner make it crystal clear that he's not part of the mob, he appears to be wrestling with the same conundrum she recently suffered through. His ogling of the pastries is near obscene. She considers getting his attention and giving him permission to follow her lead in consuming the forbidden baked good, but then he steps back and walks down a corridor lined with mingling students. Many of them eye him suspiciously as he passes.

Denise sets off in the opposite direction, through a pair of sliding glass doors onto the patio, which has assumed the atmosphere of a summer resort. She smells marijuana and chlorine. Two fully clothed guys do simultaneous cannonballs into the deep end of the pool. She should've asked Steven what he's doing because she has no idea what she's doing aside from letting her stomach dictate her future career decisions. She should talk to a few people, take some notes. But first she'll look for the photographer. Sometimes they get enough quotes while taking photos. She circles the pool, catching bits of conversation that go straight into the bloated file in her brain containing everything from the nonstop action over the last handful of days. She notices a lone figure towards the far end of the concrete area. It's Lonnie. He's seated on the hard ground with his back against the exterior wall, his hands on his bent knees, and a despondent look on his face. It's not an expression she recognizes on him. She's used to seeing him cross-legged and serene, or eager and in perpetual motion. But now he looks tormented, almost haunted.

Her instincts are again torn. Should she check on him or let him be. One good thing about the ongoing upheaval is it's distracted her from the predicament she's in with Lonnie, and also Leroy. One bad thing is she hasn't had a chance to process any of it. She retreats—they'll catch up at New Consciousness that evening.

Back inside, passively searching for the photographer, she passes a memorial to Dover alongside one of the rooms in the main corridor. Her story on Dover's memorial service, with the quotes from Edward Abbey, is framed on the wall. She reads through it and, for the first time in many months, wonders about Ethan. She hasn't seen him since their hectic encounter outside the memorial service, when she found Dover's book in his hoodie pocket. She still has his hoodie in a desk drawer at the newspaper office.

CHAPTER THIRTY-ONE
IT'S HARD TO TALK FREELY WITH SOMEONE WHEN YOU KNOW SOMETHING OF THEIR FUTURE

Ethan awakens with a throbbing headache. He's lying on the grass next to a tree, his head resting on his forest green fleece and his hands shoved between his knees. He remains still, inhaling the crisp dawn air, as images of the night before replay through his mind. He emerged from his encounter with the ATM, or rather the portal occupying the space where the ATM should've been, completely drained and with just enough awareness to stumble into the adjacent park and pass out under a tree. He'd landed, hands and knees, on the pitted sidewalk in front of the pre-burned Bank of America, a beige brick building with tall front windows and long, cement planters housing spiky yuccas. It was less jarring than the ocean portal time slip, but that might be because he's getting used to it.

The sound of scampering in the branches above propels him to alertness and he reaches into his pants pocket and pulls out his phone, knowing full well that it'll be dead but still unable to break the habit. Sitting up in the damp, trampled grass, he rubs the back of his head. The park is littered with trash and muddied from overuse. It must be all the protests. He takes out his wallet and opens it. He's been lugging around a number of old bills and coins for weeks, as if waiting for a bet to be resolved. A bet he just won. Most of the currency isn't quite historic enough to be contemporary, but he doesn't think any of the student employees who'll be exchanging it for goods and services will notice.

Getting up, he walks stiffly over to a row of bushy trees along the park's perimeter and relieves himself. He craves coffee, and wonders if anywhere will be open. He follows the sidewalk as it curves around the park. Nothing promising. As he's about to turn back towards the beach, an illuminated window, a dehydrated-urine color spilling from it into the morning mist, catches his eye. He rounds a corner and approaches the small storefront with a blocky handmade sign promoting it as I.V.'s only 24-hour establishment.

The greasy aroma that envelops him as he enters activates his hunger. A short, dark-haired kid finishes shaping a tray of donuts, inserts it into a tall rack, and wipes his hands on his apron before approaching the counter. The chef's hat he's wearing is humorously large and puffy, like a thought cloud shoved into a round hole.

"Wow," the guy says, looking up and adjusting the hat with some annoyance. "You don't look so hot." His face twitches before continuing. "It's not the police out there again, is it? I thought it was quiet last night."

"Oh no," Ethan says. "I just, uh, had a little too much to drink and passed out in the park on my way home."

"I see," Lonnie says. "You'd better be more careful, it's nutso out there these days. Anyway, some food'll help you get back on your feet."

"Sure, yeah, I'll take a couple donuts. And do you have coffee?"

"We sure do." Lonnie indicates with his stubbled square jaw towards the stainless-steel coffee percolator. "I always brew a fresh pot at 6 a.m."

"So, uh, what's the date again?" Ethan asks as casually as possible as Lonnie fills a Styrofoam cup with watery brown liquid.

"Hard to keep track these days, right?" Lonnie reaches under a stack of white paper bags at the end of the counter and pulls out a newspaper. "Let's see. This is from yesterday, so today must be February 25."

"Figures," Ethan responds.

"What figures?"

Ethan waves a hand through the steamy air. "Oh, nothing."

"Have we met?" Lonnie asks, a familiar sense coming over him.

Ethan shakes his head, not even bothering to give Lonnie a closer look. "Nah, I don't think so."

Lonnie pushes the donut bag and coffee across the counter and Ethan pulls out a couple bills. Lonnie quickly glances at the grimy money before shoving it into the register and making change.

"You sure you're OK?" he asks Ethan as he hands over the coins. "You look a little, I don't know, shell-shocked. Have you ever tried meditation? We could attempt a little session now, before business picks up. I've found it helps with hangovers, too."

Ethan inspects Lonnie to determine if he's joking. His crooked smile appears entirely sincere. "Um, no thanks," he says. "I'll be fine once I get a little food in me." He picks up the bag and asks if he can take the newspaper with him.

"Sure," Lonnie says. "But the new one will be out real soon, it might already be."

"It's OK," Ethan says, pushing the door open. "I've got some catching up to do anyway."

The morning feels different now that Ethan knows that night the Bank of America will be burned to the ground; no longer just calm but calm before a storm. Everything from the budding trees to the rows of parked bikes to the trash lining the curb is bestowed with significance, as if already frozen in history. Reaching the beach, he sits in an overgrown vacant lot along the bluffs that he's pretty sure is the site of a three-story apartment building in 2024. The sun is quickly burning away the morning dew and his mind is similarly clearing up. The coffee, while mild in flavor, is at least reasonably caffeinated. The confrontation that's been brewing on campus for months is about to reach a boiling point, sending Isla Vista into a months-long crisis and turning it into a police state. He's glad he made it back in time. There's going to be a lot to see.

He takes stock of his physical well-being and, now that the headache has subsided, identifies no aches or pains. Aside from scuffs on his palms from the fall to the pavement the night before, he's in good shape and seemingly cancer-symptom free. He thinks of his dad, who's somewhere out East living out his childhood. What would it be like to see him as a fresh-eyed kid with a mind blazing neural connections rather than atrophying them? He's seen photos of his dad from then, from now, all knobby kneed and crew cut. They're warming at first glance but disturbing thereafter. They make him feel like his existence is solely due to happenstance. Like existence is just a brief snapshot in time. The idea of castrating his young father bursts into his mind. He shakes the perverse thought away, thrusting his head side to side like he's got water in his ears. Disgusted, he leans back on the sand and lets the sun beat against his forehead. The donut kid's suggestion of meditating doesn't seem so bad if it'll help clear his mind. Before long, his filthiness starts bothering him. He heads towards Leroy's place to see if he can take a shower. On the way, he decides to tell Leroy his apartment is being fumigated and he can't go back for a couple days.

"Ethan? Is that you?" Leroy asks, answering the door with his eyes shielded from the sun by his free hand. Ethan tells Leroy his story and Leroy somewhat reluctantly lets him in. His place is dim. Books and clothes occupy portions of furniture and patches of floor. Ethan is grateful Leroy doesn't ask why he doesn't have a bag in tow. His head is already in the clouds, he thinks, he's destined for academia.

"So how are things with you and Denise?" Ethan asks upon emerging from the shower and clearing a space for himself on the couch. Leroy is across the room, seated at his desk with his head in a book.

"Things are fine," he says, raising his eyes and partially turning towards Ethan. "I haven't seen her in a few days."

"Is she out of town?"

"No, she's just busy. We both are. I've got a draft of my final thesis due in a couple weeks and she's all caught up in newspaper stuff."

"Yeah, it's been crazy around here lately. Right?"

Leroy swivels around to face Ethan. "It sure has. To be honest, I never thought UCSB students would take things this far…I mean, we're a laid-back beach school full of middle-class kids, most of whom have things pretty good. But here we are." Leroy doesn't look too pleased about being here.

"Have you been participating in the protests?"

"No. I've been drawn into a couple gatherings just by circumstance, you know, passing through. I support what they're doing—at least the parts I understand—but I've got other stuff going on, too. It's just…it's obvious a lot of people are just along for the ride. They've found a convenient outlet for the anger they have towards their landlords or their job prospects or whatever else. I mean, does anyone even remember this was originally about Bill Allen not getting tenure? If only the people in charge of that department had listened more to the students from the start. I don't understand what's so hard about that. But no, it's all about playing politics and keeping power, right? And suddenly, everyone is all swept up with the national fever over the draft and women's rights and down with the man, and…well, as I said, here we are."

Ethan stares at Leroy's desk, his mind struggling to process like an overtaxed computer. It's hard to talk freely with someone when you know something of their future.

"I saw in the paper that some famous attorney is speaking this afternoon at the stadium," Ethan says after a pause long enough to change the subject. "I think I might go."

"Denise will probably be there, knowing her," Leroy says. "Who is it?"

Ethan wants to tell him it's the defense attorney from Aaron Sorkin's "Chicago Seven" movie but stops himself.

"The lawyer who defended those guys who disrupted the 1968 Democratic convention in Chicago, William Kunstler, I think," he says instead. "Apparently some people think he's going to try to rile us all up."

"Interesting," Leroy says. "I've heard of him, he's pretty radical. Maybe I'll take a break around then." He then turns back to his books. Taking the hint, Ethan gets up and thanks Leroy for letting him shower. After a brief goodbye, he's out the door.

The next few hours pass uneventfully. Ethan naps again, eats again. Seeing Leroy was anticlimactic but natural, like catching up with an old acquaintance. By the time he starts towards the stadium, located on the north side of campus away from the ocean and bordering Goleta, he's part of a steady stream of people. He attempts to gauge the vibe, to determine if perhaps the mood of the crowd portends the violence to come, but aside from a scattering of overzealous, strung-out hippies and jaw-clenched, hardline activists, most everyone appears relatively at ease.

Ethan finds a spot near the back of the crowd and waits. He shuts his eyes and observes the sunspots forming on the interior of his eyelids dance to the ambient noise of the gathering. His mind is sober and blank. The many worries typically careening through it appear to have been left behind in the future. The introductory speaker steps to the microphone and addresses the several thousand people, who cease milling and direct their attention to the stage. The mic is soon handed over to Kunstler, who has a prominent forehead and a generous mouth, as if designed for public speaking.

Kunstler delves right into the lessons of the Chicago trial, which is the subject of his speaking tour.

"This is no time to be frightened of Chicagos, no time to be frightened by persecution, no time to be frightened by the color of your skin," he says. "The natural course of events in civilized society is routine protest, resistance and ultimately—if resistance doesn't succeed—revolution."

Kunstler's declaration meets with resounding applause. The moment overwhelms Ethan. He can't seem to wipe away the shit-eating grin that's taken over his face.

"I have never thought that breaking windows and sporadic violence is a good tactic," Kunstler continues. "But on the other hand, I cannot bring myself to become bitter and condemn young people who engage in it."

Even more rapturous applause follows this statement, which Ethan knows to be the one many will point to later as inciting the impending violence.

Ethan's heart is floating in his chest and his head is abuzz. He'd forgotten what it meant to feel this good; to feel unadulterated goodness, like after a first slow dance with a crush or catching fireflies on a prepubescent summer evening or waking up bursting with excitement for the day ahead. Only the sight of Denise pushing her way through the crowd brings him down to Earth. She appears distressed. He calls her name, but his voice is drowned out. Making his way towards her, he sees Leroy following close behind. Emerging from the most jampacked section of the audience, he watches them stride away from the stadium engaged in a heated discussion. Typically, he wouldn't interrupt such an intense conversation, but he's riding such a high—and inhabiting an almost dreamlike state of being—that he doesn't hesitate to approach them.

"Hey, that was quite some speech," he says when he's just a few feet behind. Leroy and Denise freeze mid-conversation.

"Ethan?" Denise exclaims. "I thought you'd disappeared for good. I haven't seen you since Dover's memorial."

Ethan is flattered that she's thought of him at all, and he reddens a bit. "Yeah, I've been here and there…did a semester abroad."

"You did? where?" Denise asks.

"Um, Hungary."

They both look at him like he's crazy.

"Just kidding, France. Paris."

"Oh, that must've been amazing," Denise says, but she's not fully present. Leroy remains silent.

"Sorry, am I interrupting something?" Ethan asks.

"No, no," Leroy says. "Denise is just a little upset at me for speaking my mind."

"You said if there's any more violence that the newspaper should be held partly responsible," Denise shoots back. "You said our coverage is inflammatory and we're giving voice to the most extreme elements of the movement."

Leroy crosses his arms. "I'm sorry if that offends you, but that's how I feel."

"Leroy," Ethan says. "Don't you see? What's going on here is amazing. It's a special moment in time."

"What? Mass student agitation," Leroy says. "It doesn't seem so special to me. In fact, it's happening more and more across the country and it's scaring a lot of people. I was all for the effort to bring accountability to the Bill Allen situation, but now—now we're out of our depth."

"What's this depth you keep talking about?" Denise asks. "Are we supposed to remain shallow? Like, just, ignore societal wrongs because they're so deep? Is that what you mean?"

"You know that's not what I mean. It's just, we're only college students. We're not equipped for this." Leroy gestures at the surging, almost stampeding, students exiting the stadium now that Kunstler is done speaking. "I don't think this is going to end well. I don't think this is headed for progress in any meaningful way."

"Well, you seem to be in the minority there," Denise says. "And as a matter of fact, to me, that sounds like shallow thinking."

For the first time since Kunstler started speaking, Ethan turns pensive. They both make good points. There's something to be said for living in the present, though, for living shallowly. Depth is where death lurks, and Ethan doesn't want to go there. His mindset jeopardized, he prepares to join the procession back to the park, where there's a gathering planned, and where shit will hit the fan. But before he can, Denise asks him to accompany her to the newspaper office to collect his sweatshirt, which she's been holding onto for months.

CHAPTER THIRTY-TWO
MIST FROM A FOUNTAIN OF YOUTH

Paul observes rain drops descend diagonally across the bus window on his way to meet Leroy. He knows there's an explanation to the way they zigzag across the window, some combination of acceleration and wind speed, but it appears so haphazard, so random. Kind of like Leroy's unexpected email last week, which caused a slight alteration in the trajectory of his life, which is leading God knows where. He places his palm on the cool interior of the glass and lets the bus's vibrations echo through his body. He tries to imagine that some power within him, transmitted through his hand, is powering the bus. That he's in charge. Rain in southern California affects people in different ways. It makes Paul philosophical.

    He always appreciates it when it rains in Isla Vista, not only because the region needs rain—is perpetually on the cusp of drought, which provokes its evil sibling, wildfire—but because it changes the entire atmosphere of the place. Even the people, somewhat confused about how to conduct themselves, appear altered; some jumpy, some mired in a stupor, some thoughtful, some just soaking wet. It's like traveling to a foreign city; one no longer defined by its pleasant weather. It also makes bike riding less enjoyable, which was how Paul originally intended to commute to the coffee shop a couple miles outside of Isla Vista to meet Leroy as his email requested.

In arranging the meeting, Paul intentionally neglected to ask for details, preferring to get the story all at once. He likes to react to things that way, all of a sudden; he feels it keeps him honest. He sensed from Denise in their last conversation that the issue she'd so steadfastly avoided finally came up. Skirting around the topic as usual, she'd only divulged that Leroy and she are going through a rough patch and that Leroy is back in Santa Barbara. Paul assumes this coffee date has something to do with Denise and what's going on between them, but beyond that, he has no idea.

Arriving, Paul orders a coffee and takes a seat opposite Leroy at a darkly polished, scuffed-up wooden table, one of the only pieces of furniture with any character. The coffee shop's décor is otherwise minimalist aside from a corner display of branded merch. Paul notices Leroy's skin has a healthy glow, as if he's been active and outside lately, but his clothes are ruffled and he's partially scowling, but that's not unusual.

"So, you miss conducting your lectures and meeting with students?" Paul asks after a sip of steaming coffee. "Need me to help with the withdrawal? Going to pitch an independent project?"

"God no, that feels like ages ago already."

Leroy looks down at his tea and stirs the tea bag. Paul's about to ask if he's not a coffee drinker when he continues.

"Denise and I are going through our first, I guess, big hiccup—at least in 50 years. I know she talks to you, so I thought I'd mention it so it's out in the open. Also, I was hoping you'd do me a favor, and it's a big one so I'll be compensating you."

"OK," Paul says. "I'm interested. Can you also tell me what's going on between you two? Denise is being very closed off about it."

"Oh, yeah, filling you in will be necessary," Leroy says. "That damn Lonnie has gone and screwed everything up again."

Paul can't shake the feeling that the earth is rumbling underneath Leroy's car as he exits the mountain pass and drops into the vast arid landscape east of L.A. on his way to Palm Desert. It's been less than two months since the earthquake in Joshua Tree, and the desert scene is triggering aftershocks. He turns the music up, relishing the quality of the car's sound system. He wonders if Leroy ever pumps up the volume on it. It's hard to imagine. He'll have to ask him upon returning his car after the one-night trip to visit Denise.

He pulls into Denise's driveway before noon. Stepping out of the car, the temperature jumps 30 degrees, the sun having long since evaporated any hint of morning cool. Denise answers the door in linen pants and a flowery blouse and gives him a hug.

"I still don't know why you're going along with this little scheme of Leroy's," she says, standing inches out of the sun under the porch's gable. "Seems like an awful lot of trouble."

"I don't know," Paul says. "Now that we know the whole story—or enough of it at least—about you and your ex-husband who recently got out of prison, a little extra security seems appropriate."

"Oh, Lonnie—Lonnie's not dangerous," Denise says, her voice sagging midsentence as if something just occurred to her. "He's really not," she reasserts. "I'm truly sorry about all this drama involving him though, I just wasn't sure how to broach the subject. I should've done a better job, it's so silly. But that's how I am. Reasonably competent until I'm not. If Leroy wants to be involved with me, he'll have to get used to that."

Paul puts a hand on her arm. "It's no big deal. I mean, it is a big deal. But I get it, relationships are hard. At least that's what I hear. If I ever get past the dating app stage, maybe I'll have some idea what you're going through."

Denise shakes her head, eyes sparkling with amusement. "How's that going, by the way?"

"Oh, crappy to be honest. Zero for three so far, in second dates. I think I might be too picky."

Paul omits that he's compared each of the three girls to Samantha. And that he masturbated to porn before and after each date.

"Well, sounds like you've got a lot of options," Denise says. "I can't imagine even dipping my toes into online dating." She fakes a shiver.

"I'm sure you'll have chemistry with someone soon—and when that does happen, don't overthink it. Save the overthinking for later, after the fun stuff."

Paul wants to ask Denise about porn; tell her it's messing with his head far more than the apps. It must be having a detrimental effect on dating and sexual relationships. He wants to know what older people think about this. Do they watch porn? What kind? Old-people porn? He wants to know if she thinks he should quit porn cold turkey, because he kind of thinks he should. But so far, there's no indication he will.

"I'll do my best," Paul says, readjusting the swollen backpack over his shoulders. "Anyway, should we get this over with? Installing a few cameras isn't as much of a pain as you and Leroy think it is. Lots of people have them around their houses these days. It's almost standard, especially those doorbell ones."

Denise shrugs. "I don't doubt it. My, isn't the future glorious?" She invites him in, offering him lemonade, cheese, and crackers as he removes his shoes.

"So you haven't seen him again?" Paul asks, standing beside the kitchen counter with his mouth half full.

"Who?"

"Lonnie. I mean, like, is he OK? He just pulled up to your house after being in prison? And then he went and threatened Leroy at his hotel, basically attempting to sabotage your relationship…That doesn't sound very OK."

"Yeah," Denise says. "I'm impressed Leroy is still willing to deal with me, honestly. But I guess he's worried about my safety, even if I'm not. I do miss him. But I think no matter how he heard about Lonnie, he would've required some time and space to process—although obviously I would've preferred almost any other way than him being accosted."

Denise sips her sparkling water.

"As for Lonnie, he'll find a way through whatever he's going through. He managed to embezzle money and cook the books for his yoga business for over a decade. So he's crafty, although not as crafty as he thinks he is. And he also seems to have gotten through prison alright. Maybe resourceful is a better word, scrappy. I'm more worried about Leroy. He acts like he's got a handle on things, but he can be quite brittle, you know, just beneath his soft, and somewhat plump, surface. How did he seem?"

"He seemed like he had a love hangover, and also like his usual embittered self. And also, he looked tan, strangely."

"That's about what I expected," Denise says. "Which is good. He got that tan from all the time he spent outside by the hotel pool. I started to think he was hanging around more for the amenities than my company. Like I was providing an excuse rather than a reason. Which is what finally pushed me to confront him. His self-centeredness has always bugged me, and I'm hoping we can make some progress there, even at this late stage. I can't stand older folks who take everything personally. Like, seriously, get over yourself already."

Paul wonders if Denise has read any of Leroy's student reviews, laden with pejorative adjectives that make self-centered seem borderline complimentary. But he doesn't want to drive the wedge further between them, so he pursues another line of inquiry. "You were dating Leroy when you met Lonnie, right?"

Denise nods.

"And so, did you cheat on Leroy with Lonnie?"

Denise takes a deep breath. "I did, a handful of times."

"And how did Leroy find out?"

"He caught me and Lonnie together, just holding hands, but I felt I had to tell him. It was the night that...well, that's not important. Anyway, he got upset, but he got over it. Exclusivity wasn't the norm in college in our day. But I did tell Lonnie to back off, at least for a while. Anyway, our status was never crystal clear, not until he decided he wanted to propose to me anyway."

Paul smirks.

"What?" Denise asks.

"It's just funny, the two guys you dated in college are still fighting over you. Like, I can't imagine much in my life now being at all relevant in half a century."

"Oh," Denise says. "You'd be surprised how much the past sticks with you. In so many ways. Just this morning, for instance, The Long and Winding Road by The Beatles came on the radio and I was back there, in 1970. Transported to the passenger seat in Leroy's dingy yellow car winding up State Highway 154 one day when we decided to watch the sun set from the mountain. I had to sit down it was so vivid. Me, Leroy, Lonnie, we've all been having these flashbacks that are, somehow, more than just flashbacks. It's hard to describe, but you'll get them when you're older, I'm sure."

"Yeah," Paul says. "I think I know what you mean."

• • •

Lonnie's knees creak as he navigates the apartment complex's uneven sidewalk towards the Suburban. He'd feel self-conscious about the shape of his vehicle, that shape being heavily dented and royally scuffed up, if the other cars in the lot weren't in a similar state of disrepair. What else should he expect at a place that rents by the week. He only plans to be there a few more weeks himself, a month at most. He feels each month of his life—all 900—accumulated like tree rings in his body, stiffening his spine and robbing him of his flexibility. He knows he'd feel better if he kept to his usual yoga routine, but since getting out of prison he hasn't been able to keep to anything other than half-assed stalking of his ex. That is, until he settled on a final course of action the other night. Which came with great relief; he's no good at life without direction. Although, considering the plan, and the sum of his experiences up to this point in time, he may just not be very good at life.

Up next in the course of action is a trip to the supermarket. Driving across the strip mall parking lot towards the grocery store, Lonnie notices a donut shop. He hasn't had a donut in years, hasn't craved one. But something more innate than even hunger compels him towards the nondescript shop. Upon pulling open the glass door, he realizes the aroma is what he desired. The damp, sugar-coated air seeps into his pores like mist from a fountain of youth. For a second, he's back in Isla Vista in 1970 wearing that ludicrous chef's hat and bullshitting with anyone who walks into the shop.

He's pulled back to reality by the young Asian employee across the counter asking him what he'd like. Lonnie's flabbergasted— outraged— to see that a donut costs upwards of three dollars. He remembers when that could score a dozen of the freshest donuts imaginable. To his trained, if unpracticed, eye, the donuts in the trays under the counter look easily half a day old. Then he remembers that pretty soon he won't have much use for money. He orders a dozen donuts, telling the kid to give him twelve different kinds. He wants to ask him about the protests on campus and get the latest news about the war. Or better yet, throw on an apron and join him in that saccharine world behind the counter. He whacks himself upside the head in frustration. He needs to stay focused, at least until things get underway. He'll have plenty of time to slip into asinine reflection later. The clerk looks at him askance.

"Something in my ear," Lonnie says before paying and exiting the mirage into his past.

Back in the car, he scarfs down two donuts, one slathered in chocolate, the other blueberry and cakey. He reclines in the oversized driver's seat as his body grasps the metabolizing task it's been assigned and siphons energy from the rest of his system to aid the process. His plan is foolproof. Simple, as the best plans are. No extra fat. Lean and mean. But it lacks an element of engagement, a signature of some kind. It's too hermetic. As in Frankenstein—the original version, one of the books he read in the prison library—the monster can't simply disappear into no man's land. He needs to leave a trail: To be followed, to be known, and to share the pain of existence, as much for himself as his creators. There's no dignity in crawling into a hole and disappearing, it's inhuman. He mulls it over, but nothing strikes him. Eventually, he goes to the market, returning with a dozen cartons of orange juice. He read that Gandhi drank citrus during his hunger strikes, which lasted up to three weeks. If he's still conscious after that long, he'll turn to pills.

He's given Denise space since their little tête-à-tête and the less innocuous meeting with Leroy the next day, but he hasn't stopped driving by her house. Every day for over a week he's cruised the Suburban down her block, usually after dark so there's less chance of her noticing. He realized in prison, a little too late—he's always a little too late to realize things—how much she'd anchored him all those years, even the latter years when they weren't so much a couple as cohabitants. If he's no longer quite anchored to her, he's still tethered, and so he passes by nightly as if in orbit. Initially upon being released, he tried to imagine what she would want him to do, but he's never been good at putting himself in other people's shoes. He only knows one way; his own, and, well, that way is still mostly a mystery to him. This is the unpleasant fact that's been weighing him down the last few weeks. He's an old man and he still can't explain why he does what he does, why he acts the way he acts. All those years, decades, of meditation; they pieced his thoughts together, but the puzzle was never even close to solved. So, when the notion of a hunger strike came to him while he was taking a shit, he didn't scrutinize it much. If the puzzle ends up unfinished, so be it.

Even though the sun is still settling into its daytime throne high in the sky, he heads for Denise's. He parks along the street in front of her house and starts in on another donut, this one jelly filled. Her car's not in the driveway. He grimaces at the thought that she might be attending a yoga class at his former studio. Then he notices something different, something he wouldn't have noticed before his time behind bars. But an awareness of when you're being watched—not just surveillance, but even eyes on the back of your head—develops quite rapidly when you're incarcerated with hundreds of people you don't trust, including the guards. Several newly installed security cameras ring the exterior of Denise's house. One in front of the doorway, one facing the driveway, and one a little higher up, looking directly towards him.

So Denise doesn't trust him, is feeling a little insecure. Well, she always was somewhat insecure; that's what he liked about her, or at least it was a quality that pleased him, that he used to his advantage. An idea strikes him of how he can use these cameras to his advantage, to lend his mission that sharp edge that cuts into the rest of the world and makes his pain known. He's happy with the shrewdness of it. Simple, but sensible. And requiring little additional preparation. He takes another donut and fingers the hole.

CHAPTER THIRTY-THREE
BURNING AND NUMB

Denise hands Ethan the hoodie that's been folded in her desk drawer for the better part of a year.

"I've been meaning to ask you for a while," she says. "How did you end up with *Desert Solitaire* in your pocket? It was Dover's, as you must know."

Denise's question catches Ethan off-guard. He's still floating on air from Kunstler's speech, and this threatens to reinstitute gravity.

"To be honest, I took it," he says. "I knew Dover was reading it and I wanted a memento."

"You knew Dover, then?" Denise asks.

"Oh yeah, I, uh, I worked at the Faculty Club for a while." Ethan smirks preemptively at the coming falsehood. "Pool boy."

"Wow, like a lifeguard?"

"Yeah, that was part of it."

Denise takes the book out of the same drawer and fingers the spine where Abbey's name is written.

"Well, this book helped flesh out my coverage of Dover," she says. "And it made me feel more confident writing about the environment. You know, just seeing how someone else does it. Of course, he's a much better writer. It was more, like, it made me understand that the environment is an emotional topic, and if I'm feeling angry, or helpless, or whatever, it's OK if that shows through in my writing sometimes.

"Yeah," Ethan says. "I haven't read the book yet, but it sounds intense."

"Oh, you should, if for no other reason than that Dover clearly loved it. Also, it gave me a whole different impression of what a desert is, how beautiful and full of life it is. Yeah, I'd really like to visit. Especially some of the spots that Abbey says will soon be overrun by tourists and development."

"I bet you would," Ethan says.

"Huh?"

"Never mind. I'm sure you'll get to spend plenty of time in the desert."

Denise looks unconvinced. "I think part of what I realized during the oil spill is how estranged I am from my surroundings. Like, I owe everything to nature and I totally take it for granted. Even though I knew, before the oil spill, that pollution is rampant, and we're addicted to oil, and all that, I wasn't able to acknowledge it until catastrophe struck. It's like, if your mom or dad was sick and you waited until they were admitted to the hospital to even say anything because you're too busy or too subconsciously scared or whatever."

Ethan takes a deep breath. He's losing track of which world he's inhabiting. His throat hurts when he swallows. It could be strep throat or something worse. And between his toes, something oily. Athlete's foot? Gangrene? He folds the hoodie under his arm. He needs to stay present.

"I was gonna follow the rally back to I.V." he says. "You interested?"

Denise pivots towards her desk. "I've got a few things to finish up, but if it's still happening on my way home, I'll stop by."

Ethan goes to the door of the subterranean office, through which a shaft of yellow light pours onto the room's many uneven surfaces. "Oh, I'm pretty sure it'll still be going on."

Steven cringes at the piercing sound of glass breaking. "This is not looking good. I knew that speaker went too far. These kids are already primed for violence, of course they're going to take his words literally."

Becca's head swivels around next to him. Downtown Isla Vista, at the center of which is Perfect Park, is overrun with students, and some nonstudents, and some mix of those present are instigating violence by shattering the windows of local businesses.

"Shit," Becca says. "Was that the Finear Realty storefront? They're a big advertiser with us. I've already been getting a mouthful from advertising that local businesses are threatening to cut off their ads because they think the paper is helping escalate the chaos."

"I can see that," Steven says. Becca gives him a cold stare. They forge ahead in the direction of the vandalism. "It looks like they might be targeting the realtors," Steven says.

"Impressive," Becca utters. "That there's discernment anywhere amidst this."

A yell percolates through the crowd that stops them and those around them in their tracks: "The bank is on fire. The bank is on fire." The slow-moving mass reorients towards the bank on the opposite side of the park. Becca hears someone call her name. Looking over her shoulder, she spots a young man with a short, dark beard and a polo shirt eyeing her suspiciously.

"Yeah, you," he says. "You're the editor of the paper, right?"

Pushing against the onrushing crowd, Becca approaches the guy, who appears upset.

"Yes, I'm the editor of the student newspaper," she says. "Why do you ask?"

"Are you happy with what you've accomplished?" The guy waves his hands around, indicating the scene. "This is what you wanted to happen all along, right?"

Becca takes a deep breath and yells to make herself heard. "I'm sorry you feel that way. We try to give voice to all the opinions on campus, even if some of them strike people as extreme."

"That's bull and you know it," the guy says, stepping towards her. "If I wanted a radical college experience, I would've gone to Berkeley. This is supposed to be a nice place."

"I see," Becca says. "Well, I'm sorry if it doesn't meet your standard of civility. Feel free to write a letter to the editor for possible publication."

The man's face contorts. "Bitch," he yells as he pulls back his arm. But as he's about to release his hand, Steven charges into his chest. The two of them stumble back several yards, eventually falling onto the trampled ground.

Even though Ethan knows the bank will burn, it still catches him off guard when the fire erupts. He's eavesdropping on a trio of side burned students debating how the new Beatles' single "Hey Jude" compares to the rest of the band's catalog when their attention turns to a flaming trash can just inside the bank's doors. The three guys remind him a lot, in an annoying way, of three of his roommates back home. He never understood the satisfaction they derived from dissecting the latest War on Drugs or Tame Impala track. He's tempted to disrupt the conversation and announce that The Beatles will soon break up. The trash can bursting into flames brings him relief. He's glad the real action is underway—even though it's much earlier in the night than he expected, not even dark yet—because the occasion is becoming dispiriting. He'd expected organized chants or marching hand-in-hand or something more inspiring, but it's mostly aimless milling punctuated with outbursts of violence. He's lost interest on several occasions and reflexively reached for his phone, for a screen to scroll, for active distraction.

And then there's the way Denise's reckoning with the oil spill reminded him of his father. He remembers how during the spill his instinct was to encourage people not to give way to despair. How come he was able to deal with that so much better? Maybe because he was forced to face it. He wishes facing things didn't require so much force. Had he really dealt with the spill better, though? Or had he simply protected himself by remaining emotionally distant? Why couldn't he ever get his emotions to be exactly the right distance away. They were either painfully, blindingly near or so far off as to be nearly imperceptible.

Approaching the bank, he realizes the flames are a false alarm; just a preview of what's to come. The trash can is quickly extinguished. The density is making him uncomfortable, like he might somehow lose himself in it. He works his way across the park hoping to avoid any impending melee with the cops and arrives at an opening. Pausing to catch his breath, he identifies the cause of the bubble of space—two guys are wrestling on the ground a few yards in front of him. Or more accurately, one guy, the bigger guy, has the smaller guy pinned and looks like he's about to smack him. A woman joins the scuffle, pulling the top guy's shoulder back. Ethan is about to file the confrontation as another disheartening development in the evening's action when he recognizes the woman's face, recalling her from Dover's memorial. She helped him escape, along with Denise. Taking a closer look at the two guys, he also recognizes the one on the ground; it's the guy he swapped jackets with.

Some volatile mix of obligation, exhilaration, anger, and frustration compels him to barrel forward into the large guy's ribcage, pummeling him over. The two of them roll to the ground next to Steven, who jumps up, eyes wide in disbelief. Becca, thrown back into several passersby due to Ethan's charge, recovers her footing, apologizes to those who broke her fall, and goes to Steven's aid. She brushes his ruffled hair back into its neatly parted position and inspects him for damage. Before she can finish, Steven yells, "Hey, that's enough." Becca turns to see Ethan straddling Steven's former aggressor and punching him in the face, three, four, five times. Blood is flowing from the guy's nose and he's no longer fighting back. His arms rise to meet Ethan but slump down without any force of impact. Steven races towards Ethan, grabs his biceps from behind, and pulls him away. Becca joins Steven and, each holding one of Ethan's arms, they retreat across the street.

"Jesus Christ," Steven says as they step into an alley. "What got into you back there?"

Ethan's eyes flash between Becca and Steven but his mouth doesn't move.

"I know you were trying to help, but you went way too far with that guy," Steven continues. "I mean, you just can't punch someone in the face like that, it could cause brain damage."

Ethan looks down at his hands and clenches them into fists. His knuckles are red and pain shoots through his right wrist. But the pain feels good, for once.

"This is all so out of control," Steven says, wiping his forehead. Becca yanks Ethan's arm, forcing him to look at her. "You're the guy who was getting chased by the police at Dover's thing, aren't you? What's the deal, does trouble just follow you around or something?"

Ethan shrugs, avoiding eye contact. "I don't know what happened back there," he says. "I lost control. I wasn't myself."

"That guy may have been an asshole—and the instigator of the whole thing—but he was going to slap Steven, not knock his lights out," Becca says. She looks over her shoulder at the sliver of street visible from the alley. It's crawling with people. "We should get back there to make sure he's OK, and also to ensure it doesn't get misconstrued as police violence or something. Who ever thought I'd owe that guy an apology."

Steven nods, although Becca can tell he'd rather not.

"Are you cooled off now?" Becca asks Ethan. "I'd lay low for a while if I were you. Since you were ostensibly trying to help, and since you're Denise's friend, I'm not going to make this into a bigger thing than it has to be. But you'd better get a grip on yourself, man."

"Yeah," Ethan says, flexing his right hand, which is both burning and numb. "I'll get a grip."

"Good," Becca says. "This is already turning into a circus without your help."

Loud sirens and stern directives from a fuzzy megaphone permeate the air. With a final weary look at Ethan, Becca takes Steven's hand and leads him back towards the commotion. Rather than look at what's coming, Steven focuses on his hand held within Becca's as they turn the corner.

Ethan leans on the cool brick wall of the building bordering the alley and cradles one hand within the other. He half listens to the uproar caused by a flank of officers sweeping the premises and hardly registers the gurgling mayhem of fleeing students. He wants to escape with them, but he can't summon the strength. It's like he's destined to remain present as the long, fateful night incrementally unfolds. His bloodied hand reminds him of a heart. Something clicks in his mind and everything else tunes out. His heart aches. It really does. And this ache, it's not going to go away. But it's not going to kill him either. In fact, it's a sign that he's alive. His heart beats, and it aches. If he can remember that he thinks he'll be alright. He wants to go home and, as if someone or something is reading his mind, he experiences that familiar inner tug indicating how to make it happen.

He emerges from the alley to a much-diminished crowd, but one engaged in rock-throwing back-and-forth with the police. He wanders around the perimeter of the confrontation, occasionally picking up a stick or a rock and wielding it, but never going so far as to hurl anything. He's not sure how much time passes, but the next thing he knows an abandoned police car is being overturned and burned.

Later still, while seated on the curb, he notices the short guy from the donut shop stomp by, apparently caught up in some dilemma of his own. Ethan overhears the guy mutter, "What are they up to now?" as he passes.

"Hey," Ethan calls out. Lonnie snaps around and glares at him.

"You're the guy from the donut shop, right?" Ethan asks.

"Yeah," Lonnie says. "So?"

"Where are you going?"

"None of your business." But something about Ethan's appearance—his stretched and dirtied clothes, his inscrutable expression, the blood on his cuffs—makes Lonnie reconsider. "Sorry, I'm just in a rush. I saw this guy, a former friend, drive down a side street a few minutes ago and I'm trying to track him down."

"Why?" Ethan asks.

Lonnie huffs in exasperation and throws his arms in the air. "Because look around, this is basically a war zone. And, well, I don't trust him."

"I see," Ethan says. A detail about the bank burning from an article he read comes to him. "What kind of car is he driving?"

"What? What kind of car? I don't know, I think a Ford Falcon."

Ethan nods. "Yeah, he's up to no good."

"What do you mean?" Lonnie's voice escalates, spittle spreading from his lips like buckshot as he approaches Ethan.

"Tear gas," Ethan says. "Someone in that car is going to throw tear gas into the crowd. And after that some people, probably the same ones, are going to make a pile of furniture in the bank, pour gas on it, and burn the bank down."

Lonnie grabs hold of Ethan's fleece collar. "What the devil? Are you working with Russell or something?"

"Nah," Ethan says. "I just know."

Lonnie releases Ethan with a shove. "You're crazy, man," he says. "This whole town's gone berserk." He shuts his eyes and takes a long, deep inhale followed by an equally measured exhale. Ethan watches him and is about to join the breathing exercise when a loud pop goes off across the park and a murky substance fills the air. A car's wheels screech away in the opposite direction.

"That's got to be it," Ethan says, his eyes still closed. Lonnie's eyes shoot open, and he watches the scene with increasing apprehension. "If you hang around a while, you'll see the bank burn," Ethan says, his eyes slitting open. "I believe the flames will be 30 or 40 feet high. And you might even witness someone jump into that fire." Ethan's entire face brightens cryptically as he utters the final phrase.

"You're weirding me out," Lonnie says, retreating. "I'm getting out of here."

But before he can split, a voice from behind calls both their names. They turn simultaneously towards Denise.

"Lonnie, Ethan, do you guys know each other?" She calls out as she approaches. Neither of them responds. "Never mind," she says. The three of them watch the frantic exodus taking place across the park where the gas cannisters went off. "Who the hell is launching off tear gas?" Denise asks. "I'm starting to worry there might be a bomb around—maybe it's the same people who attacked the Faculty Club."

Lonnie recoils at mention of the Faculty Club before composing himself and taking Denise's hand.

"Should we get out of here, then?" he asks. "It'll be quiet at my place out in…" But before he can finish, Denise yanks her hand back from his, her gaze fixed straight ahead. Lonnie follows it, confused, until he too stiffens and his eyebrows furrow.

"What are you doing here?" Denise calls to Leroy, who's halfway down the block.

"Well, the whole town is in such a state of agitation that I couldn't focus," Leroy says, silhouetted by eerie light filtered through the haze and smoke. "Plus, I wanted to make sure you and Ethan were OK. But I guess that wasn't necessary."

Denise looks from Lonnie to Leroy and back. "I'd better go with Leroy now," she tells Lonnie. He gives her a nod, and Ethan can hardly believe it—he winks at her. She squeezes his shoulder before heading towards Leroy, who's already turned his back on them.

Once Denise and Leroy are out of sight, Lonnie turns to Ethan. "How do you know Denise?" he asks.

"Oh, well, um, we…I dated one of her friends, sophomore year," Ethan says. Lonnie eyes him questioningly. "And I suppose you know Leroy through that same scene?"

Ethan nods.

"That guy's got to loosen up," Lonnie says. "He also needs to realize that Denise wants something other than what he's offering. Maybe you can talk some sense into him."

"Talk sense into Leroy?" Ethan says. "I doubt it."

Lonnie chuckles, but the lighthearted moment is interrupted by another tear gas raid.

"Aw man," Lonnie says. "We got to keep the cars out of here. I'm going to go help those people barricade the road. You want to come?"

"Why not?" Ethan says. "It's about time to get close to the bank anyway."

A half hour later, Ethan and Lonnie are part of an amorphous group of students centered around a makeshift traffic barrier composed primarily of overflowing trash cans, but also several benches, miscellaneous large receptacles, and even a few tree branches. Lonnie is expounding on the merits of his meditation practice to Ethan, how it's helped him keep his head amidst all the internal and external tumult, when Ethan, only partially listening, bumps him with his elbow.

"Hey, is that the Russell guy you mentioned?" Ethan asks, pointing towards the bank. Lonnie shuts up and his eyes narrow. He climbs atop a trash can for a better view. "Oh yeah, that's him."

"Looks like he's up to something, doesn't it?" Ethan says. Lonnie doesn't respond. His attention is locked on his former accomplice, who disappears into the bank, but not before Lonnie spots the gasoline cannister in his hand.

Lonnie jumps down from the trash can and starts towards the bank, but Ethan grabs his arm. "Let him do it," he says. "It's already history." Lonnie attempts to pull himself free but Ethan's hands, which are swollen and red, won't loosen.

"A few hours ago, I was ecstatic to watch this happen," Ethan says. "I thought I might locate some emotional core here, some way to harness into life rather than freefall through it. And maybe I have, even if it's gonna hurt. To find out though, the bank needs to burn. When the flames reach their peak, I'm going to jump right into them."

Lonnie ceases his struggle. "What did you just say?"

"I said I'm going to jump into the fire, but don't worry I'll be OK."

"How could you be OK after jumping into a fire?"

Lonnie's hand wraps around Ethan's arm so they're both grabbing each other.

"I just know," Ethan says, pulling Lonnie closer. "And now I'm going to do you a favor like a friend once did for me."

The next thing Lonnie knows, Ethan's bruised fist is rushing towards his face.

CHAPTER THIRTY-FOUR
CLOUDS YOU'RE THINKING

"I still can't believe Denise married Lonnie," Ethan says to Paul. "It just doesn't compute."

"Yeah, I know," Paul says. "Apparently he's got some, like, mysterious, guru-like powers of persuasion, at least that's how Denise described it to me."

They're sitting in Paul's apartment, watching a live feed from the cameras Paul installed at Denise's house. A butterfly flutters across one of the videos.

"Let's go out to the balcony for a bit," Paul says. "Nothing much happening here. Then I think you'd better go home and get some more rest."

After jumping through the portal that emerged within the heart of the flames engulfing the Bank of America, Ethan passed out, once again in the park, but a quiet, reasonably well-kept park rather than one resembling a war zone. The distant mutterings of homeless people were music to his ears as he fell asleep to the welcome thought that he was back in the right century. Rising just before dawn, he went to Paul's where he recounted his marathon one-day trip to 1970 over several cups of coffee. Ethan thought the climax would come at the end of the story, when he jumped into the flames, but for Paul, it came when he heard Lonnie's name, and then he climaxed again when he heard Ethan punched Lonnie's lights out. He'd been speculating a lot about Lonnie as a youth, and now he had first-hand intel, well, fresh first-hand intel, since Denise's was eroded by decades of wear and tear.

On the patio, Paul attempts to extract more information about Lonnie, but Ethan is fading.

"It's pretty funny, don't you think," he says, not ready to let the conversation wind down quite yet. "That you had to punch Lonnie to get back here, and I had to punch you last time. I guess I'm confused why you didn't want to stay. What was the rush?"

Ethan removes a pair of sunglasses he borrowed from Paul. There's bags under his reddened eyes and his hand is black and blue, but he's smiling.

"I don't know," Ethan says. "I guess I had a change of heart."

"Well, happy to hear it. It would've been a shitshow here if you just disappeared for good." Paul looks out over the cozy half-acre park. Daffodils bloom along the fence and the buds on the impenetrable, dark-leafed bushes look ready to burst. "Plus, you know, friends."

Ethan leans back in his chair. "Yeah, plus friends. And family."

In the ensuing silence, Ethan absentmindedly unzips the inside pocket of his hoodie. He reaches in, pulls out a faded piece of cardboard, and tosses it next to a row of bottles waiting to be recycled.

"Hold on," Paul says, sliding from his chair and kneeling towards the item. "This is the hoodie you wore last time, when we went to the Faculty Club, right?"

Ethan nods. "Yeah, I tied it around my waist after Denise gave it back."

Paul retrieves the piece of cardboard and inspects it. "And this is the bit from the bomb parcel that I wanted to save. Haha."

Ethan mines his muddied brain for the cardboard's significance.

"Don't you remember?" Paul asks. "If I can get this DNA tested, there's still a chance it could identify the bomber. It looks like the tape yanked a small clump of hair out, which is good, because that means it might still have the roots."

After Ethan departs to crash at his place, Paul texts a police detective he once cold-called with several questions about local gang culture, and who subsequently asked him to tutor his kid in AP History. Paul successfully ushered the unmotivated child through the course with an A-, and the detective told Paul he owed him one. Paul is now ready to make good on that offer.

Feeling the effects of Ethan's early wake-up call, Paul lounges on the couch with Denise's video feed playing in the background. His mind wanders to Samantha. The weekend they spent together in the desert keeps growing in stature, only a few months old and already it's being mythologized. He glimpsed the potential for something higher, a higher plane of existence, in those cracked-open hours after the earthquake. The two of them forged a personal connection there; of a quality and nature he has trouble imagining developing from the algorithmic confines of his dating apps. At the time he didn't assume it was sexual, but in the weeks since his penis has made clear it is. He feels it prick up underneath his sweatpants. He refuses to masturbate to her memory though, to tarnish his image of her that way. He's already asked Ethan too many times about when she might visit next. He might have to come up with an excuse to go to L.A. if he can't shake the feeling, which he doesn't want to do. He wants to grip it tightly, follow it wherever it takes him.

As he prepares to bring up porn, he hears a car pull into the video feed. He doesn't pay much attention until it idles in front of the house for a while, at which point he glances up. The vehicle is partially obscured by the front entry gate and adjacent palm tree, but Paul thinks it might be a green Suburban. Curiosity piqued, he sets his phone down and zooms in on the driver's side window, but something unexpected obscures his view of the driver. At first, he thinks there's a branch in the way or an unusual glare, but then realizes he's looking at letters. There's black writing across the window. He mouths the words as he reads, "Hunger Strike Day 4."

Paul steps back from his computer. The message is clearly intended for whoever's monitoring Denise's house. As he's working out what to make of it, a hand inside the car wipes the window clean and then the Suburban takes off. Paul looks at the time; 12:06 p.m. Before he can arrive at any conclusion about what to do next, his phone rings. It's the detective asking him to bring the evidence downtown.

In his large lecture the next day, no one thinks anything of it when Paul slinks off through the rear door just before noon. Sitting in a musty alcove on a sticky bench, he opens the feed to Denise's house. The Suburban pulls up at 12:02. This time the message on the window reads, "Hunger Strike Day 5." Three minutes later, the same unhurried hand rubs away the text and the Suburban pulls away. Paul replays the video, hoping to get a better look at the driver. The man is a senior, small in stature. His expression is tranquil, but his eyes burn with fire. It's easy to imagine his head spontaneously combusting. Paul has no doubt it's Lonnie.

Quite disturbed by the situation, Paul considers contacting Denise, or Leroy, or even Ethan, at least to talk things through. But he hesitates, waiting another day, and another. His frustration spills over into his thoughts about Samantha and he loses hope of any prospects there. He immerses himself in the dating apps and then flakes out on two dates. The stress of bailing eats away at him. He hates flaking, it makes his skin crawl. He has trouble falling asleep at night, his attempt at dating having gotten nowhere in months, having possibly gone backwards. He feels like he's at the end of a rope which may or may not be tied to anything.

Day eight is a Friday. He's not sure Lonnie will be able to drive for much longer if he's really fasting. Plus, the guy is clearly crying out for help. The urgency of the situation forces Paul into action. Instead of asking Leroy to borrow his car, which would reveal that something's up at Denise's, Paul promises Greggy he'll help him test out of his senior year writing course if he lets him borrow his truck. Greggy eagerly accepts. If he needs a car while Paul's gone, he can just ask his parents to bring the spare sedan up from Ventura.

Paul departs for Palm Desert just before dawn the next morning and is staked out a few houses down from Denise's by 11:30. He watches, slumped low in the driver's seat, as Lonnie drives past to perform his daily ritual, and follows behind once he's through with it less than five minutes later. Lonnie's driving is sluggish and erratic and Paul's pretty sure he can tailgate him without drawing suspicion. After fifteen minutes, Lonnie pulls into a dingy apartment complex and jerks the Suburban to a stop diagonally across two parking spots. The door swings open and Lonnie weakly stumbles out and shuffles the 30 or so yards to his apartment, bent over as if he's queasy. One of his shoes is untied and his linen pants hang loosely around his waist. Paul waits a few minutes before knocking on the door.

When Lonnie doesn't respond, Paul turns the handle. It's unlocked. He cautiously enters the musty apartment while calling Lonnie's name. The beige shag carpet seems to sap all the color from the room. Unfortunately, it doesn't do the same for the odor, a mix of patchouli, stale sweat, and citrus.

"Over here," a frail voice beckons from down the hallway. Paul peeks into the kitchen. A glass with some crusty orange juice remnants clinging to the rim is the only thing on the counter. He opens the fridge. Several half-gallons of orange juice occupy the top shelf. There's no sign of anything edible besides an empty donut bag in the trash can. He proceeds down the hallway and into the bedroom. Lonnie is sitting cross-legged on a coarse blanket folded in thirds. Leaning against the wall, he looks up at Paul with gaunt eyes.

"I was starting to wonder if anyone was going to notice," he says. "I guess you didn't bring Denise."

Paul shakes his head.

"She doesn't want to say goodbye to me."

"If I told Denise, she'd definitely call the police and your hunger strike would really be over."

"Maybe, maybe not," Lonnie says, no longer observing Paul. "Denise isn't so by the book; she may honor my wishes. And she can keep a secret."

"You mean like the secret that you're responsible for Dover Sharp's death? That you killed Dover Sharp."

Lonnie ceases rubbing his fingers and thumbs together, his hands resting on the inside of his knees, and looks wonderingly at Paul. For a second, Paul thinks maybe the test was wrong, the hair sample too aged.

"That has nothing to do with this," Lonnie says eventually. "I spent years coming to terms with that. Years of alternatively hating myself and forgiving myself…" Lonnie trails off and looks towards the square of faint blue sky visible through the window across the room. "Not much better than my view in prison."

"So you admit it?" Paul asks.

"Denise told you, then?" Lonnie replies with his own question.

Paul shakes his head.

"Then how do you know?"

"Let's just say I have pretty solid evidence."

"Oh, fuck it," Lonnie says, half raising an arm and pointing towards the hall. "Can you fetch the pill box from behind the bathroom mirror? You can have the rest of my money if you leave me be."

Paul makes a point of stepping into the room, sitting on a wooden chair by the wall. "How did you do it?" he asks. "Come to terms with killing someone."

Lonnie looks hard at Paul. "Why do you want to know?"

Paul isn't sure, but it feels relevant to him somehow. He also wants to steer the conversation away from suicide. "I'm just curious. Seems like a hard thing to do."

"Oh, pffft," Lonnie exhales. "After Dover died, I got into meditation, transcendental meditation. Everything good and peaceful that happened in my life came from that, but eventually my demons overpowered it. Still, meditation helped me control my actions—my impulses, my feelings too—even if it never got me all the way to understanding them."

Paul nods.

"But I appear to be incapable of pulling myself together like that anymore, meditation or not," Lonnie continues. "I can't obtain that inner peace, which is why I ended up at this juncture. And now that someone other than Denise knows I'm guilty of murder, well, there's even more reason to believe I'll only ever find peace in the next world."

"Listen," Paul says, standing up. "The only way I'm going to leave you here is if I turn you in first. But there's another option. It would require leaving this depressing apartment and going on a road trip. And with a little luck, it could end up making Denise very happy, which, if you really do still love her, should also make you happy."

"How do you know so much, anyway?" Lonnie asks.

"Let's just say I'm your guardian angel," Paul says with a wink. Lonnie smiles through chapped lips and emits a croak of a laugh before doubling over in pain.

"You bastard," Lonnie says. "I can't laugh in this state."

They share a moment of contemplation.

"You look familiar," Lonnie says.

"If you come with me" Paul says. "I'll explain why that might be."

A look of recognition enters Lonnie's eyes and he nods his consent.

"One more thing," Paul adds. "Why did you do it? Murder Dover, I mean."

"The truth, the sad fucking truth, is I did it over a girl," Lonnie says. "He got in the way of me and a girl, so I killed him."

Lonnie sits a little straighter on his folded rug, finding relief in venting the sordid fact.

"Over a girl?" Paul asks, incredulously.

"Yep, my libido got the best of me. Wasn't the first time, nor was it the last."

They set out the next morning after Paul's best attempt at nursing Lonnie back to life. For breakfast, he's able to down an entire glazed donut administered in small morsels and a few sips of coffee, which Paul takes as adequate evidence that he's road ready. A couple hours into the drive, as they're whizzing by the whitewashed rocks and snarled shrubs of the Mojave, Lonnie asks Paul to explain "everything."

"Everything?" Paul asks.

Lonnie nods. "Including why the hell we're heading into the middle of nowhere."

Paul inquires if Lonnie already guessed why he seemed familiar.

"I think I threatened you with a knife back when we were both young," Lonnie says. "Which was a very long time ago for me but just a few months ago for you, I guess. Makes me think you've also taken part in this time travel phenomenon, or at least know about it somehow."

"Bingo," Paul says, and for the next half-hour all he does is talk, sip Mountain Dew, and intermittently take a bite from a 5 oz. bag of teriyaki beef jerky.

"Hard to believe," Lonnie says after Paul finishes up his recounting with his tracking of Lonnie's hunger strike.

"What's hard to believe?"

"How different life is viewed through the rear-view mirror than the front dash."

Paul glances at Lonnie, who is in fact looking through the passenger's side mirror. He wasn't anticipating any specific reaction to his words, but is surprised by Lonnie's pensive reflection.

"Well, you might still have some good years ahead of you," Paul says.

Lonnie doesn't respond.

"What do you think you might want to do next, then?"

"Oh, I dunno," Lonnie replies. "I might want to not talk about it now."

Paul shuts up and after a few minutes plays The Beatles on the truck's stereo. Lonnie tells him to turn it off, that he hates The Beatles. Paul insists, and Lonnie gives in, his energy depleted. They traverse the desert to the tunes of John, Paul, George, and Ringo. Having not been out of California in a decade, and having never been to Nevada, Lonnie watches the world pass by with increasing awareness, his mood incrementally improving with each milepost along with his opinion of The Beatles.

The next day, after a ten-hour drive split up by an overnight stop in Vegas, including a grueling evening at a hotel buffet helping Lonnie down an array of the blandest foods on offer, Paul eases the truck into a dirt pullout a dozen yards from the rim of Lake Powell. The sky is big and blue, the earth is rocky and sandy, the water is low and murky, and there's not much else to look at. Paul has just about had his fill of desert, but at the same time he can't stop inhaling deeply of the pure, dry air, which hits him like a small dose of nicotine, nor can he keep himself from staring into the boundless horizon, mesmerized by the way it ebbs and flows like an earthen tide. He turns to Lonnie, who's got his feet up on the dash and is gazing lazily out the window.

"This might be it," he says. "Or at least it's as near as I could pinpoint based on Denise's description."

Lonnie grunts.

"Let's get out and poke around. We'll set up the campsite later."

Emerging from the car, Lonnie stretches his arms out to their maximum reach for the first time since being dragged out of his bedroom half-starved and smelling like sour orange juice. His ears perk like a rabbit, and a light breeze cleanses his dour face as he watches Paul approach the partially filled man-made lake. When Paul returns from his reconnoitering a few minutes later, Lonnie's hands are pressed together in front of his chest in a sun salutation position. His eyes are closed and his face is devoid of tension.

"The water is really low, but we already knew that," Paul says. "I checked out the level history, and it's about ten feet lower now than it was on the date Leroy tossed the ring."

Lonnie nods twice but otherwise doesn't move a muscle.

"You can get back into that in a minute," Paul says. "Let me show you what we're looking at first." Lonnie releases his pose and Paul guides him to the rocky cliffside overlooking the water. He points to three outcrops above the waterline but far beneath the top of the chalky bathtub ring staining the entire lower cliffside. "See those sort of little pits. They're sandy enough that the ring might be buried there."

"Seems pretty unlikely to me, but OK," Lonnie says.

"I'm going to attach the rope up to the truck and scoot down there with my metal detector," Paul says. "We're not supposed to climb here so remember if anyone comes by just play dumb. I don't think we'll get worse than a ticket."

"Sure," Lonnie says. "I'll tell them you wanted to dip your toes in the water."

While Paul plays metal detectorist for two hours, Lonnie fulfills his role of innocent bystander with three different sets of passersby. A group of teenagers who ignore him; a young couple whose SUV is brimming with climbing gear and who give him a conspiratorial salute; and an overweight, balding man in a beat-up sedan who gives him the stink eye before turning and going the other way.

Paul finally ascends as the sun dips low in the sky. He's plastered with dust and sweat stains bloom from his underarms and across his belly. "Nothing but junk," he says. "Interesting junk, but still junk."

"Thought so," Lonnie replies.

"I'm exhausted." Paul wipes his forehead and drinks plentifully from a large water bottle. "Let's set up camp. I'll try tomorrow at one other spot and then that's it."

Paul pitches two $30 tents on a campsite a mile away adjacent to a playful pile of boulders and partially shaded by a pair of sinewy junipers. After a meal of day-old sandwiches and potato salad, Paul builds a fire. Lonnie takes the initiative of tending to it, clearly enjoying stoking the flames. Paul is warmed by the promising change in Lonnie's demeanor, whose unshaven pallid skin takes on a healthy sheen under the starlight. After rinsing their hands and faces with bottled water, they turn in early. Paul initially passes out but wakes up before falling into a deep sleep. He lays still, just able to make out the steady pattern of Lonnie's breathing. After a few minutes, he removes his laptop from his backpack and opens up a porn video he downloaded in anticipation of not having internet access. He's got his hand on his cock when Lonnie's voice interrupts the video's quiet moans.

"You're watching pornography right now?"

Paul slams his computer shut and yanks his pajama pants up over his engorged penis.

"Dude, what are you doing here?" he yelps, sounding both angry and helpless.

"I had to pee," Lonnie says. "I pee like ten times a night."

"Fuck," Paul says. "Yeah, I'm watching porn. I watch a lot of porn."

"That doesn't sound very healthy," Lonnie says. "I mean, it's gross."

"Porn grosses you out?"

"I guess so," Lonnie says. "Not really my thing. Why don't I go relieve myself and then let's meet out here."

Cursing himself, Paul calms down and exits the tent. They gather around the ashen firepit. The Milky Way hangs like suspended ejaculation in the night sky. The night is calm, undisturbed, a near-perfect pocket of time and space. Somewhere else, at other campsites, romance is in the air. The boulders peek down at them like dormant Wild Things, waiting to be animated.

"I wonder," Lonnie says. "How all this porn would've changed the vibe of the 60s. Everything was so tactile then, almost carnal. It's like we're living in a different dimension now with different rules of engagement. Like, would I even have murdered Dover?"

"What do you mean?"

"I had so much pent-up sexual energy," Lonnie says. "Would porn have provided an outlet? A distraction, preventing me from doing what I did. I mean, there was pornography, but nothing like now."

Paul sighs. "I think it's the opposite. Porn makes it worse; it tricks you into thinking you're being sexual when you're really not. It cripples you in a way. Increases the gap between what you want and what you have. If it prevents a few murders, that's a minor side effect. I mean, a good one—a very good one—but just a tiny piece of what's going on."

"I suspect you're right." Lonnie pokes at the ashes with a slender stick. "Sounds like you're kind of addicted."

"Bingo," Paul says. "I should join a group like porn addicts anonymous or whatever."

Lonnie clears a little patch of dirt with his foot. "Perhaps, but I think there might be another way. Why don't you join me on the ground over here."

"We're going to meditate, aren't we?"

"It'll do us both some good."

"I hope you're right," Paul says, getting up. "And Lonnie, can we please never talk about this again?"

"Your secret is safe with me, young man," Lonnie says.

The next morning's attempt at retrieving the ring is no more successful, and at lunchtime Paul kicks the truck's front wheel in frustration. "Why the hell did I think the ring would still be here?"

"You wanted it to be," Lonnie says. "Wanting something badly enough usually clouds your thinking."

"OK," Paul says. "I'm not going to argue with that."

Paul goes around to the back of the truck, climbs into the bed, and lays his head on his rolled up sleeping bag. He observes a cluster of stratocumulus clouds seamlessly shapeshift as they meander across the broad midday sky. One of the larger clouds begins to pull apart, its center hollowing, resembling at first a donut, and then a ring. There's even a stud on one side where a stone would be crowned. Paul rubs his eyes. He doesn't believe in omens, but then again, he didn't believe in time travel either. Just as he sits up to point out the unusual formation to Lonnie, who's midway through a sun salutation, the Earth begins to quake. The truck bed bounces as if it's romping recklessly down a rutted dirt path. Paul grabs the side panel with both hands and watches Lonnie drop from his yoga pose onto all fours. He looks like a tiny animal balancing on a much larger animal's back. They make eye contact and hold it until the shaking stops.

"Earthquake," Lonnie says. "Second one I've been through in the last few months. This one was smaller, but it felt, I don't know, closer."

"Yeah, agreed," Paul says, looking at the sky. The ring is still there, but the stud has elongated and shifted around. It now resembles an arrow pointing at the lake. "You know what. I think I'll make one more trip down, just in case."

Lonnie follows his gaze towards the portentous cloud.

"Yeah," he says. "That's not a bad idea."

CHAPTER THIRTY-FIVE
AT LEAST THIS PLACE
IS CLEANED UP PRETTY WELL

"You spent the first Earth Day at a funeral?" Ethan asks Denise as they walk towards the UCSB lagoon trailed by Samantha, Paul, Leroy, and Lonnie. Every Sunday for the last month, since Paul and Lonnie returned from the desert, the six of them have met at Leroy's house and caught up on the events of the prior year, or the prior 50 years, depending on who's talking.

Denise fiddles with the gold ring with a turquoise stone inset on her finger and looks back at Leroy and Lonnie before answering. "Yeah, two days beforehand the police shot a young man who was trying to put out one of the fires that the rioters started."

"Right," Ethan says. "I keep forgetting that the chaos in I.V. went on for, like, months."

Denise smiles at him. "It's good you got out when you did."

It's Thursday, and Ethan and Paul should be in class, but they're taking the day off in honor of Earth Day, and as a final get-together before Denise and Leroy depart to Vegas to get hitched.

Lonnie initially refused to allow Dover to be openly discussed, but Denise said if he wanted closure—which included the inherent threat of disclosure—they'd have to address it. She also told him that it would be good for her to get it off her chest. She suspected it'd weighed on her more than she knew in the years since he told her what happened, which he only did because she'd overheard him mumbling about it in his sleep. She didn't want to suppress anything anymore; an unrealistic target, she admitted, but she never threw bullseyes anyway.

Lonnie eventually relented, figuring that everyone already knew his darkest secret, and they decided to pay tribute to Dover on Earth Day. Lonnie also announced his intention to take a road trip to Utah to visit the desert sites that Dover never got to see, which they all encouraged.

The lagoon air is more humid than on campus, and Leroy and Lonnie openly perspire as they march up the hill towards the flat bluff overlooking the ocean. A rocky expanse about the size of a football field opens before them, half of it blanketed by an invasive coastal succulent and the other half covered in black tarps meant to kill off the succulent. A bright red couch sits facing the ocean at the far edge of the main lookout point, most likely lugged there by a group of inebriated students at some wee hour of the morning. Lonnie and Leroy plop down on the couch with relief while the others perch around it. The Channel Islands rise from the ocean in the distance like the spine of a fossilized beast and the Santa Barbara harbor is visible to the southeast.

"What a perfect day," Denise says, her eyes on the horizon before turning towards Lonnie. Lonnie nods her way and gets up from the couch. Ethan reaches into his interior jacket pocket and hands Lonnie Dover's copy of *Desert Solitaire*. Lonnie holds the book against his chest, and they all stand silently for a minute, observing, listening, communing.

"Dover," Lonnie says at length. "When last you were here, this place was suffering through an oil spill, one brought on by greed and recklessness. Well, look at it now. A lot has gone wrong since then, but at least this place is cleaned up pretty well. I like to think now that you're part of nature, here, somewhere, and that you've felt some of that return to life."

Standing by herself behind the couch, Samantha observes Lonnie's back. Ethan and Paul invited her to their weekly meetups, and she's attended each one, taking it upon herself to act as notetaker. She was the most reluctant to let Lonnie off the hook for what he'd done, but the battle wasn't hers to wage. She still thinks he's full of shit, but shit can be used to make fertilizer. What she's enjoyed even more than the discussions are the group meditation sessions afterwards. The bubble of calm she creates there is impermeable to carbon, and she keeps it intact for as much of the workweek as possible as she goes about the Herculean task of healing the atmosphere.

Paul joins Samantha, who called in sick that morning to accompany them. Their youthful bodies glow in the diffuse ocean light. He asks her if she's going to stay for dinner. She shrugs her shoulders. She knows Paul's building up to asking her out, and she's curious to see how she'll respond.

Leroy pushes himself up from the couch with a grunt.

"A perfect day indeed, even a bit unseasonably cool," he says. "Not a hint of climate change in it." Denise bites her lip as he turns to Lonnie. "You know, there's studies—buried by the establishment scientists of course—showing that there's actually more plant matter now; that more carbon might be doing good for a lot of ecosystems."

In unison, Denise, Samantha, Ethan, and Paul tell Leroy to shut up. Ethan takes a picture of the view and sends it to his dad along with the message, *looking forward to your visit*. Beyond the mountain behind them, a cloud of smoke unfurls. The chiming of Storke Tower is barely audible over the ocean's lapping.

THE END

ENDNOTES

[I] "The Place is Here, the Time is Now." El Gaucho, Monday, Jan. 27, 1969, p. 4. https://www.alexandria.ucsb.edu/downloads/37720d98f

[II] Kieffer, Joe. "Union Oil's Hartley's – 'Distinctly' Executive." El Gaucho, Thursday, Feb. 13, 1969, p. 1. https://www.alexandria.ucsb.edu/downloads/qz20st80q

[III] Boggs, Larry. "700 Demonstrators Fight Off-Shore Oil Drilling." El Gaucho, Tuesday, April 8, 1969, p. 1. https://www.alexandria.ucsb.edu/downloads/3j3333419

[IV] "House-Made Bomb Damages Faculty Club." El Gaucho, Noon Edition, Friday, April 11, 1969, p. 1. https://www.alexandria.ucsb.edu/downloads/ws859h08v

[V] "Editorial." El Gaucho, Noon Edition, Friday, April 11, 1969, p. 1. https://www.alexandria.ucsb.edu/downloads/ws859h08v

[VI] Wagner, Dave. "Legalize Reality…" El Gaucho, Thursday, Nov. 6, 1969, p. 1. https://www.alexandria.ucsb.edu/downloads/qn59q4962

[VII] Plevin, Steve. "Professor may be fired by tenured," El Gaucho, Thursday, Nov. 6, 1969, p. 1. https://www.alexandria.ucsb.edu/downloads/qn59q4962

[VIII] Probst, Jeff and Kestler, Denise. "Students Demand Public Hearing," El Gaucho, Wednesday, Nov. 12, 1969, p. 1. https://www.alexandria.ucsb.edu/downloads/qn59q4962

[IX] "(a thought-feeling)." El Gaucho, Thursday, Jan. 22, 1970, p. 1. https://www.alexandria.ucsb.edu/downloads/9306t039p

[X] "An Unacceptable Response," El Gaucho, Monday, Jan. 26, 1970, p. 4. https://www.alexandria.ucsb.edu/downloads/6m311q20w

[XI] Flacks, Richard; Whalen, Jack. "Beyond the Barricades: The Sixties Generation Grows Up," Temple University Press, 1990. ISBN 13: 9780877227076

[XII] "Peace, Togetherness: it was a beautiful victory." El Gaucho, Thursday, Feb. 1, 1970, p. 4. https://www.alexandria.ucsb.edu/downloads/b8515p31j

ABOUT THE AUTHOR

Philip Reari (pen name for Ari Phillips) is a Washington, D.C.-based writer and editor working to reduce industrial pollution and enforce environmental laws. Previously a climate reporter, his work has been published by Dissent, Grist, Huffington Post, Mother Jones, n+1, Wired, and many others. His first book was shortlisted for the Santa Fe Literary Awards.

Prior to settling in the District of Columbia, he lived in four western states, two eastern ones, and a few foreign countries. He studied philosophy and art at UC Santa Barbara and journalism and public policy at UT Austin. He enjoys a refreshing walk or bike ride, believes his thumb is somewhat green, and watches too much soccer. His family alternately refer to him as a domestic god and a trash monster.

NOTE FROM PHILIP REARI

Word-of-mouth is crucial for any author to succeed. If you enjoyed *Earth Jumped Back*, please leave a review online—anywhere you are able. Even if it's just a sentence or two. It would make all the difference and would be very much appreciated.

Thanks!
Philip Reari

We hope you enjoyed reading this title from:

BLACK ROSE writing™

www.blackrosewriting.com

Subscribe to our mailing list – *The Rosevine* – and receive **FREE** books, daily deals, and stay current with news about upcoming releases and our hottest authors.
Scan the QR code below to sign up.

Already a subscriber? Please accept a sincere thank you for being a fan of Black Rose Writing authors.

View other Black Rose Writing titles at www.blackrosewriting.com/books and use promo code **PRINT** to receive a **20% discount** when purchasing.

Printed in the USA
CPSIA information can be obtained
at www.ICGtesting.com
LVHW092131230724
786294LV00003B/5

9 781685 134488